DONATED BY

JOY & PAUL GOLDSTEIN

American Journeys: From Ireland to the Pacific Northwest (1847-1854)

Book 1

Richard Alan

Village Drummer Fiction
www.villagedrummerfiction.com

This book is a work of historical fiction. Wikipedia was a constant guide to finding the outline of the historical knowledge needed and a resource toward the more specific details of the times described. However, any names, places, characters, or incidents are products of the author's imagination or are used fictitiously.

ISBN: 978-0-9912342-2-6 (print edition)
ISBN: 978-0-9912342-3-3 (eBook edition)

Also by Richard Alan

Meant to Be Together series:

Finding a Soul Mate (formerly called Meant to Be)

The Couples

Finding Each Other

Growing Together

Dedication

This book is dedicated to my life partner Carolynn, without whose love and amazing skills this series would not have been possible.

As Americans, we all owe a debt of gratitude to those pioneers who came from other parts of the world in the 18th and 19th centuries. Their thoughts, strength, values, and courage molded this country.

Contents

AMERICAN JOURNEYS: FROM IRELAND TO THE PACIFIC NORTHWEST (1847-1854)

Book 1

Chapter One: Myra McCormick

"Myra, I'm cold," my shivering three-year-old sister said while seated on my lap.

A pestilence entered many homes when the Potato Famine destroyed the mainstay of the Irish peasants' diet and showed no sign of abating. Now, two-years later, the elderly and small children were particularly susceptible to any illness which, in their weakened state, could overwhelm and kill them.

Seated near the hearth of our cold, musty, one-room shack, I wrapped my arms around Ciaran, holding her against my starving body. In what would prove to be a futile attempt to ward off her coming death, I wrapped another blanket snugly around her. Ciaran's sunken eyes and deathly pallor burned a permanent place in my memory.

Surely my mother would have liked to hold Ciaran but she was busy trying to comfort five-year-old William who had so little strength left, he was barely breathing. My father sat in the corner of the room, leaning forward with elbows on knees and hands covering his face. His anguished sobs rent the air. Our once strong and proud father could no longer provide for or protect us.

"Don't worry, Ciaran," I told her. "Soon the angels will come and take you to an amazing place where you'll be warm and have all you want to eat."

"I don't want to go," she said as a tear ran down her cheek. "I want to stay."

I held her emaciated body to my chest as I tried to stem my tears. Ciaran coughed a few times and wiped a tear from my cheek. "Don't cry, Myra. Remember when you brought food home?"

With the words sticking in my throat, I replied, "Oh how I wish I could bring more, pretty girl."

***

Six-months prior, fifteen-year-old Myra was talking to her similarly-aged neighbor and best friend, Kathleen Devlin. It was just after dark and they were speaking in low tones, kneeling in a clover patch near their home in a small village outside Cork, Ireland.

"Lord Heath gave me this," Kathleen said as she opened a burlap bag.

Myra's eyes bulged. The bag held cabbages, onions, and sausages.

"I have a sack of barley as well. He's seen you around town and said he'd do the same for you."

"Why is his lordship suddenly becoming anything other than a skinflint?"

"He likes to look at young girls. Twice-a-week, I go in after dark, take my clothes off, and get a sack full of food."

Myra's mouth watered as she thought of the food in Kathleen's sack but shuddered at the thought of undressing in front of the old man.

"I'm not so hungry I'll be taking my clothes off."

"With your little sister and brother desperate for a decent meal maybe you *should*."

Myra thought of Ciaran and William crying from constant hunger; there hadn't been a decent meal at her home since the potato blight started. She bowed her head and stared at the ground. Kathleen raised Myra's chin.

"Look at me, Myra. It's easy. Once I have my clothes off, he puts his hands on me. I just keep thinking of the food. When he's done, I dress and take a sack of food back to my family. I'm the same person now as when I went in there but I have something for my family to eat. "

"Do your parents know?"

"They spend all their time trying to find a couple of scraps to feed us. They don't know and don't care to know."

Myra swallowed hard.

What is hunger forcing the Irish to become?

"Myra McCormick, please don't give me a sad look. We've been friends all our lives. Here, take half." Myra felt guilty taking the food which her friend earned in such an immoral manner… But her hunger and thoughts of having food for her family overwhelmed her and she held tightly to the life giving gifts.

"Next week, Tuesday night, you meet me here and we'll both go."

Myra scurried home. She placed the precious items on their kitchen table.

Her mother glanced at the food with her mouth open but then regarded Myra with a sad expression. Tears welled up as she walked over and embraced her daughter.

"The Lord bless you for what you've done for your family, sweet Myra."

It warmed Myra's heart to see the eager expressions on her younger brother and sister's faces as they ate their first decent meal in many months. Afterward, they each thanked and hugged their big sister.

Not to worry, little ones. If Kathleen can do it, so can I.

***

They entered the stone mansion whose walls reeked of mold. They undressed in his windowless parlor; minimally illuminated by a few oil lamps. Lord Heath leered at Myra's naked body. He watched her face intently as he instructed Kathleen to touch Myra's body. Her friend's hands were warm and gentle. She was gentle in turn when he directed her to touch Kathleen. Her childhood acquaintance was correct. Keeping her mind on the expression her little brother and sister would have when she arrived home with her bounty made this easy. It was difficult, however, to ignore the pain the first time he pushed her onto the big couch, pulled his pants down, and put his thing inside her… But, as Kathleen assured her, it only hurt the first time.

The twice weekly rendezvous continued for four months. It ended when they appeared at the usual time and were greeted by a locked door and a sign which informed them Lord Heath had moved to France. The two friends, bitterly disappointed, embraced and cried.

***

There was no keening at Ciaran's funeral; as there wasn't at poor William's a week prior. No one had the strength.

Myra and her two-years-older brother, Colin, kept an arm around their mother to prevent her from collapsing. She regarded the ornate crucifix which led the mourners into the cemetery. "Why did You let this happen? It's so unfair. They were good children and deserved better than the pain they suffered."

Myra continued to support her mother who was barely strong enough to walk home. Arriving there, a postman gave them a letter.

Colin read it and said, "It's from Aunt Iona in Philadelphia, America. She writes, 'There's plenty of work and plenty of food over here'." He looked up at his family. "She and some friends, who are listed here, have purchased passage to America for Myra and me."

"Saints be praised," her mother, Darcy, said, crossing herself. "At least two of my children can leave Ireland."

"God bless those folk. Children, this will be a fine opportunity," her father John said. "My brother must be doing well to arrange for your passage. I know you'll be welcome in his home."

Myra stiffened. "I don't want to leave you and Ma."

"This is the opportunity of a lifetime. They have plenty to eat and there's lots of work. You might even find a strong Irish boy to marry."

Myra placed her hands on her hips. "So God has a plan to send me even further from William and Ciaran. I'm angry as hell at Him."

"William and Ciaran are in His merciful hands now," Darcy said. "I'm sure they're fine."

"His mercy? Mercy would be a strong Irish boy getting me pregnant the minute we arrive and having two fine children to raise in Christ's image like Ciaran and William."

"Enough foolish talk. The ship will be arriving in one week. You need to prepare for your journey."

***

On a grey, rainy, and cool day, the family approached their home having returned from church on what would be Myra and Colin's last Sunday in Ireland. Their father took off his hat as soon as he saw Mr. Goldman and the sheriff waiting for him in front of their home. He kept his other hand on his surely knotted belly.

"I'm sorry about your children," Goldman said in a flat voice, not looking directly at John.

"I'm sure you didn't come all the way out here just to tell me about my kids."

"You owe money to Lord Heath."

John begged, "Please, Mr. Goldman. Have pity. Everyone's crops have failed. We don't have food for ourselves let alone crops to sell to pay Lord Heath. You know good and well, if you take me off the land I work and out of the home we've built, I won't be able to feed and shelter my family."

Goldman showed no emotion; as if he was not concerned about the damage he could do to their family. "Lord Heath needs to put men on his land who can make things grow and pay timely rent. This is your only warning. Find a way to pay your rent or I'll have the sheriff move you off his lordship's land."

They watched Goldman and the sheriff walk away. Myra asked her trembling father, "How can he take away our means of living? Goldman acts like he's not even human. Where does Lord Heath find such despicable men?"

"Only a heartless Jew could do Lord Heath's evil bidding," he said. "I'm told the man who preceded Goldman was a damn Jew as well. I hate them. I've never heard a good word about them. They're pure evil, I tell you."

Their father's hate-filled pronouncements reinforced the terrible stories they heard about Jews at church as well as stories from the other villagers. Myra and Colin's hatred of all Jews increased, even though Goldman was the only Jew they ever met.

Chapter Two: Journey to Philadelphia

The family was cried out from grieving over William and Ciaran, so there were few tears when Colin and Myra said goodbye to their parents. The twosome wondered if this would be the last time they'd see their folks. Enveloped in sadness, they dragged themselves up the gangplank to the sailing ship's deck. They were shown to a cabin which they would share with two young families, each with small children.

"A cabin?" Myra said. "That must have cost them a pretty penny."

"Aunt Iona wrote she thought it would be safer than steerage."

They secured their handful of belongings.

"Colin, did you note the names of those who helped pay our passage?"

"Not really. I'm just glad they did."

"A few of the names weren't Irish."

"Probably American."

"Aunt Iona wrote a rabbi's needy fund helped. Sounds like Jews."

"Nah, they only help their own kind."

"Isn't a rabbi a kind of priest for Jews?"

"Don't worry, Myra. Whoever it is, we'll work hard and pay them back … even if they're Jews."

One of the ship's crew knocked on their cabin door and announced, "Beef barley stew for dinner, ready in the mess hall. The tide's nearly finished changing so we'll be under way shortly after dinner."

The smell of barley soup and the yeasty scent of fresh baked bread quickened their footsteps as they walked to the dining area. They found two long tables with bench seating and place settings. Each table supported two large soup pots and dark loaves of savory olive bread.

Colin lifted his bowl and ladled in a helping of the savory stew.

"Meat, lots of it," he said.

"And carrots, parsnips, and onions," Myra said after giving the rich soup a stir and filled her spoon.

"Take all you want," one of the cooks said. "I hear you Irish been having a tough time the last couple of years."

"Thank you, sir," Colin said as he hastily scooped up more of the rich stew.

"Not too fast," the cook warned. "You'll make yourselves sick. There's plenty more and there'll be another meal at dusk."

After ten minutes of rapid eating, Myra said, "Colin, my belly's stuffed. I forgot what it felt like to be full."

"I as well."

The dining area tilted. "We're under way," a tablemate said.

An hour later and they were sailing onto the Muir Cheilteach when they heard thunder. The rain falling on the deck above their cabin multiplied to a steady tattoo. The ship's rolling and pitching motions increased as the ship plowed into wave after wave.

"Colin, I'm starting to feel sick."

"You look a bit green. Maybe you should get to the head."

Myra left their cabin and found a line at the head with some already vomiting in the corridor.

"Head to the deck, lassie," a sailor said who was using a swab and bucket to clean up after those suffering seasickness. "You'll get your sea legs in a day or so."

She ran onto the deck which was tilted at what seemed a crazy angle. A stiff wind blew as Myra ran uphill to the rail.

Another sailor yelled, "Mum, not into the wind."

Myra reached the rail, leaned across it just in time as her stomach wretched her meal over the side of the ship. Unfortunately she was on the windward side of the ship so much of her meal was now on her face and clothing. A sailor brought over a pail of water and a rag. Myra spent the rest of the trip staying near a bucket.

"No sea legs for me," she told Colin.

***

During one of their twice daily visits to the sailing ship's breezy and gently rolling deck, they celebrated Myra's seventeenth birthday on the third of June in 1847. A bright yellow sun embedded in a deep blue sky greeted her eyes and warmed her skin. Salty sea air filled her lungs and occasional cold ocean spray gently misted her. The sounds of the journey included the wind whistling around them, the moaning of the rigging and spars as they strained to power the ship out through the Celtic Sea and into the Atlantic, and the plaintive cries of the gulls who circled high above their ship.

***

The McKinneys welcomed Colin and Myra to the bustling city of Philadelphia. Due to weeks of seasickness, Myra's appearance still showed the deprivation she suffered in Ireland. Even though Colin became more accustomed to the ship's constant motion, he evidenced grey skin which was pulled taut against his six foot frame. Their eyes were haunted by sadness.

After a few meals at her Aunt Iona's home and with the opportunity for a better life in her future, Myra tried to be optimistic but her emotions were weighed down by guilt.

William and Ciaran should be alive and able to accompany us. Maybe, if I tried harder, I could have found someone else to please to procure more food.

They gathered in Thomas and Iona McKinney's living room with the McKinneys' friends and neighbors.

"Uncle Thomas," Colin said. "Our first meal on the ship was barley soup with meat in it. That's the first meat we've eaten in—" he turned to his sister who shrugged "—we don't remember how many months. When our little sister and brother died, we knew we must get out but didn't know how. The Lord bless you and your friends for paying our passage. We'll certainly repay your kindness as soon as we can find work."

"You've been through so much pain. I'm sure better times are ahead," Hannah Kaplan, the McKinney's neighbor, said.

"It was indeed painful to lose Ciaran and William. Precious Ciaran died in my arms," Myra said, remembering the sad day. She took a deep breath before continuing. "She was so weak she couldn't even take a sip of water. Her eyes glazed over and her breathing slowed until it stopped. My angelic little sister who was so full of laughter didn't deserve such a cruel fate."

There were few dry eyes among the listeners as they heard additional stories of the terrible loss of life by starvation on the small island.

"If people get the slightest illness, it can kill them because they have no strength to fight it," Myra explained. "While people are starving, the Brits are allowing food to be exported instead of demanding it stay in Ireland and be used to feed the hungry. What are they thinking? How can they be so cruel?"

"A hatred of the Brits is building which is going to explode one of these years," Colin said, clenching his fists.

"Calm down Colin… You're in America now. Rest the balance of the week," Mr. McKinney said. "Get your strength back and next Monday you come with me to the forge. I'm sure they'll find something for you to do."

"Thank you, Uncle. I'm a hard worker. You'll see."

"I can train you to be a seamstress in my shop, Myra," said Mrs. Lombardi, another neighbor, when she stopped by.

"Bless you, ma'am. I can start any time."

***

Iona and her neighbor, Hannah Kaplan, took the new arrivals shopping.

They listened to numerous languages and saw signs in store windows painted in just as many languages. The air was filled with the scent of fresh bread as they entered a Polish bakery. Hannah bought each of them "just out of the oven" round bread which were split in half and spread with fresh churned butter and strawberry jam. Myra thought the little round bread was delicious but considered the hole in the middle wasteful as it should have been filled with more of the delectable, chewy warm bread. They visited a butcher, and there were flower, fruit, and vegetable vendors on the street loudly hawking their wares. These sights and sounds, combined with those of the iceman, milkman, and the fishmonger, pushing their carts through the neighborhood, were to become a daily part of the panorama of their young lives.

Colin and Myra were grim as they saw the huge mounds of food available in the stands at the local market. Myra was staring at vendor's tables loaded with bushel baskets piled high with apples, cabbages, onions, carrots and parsnips, potatoes, and corn. She collapsed to her knees; put both hands over her face and sobbed.

"It's not fair," she said in between sobs. "A few cabbages and my precious sister and baby brother might have lived until we could bring them over here to this land of plenty."

"They've just arrived from Ireland," Hannah told one of the vendors as they watched Colin and Iona help Myra to her feet.

She bought a dozen apples from him but watched as he added six more to her shopping bag, plus two large cabbages, and a handful of carrots. He wouldn't accept payment for the extra items.

"Surely, they look like they could use more to eat," he said with pity in his eyes.

On the walk home, Colin said, "Aunt Iona told me you and your husband put up part the money which brought us over here. Thank you."

"I'm glad we were in a position to help."

"I've never met Jews before except the vile man who collected taxes for cruel Lord Heath," Colin said. "He was also the one who told the Sheriff which farmers to throw off the land they worked. The stories Myra and I heard about Jews told me they wouldn't help anyone but their own kind."

"You watch your tongue youngster, unless you want your ears boxed," Iona said, glaring at them. "She's not only my neighbor but good friend as well."

"I'm sorry if I offended you, Mrs. Kaplan," Colin said, "but we've been wondering about it since we met you folks."

"I'm sorry as well," Myra said. "You've been most kind. Are you Jews different from the Jews in Ireland?"

Hannah said, "I'm a Jew from Ireland myself as is my husband. You children have been through so much. I'm sure it will take a while for you to come to grips with what has happened and adjust to life in the States."

"Nothing but death in Ireland," Myra said angrily through gritted teeth. "And so much life here. I can't wait to have children so I can name them after my departed brother and sister."

"Please wait until you have a husband," Iona said, and she, Hannah, and Colin laughed.

***

"Myra," Aunt Iona said just before church started, "a young man saw you at church last week and his mother told me he'd like to meet you."

"Who is he? I may have seen him."

"His name is Sean Coughlin."

"Surely I've seen him. He's huge. You can't miss him."

"I was thinking of inviting his family for Sunday dinner today. You'd have a chance to talk to him."

"I'd like that."

***

Sean Coughlin was a good looking, tall, and muscular man.

I'll bet he wouldn't hesitate to defend his family.

Myra sat next to him at dinner.

"Sean was an altar boy for a number of years," his mother said.

"I was."

"Sean, tell Myra about your job at the docks."

"I work the docks."

"What do you do there?" Myra asked

"Unload ships."

"He's a hard worker and he's sure to get promoted one of these days," Mrs. Coughlin said.

Myra glanced at Sean's sister, Kelly, who was her age. She hadn't uttered a word since they exchanged greetings.

"Kelly, sit up straight. Kelly was quite sickly while growing up which is why she has nothing in the way of a woman's body."

"Mother, please don't embarrass me."

"You never speak up for yourself so someone has to." Kelly blushed and returned to staring at her lap.

"Kelly, how do you fill your days?" Myra asked.

"She helps me around the house and helps with the laundry I take in," her mother said.

"What would *you* like to do, Kelly?" Myra asked.

"Become a teacher." She showed the faintest of smiles.

"A teacher," her mother said laughing. "You can't even read. After all the years I suffered while getting you through a sickly childhood, the only thing you're qualified to do is help me with my laundry business."

Myra turned to Sean. "Do you live with your parents?"

"Yes."

"We have a large enough home, when Sean takes a bride she could come and live with us until they have enough money to be on their own."

Myra smiled. *Surely I wouldn't look forward to living under your thumb, Mrs. Coughlin.*

After the Coughlin family departed, Iona asked Myra about Sean.

"He's nice but never constructed a sentence with more than a few words."

"It doesn't take much vocabulary to unload ships."

"I was hoping to find someone who was a bit more educated."

"I understand, dear, but please remember, you don't want to be too picky. Your reputation will suffer and no one will want you."

"I believe Sean wants me. He spent so much time staring at my chest, I doubt if he'd recognize my face."

***

Myra started her career as a seamstress at Mrs. Lombardi's by pulling threads and learning various stitches. She watched Mrs. Lombardi design clothes and started to make suggestions.

"You've got a keen eye," Mrs. Lombardi told her. "You'll be designing one of these days."

Colin found a job at an ironworks. It was hot, sweaty, back-breaking work. The two jobs allowed Myra and him to rent their own apartment. They worked long hours at mind-numbing jobs. Their only relief came on Sunday with church and dinner at Aunt Iona's.

***

Six months later, another boy arrived to get to know Myra. James was educated, a teacher, and skinny as a reed. Myra imagined a stiff breeze would blow him over. They sat in the McKinneys' parlor.

"What's your favorite subject to teach?" she asked.

"History, without a doubt," he said while adjusting his thick glasses. "In school I majored in early German history. I received a special merit award from my college for a paper about the Visigoths."

"Visi … whats?"

"They were members of Germanic tribes who, among other things, sacked Rome in the year four-ten. They settled in southern Gaul. They considered themselves like the Hebrew tribes who wandered the desert for forty years."

"I see," Myra said, trying not to yawn. "I'm sorry, James. Thank you for visiting but this won't work."

She told Aunt Iona, "I know I said I wanted a man who was educated but there has to be more to an educated man than… Visigoths."

***

"This will be a fine looking wedding dress when we get it finished," Myra said to the Lombardis' daughter, Anna. They were working at the Lombardis' dress shop, located in the living room of their home.

"After so many weeks of our hard work, it better be fine," Anna said as she stepped back to admire their work. "You should be proud as it's actually your own design."

"I am."

"Have you heard from your folks lately?"

"I received a letter from Ireland last week. Ma writes every few months. It's been a year since we arrived here, you know, so it was good to hear from them. I'd written a couple of months before and told them me and my brother were doin' well, we have our own apartment, we both put on weight, and we're feeling fine. I suggested they accept my aunt and uncle's offer to come over here but Father thinks it'll be too big a change. My uncle told him he could have a good job with a friend in Boston but I think he's too frightened to leave. Ma won't leave without him and, besides, I don't think she could stand to be far away from my sister and brother's graves."

"Their death was so tragic."

Myra sighed deeply. "I feel the pain of their loss every day but try not to show it. Having lost them, I have a burning desire to compensate for their deaths. Since I've become healthy again, my body aches to have children."

"You'll need a man for that."

"Not just any man." Myra looked up from her work; imagining her future partner. "I want an intelligent man, a kind man who loves children, has a sense of humor, and I wouldn't mind if he was good looking… A strong man who's willing to defend his family at a moment's notice."

"Listen to you." Anna laughed and returned to sewing. "We all want the same but we'll take what we can get."

"Not me. I owe my brother and sister who didn't even live long enough to have their first Holy Communion. I keep racking my brain trying to think of something else I could have done to save them."

"They starved because there wasn't any food. What else could anyone have done?"

"I'd have done anything for them and, in fact, I did as long as I could."

"You're a good woman so I'm sure you did everything possible, just like I would in such an awful situation."

"I'm not such a good woman," Myra said, keeping her gaze on her sewing.

Anna stopped working and regarded Myra with a quizzical expression. "What do you mean?"

"Wealthy Lord Heath owned a large home near us and owned all the property around our village. My best friend, Kathleen, told me he wanted to see us naked and would give us food to take home if we did."

"You didn't."

"One thought of me starvin' brother and sister and I did."

"Did you have to…?"

"He was an old man so he couldn't do it often and didn't last long when he could." Her body shuddered as she wrinkled her face at the memory of his fat, sweaty, and smelly body banging away on top of her. "That evil bastard mostly asked us to do things to each other while he watched."

"I'm so sorry for you. Didn't you worry about…"

"We were so hungry I didn't worry about gettin' with child." Myra sighed. "It was humiliating at first but Kathleen was my good friend and we quickly discovered we could do things to get ourselves in a state of desire making it easy to do whatever the old man wanted."

Anna, sitting motionless, stared at Myra for a long time before starting to work again.

"You don't understand, Anna. Hungry people will do anything. Food was more precious than money because you can't eat money. It only lasted a handful of months with that filthy man anyway; after which he left for France."

"Did your family know what you were doing?"

"Everyone was busy looking for the next scrap to eat; they didn't have time to worry about how I brought food home. I think my folks knew. It wasn't enough anyway."

They were interrupted by a knock on the front door.

"I'll get it, Ma," Anna called out.

"Hello David," she said, welcoming David Kaplan to her home. "Ma will have your shirts done in a few minutes. She said for you to have a seat and I'll get you a coffee while you wait."

After he left, Anna continued conversing with Myra. "There's a good looking man for you. He's so smart; he took college entrance exams two years earlier than most. He just finished his first year of college in Boston this past spring."

"How old is he? He looks little more than a boy."

"He's seventeen. I saw him at the ocean last summer and, believe me, he may be a little less than average in height but he has a man's body."

"What kind of person is he?"

"He's gentle and tough at the same time. I remember he and his sister Sarah stood up to bullies who were harassing a handful of little kids at the beach. His expression informed the bullies, who were mostly bigger than him, that he'd rip them apart if needed. Of course, I'm sure it helped his powerfully built sister stood next to him. But don't get your hopes up, you don't want to fall in love with him. Besides being one-year younger than us, he's a Jew."

"Kind, nice looking, strong, and smart … good qualities… A Jew is he? I don't care about love. I don't really want him anyway … just his stuff."

"Myra McCormick, how can you say such a thing?"

"I couldn't save them but now my body is healthy again. A man like David could help me bring William and Ciaran back to life."

Anna's jaw dropped.

"Ignore me, Anna. I'm just daydreaming."

Chapter Three: A Weekend Visit

"Good evening Mrs. Kaplan," Myra said when she appeared at the Kaplans' door, late on a Thursday in mid-summer after an hour and thirty minute walk from her apartment.

"Good evening to you, too, Myra. What brings you to our side of town?"

"I have clothing to assemble at our apartment which I'll be working on tomorrow through Sunday but the work requires stitching leather. My wrist is sore and I'm having trouble pushing a needle through the material. I was wondering if David might be available to help, since he helped Mrs. Lombardi sew bridle leather earlier this summer."

"He's working with his father tomorrow but would be available after four. Let me ask him." She called David to join them.

"I'd pay you for whatever pieces you sew together."

"That'd be fine," David said. "I'll have more money to take back to school." He turned to his mother. "I'd have to miss *Shabbat* this weekend."

"One weekend won't hurt… Besides, it's for school." She turned back to address Myra. "He's saving to have his own apartment so he has a quiet place to study."

"A serious student are you? Excellent. Here's my address." Myra took a piece of paper out of her pocket and handed it to David.

"I'll see you tomorrow," she said. She turned slightly and, seemingly as an afterthought, added, "He can stay overnight with Colin and me, if it's okay. It'll save him a few long walks." She looked up at the sky and pulled her collar up against the cool air which generally preceded a mid-summer shower. "A few long walks in the rain from the way it looks."

"That'll be fine, Myra," Mrs. Kaplan called after her.

***

Before David arrived, Myra brushed her fiery red hair three times and checked her appearance at least as often. She wore a fitted, button-front, white shirt which emphasized her perky breasts and a tight, full length, leather skirt.

He knocked on her door at five-thirty. She forgot her carefully planned welcome when David's bright eyes greeted her with disarming warmth.

"Welcome David," was all she managed.

"Glad to be here, Miss McCormick." He quickly glanced around the small two-room apartment, observing a long table covered in stacks of cloth and leather, ready for assembly. "Lots to do I see."

"I need you to begin by assembling these belts."

They sat across the table from each other. Myra was pleased as she caught him glancing at the tight top she was wearing.

David used his deft fingers and strong wrists to combine two vegetable tanned, brown pieces of cowhide into smart looking belts.

"I sell the belts for fifteen cents each. I'll give you seven cents for each one you complete."

David's face lit up. "Thank you, Miss McCormick. That's more than fair." It was tedious work but he quickly fell into a rhythm which allowed him to complete numerous belts. "When will Colin be coming home?"

"First, call me Myra. Colin won't be home until Monday."

Surprised, he stopped working. "I shouldn't stay here tonight."

"Don't be daft. We're not children. There's plenty of room here. How're the belts coming?"

David counted his finished pile. "I have nineteen belts completed."

"Good work. You're a lifesaver, you are. I couldn't have completed this order without your hard work. If I don't get orders out on time, I won't get more work."

She walked around the table, leaned toward him, put her arms around his neck, and kissed his cheek.

"Glad I can help," he said as Myra saw him blush.

"Tell me about your college studies."

"I'm learning German. It's easy because I already know Yiddish. I need it to read books on math and chemistry. I'm learning the infinitesimal calculus, astronomy, and it seems they always have me writing papers and reading books about history."

"You're smart and a hardworking man. William and Ciaran, the brother and sister I lost, were the same."

"It must have been painful to lose them."

"It still pains me to my core."

But you, David Kaplan, are going to help me bring them back to life.

***

Before their evening meal, Myra gradually opened a couple of the buttons on her shirt. she saw David's eyes glancing at her chest as she moved around, sewed and while they ate.

I've got you hooked, David Kaplan. Now I need to bring you in.

They returned to sewing for another hour, when she said, "Enough work for tonight. Come and sit with me."

They sat at opposite ends of a small couch.

"Do you have a girlfriend?"

"Not really," he said. "My parents have been telling me about the daughter of a friend of theirs. I've only talked to her once and know little about her. I suspect they're setting up a match for me."

"Have you ever kissed a girl?"

"No."

She moved next to him, putting her hands on either side of his face and her lips on his. Myra was pleased to hear his breathing become faster while he returned her lengthy kiss.

"David, I'm sore from bending over while I was sewing. Will you please work the muscles in my back and shoulders?"

She turned away from him. He started on her shoulders and worked his way down her back. His touch was gentle but firm.

"Ooh, how pleasant. Thank you."

Myra turned out all but one of the room's lamps which she dimmed. The weather was helping her set a romantic mood with a breeze-blown light rain beating a soft rhythm on the apartment's windows. She removed her shirt and sat on his lap with her back against him. She brought his arms around her body and his hands up to cup her breasts.

He pulled his hands away. "I don't think I should touch..."

"David, a woman needs a man's touch to make her feel good; especially on her breasts. Please, be a man and do it for me."

He let her guide his hands back to her breasts which he gently caressed while softly pulling on her nipples. She leaned back against him, resting her head on his shoulder and placing her cheek against his. She closed her eyes and took a few deep breaths as his caresses warmed her body.

After many minutes of luxuriating in his soft touch she turned around, faced him, and, while kissing him, unbuttoned his shirt. From David's contented expression while he touched her, she knew he was enjoying this. She could also tell by the bulge she was sitting on.

"Time for bed," she announced, her throbbing body telling her it wanted more than touching. She reached over and blew out the last lamp. She held his hand while they walked to the bedroom where they undressed.

Myra lay down on her back. When David slid under the blanket, she rolled him on top of her. He kissed her lips and kept one hand softly caressing her breast. She reached between her legs and guided him inside her.

William and Ciaran, I know this isn't right but I'm doing this for you. I'll be thinking of you when I raise him or her.

David began thrusting slowly which caused a wave of pleasure with each movement. David brought his face down to her chest. He caressed her nipples with his lips.

She ran her hands down David's back and her fingers onto his buttocks then slowly kneaded his back muscles.

David Kaplan you're making my body feel sensations I've never experienced. Is this because you're a Jew or is this exciting because it's so wrong? Your touch and having you inside me is exciting more than anything in my life.

He moved faster, pushed as far into her as he could, moaned, and she felt his warm liquid inside her.

Immediately, she experienced something entirely new. Her muscles tightened on him in waves. She rode each wave along with the pleasant sensations which emanated from her hips and coursed through her body.

David's moaning ended; he stopped moving and gradually slowed his breathing.

"Thank you, David," Myra said, out of breath, as she kept her arms wrapped tightly around him. "I enjoyed that."

"My cousin, who's married, told me about being with a woman before I went to college. He said to go slow and be very gentle. He also told me about making a woman's breasts feel good. I hope you liked what I did. Should I do anything differently?"

Differently? Are you out of your mind? I can't imagine it getting any better than what you just did to me!

"It was fine, David."

"Will you become pregnant?"

"You don't need to worry."

He rolled off her. She turned away from him, onto her side. He brought his body against her, spoon style, and wrapped an arm around her.

Lord Heath never held me afterward. David's embrace is so comforting. Is this what it's like for other women or is there something different about this Jew? Surely I'm sinning by enjoying this. One day there'll be a terrible price to pay.

She pulled his hand up to cup her breast. He kissed her neck. A little soft kiss and it started building a fire in her as surely as if he'd placed a flame in kindling. Myra twisted and brought her breast up to his lips. They began again. Slower this time and, as they finished, her body convulsed more intensely than the first time.

They fell asleep in each other's arms.

When she awoke the following morning, he was on his back and her arm and leg were across him while his arm was still around her.

"Good morning, Myra," he said as he tightened his embrace.

"Morning."

She moved to kiss his lips. While doing so her leg brushed against him and she knew he was ready again.

"I'm too sore to take you inside me but let me take care of you." She slid her hand onto him and stroked.

"Myra, you don't have to... Oh..."

David closed his eyes. She gradually moved faster and faster, until she felt his liquid run down her hand.

"Thank you, Myra."

"We have lots of work to do. Let's get washed up and I'll prepare us something to eat."

She thought she would prepare a bath and make breakfast for them but found David helping. Myra was surprised as her father and brother never lifted a finger around the house. "Men shouldn't do women's work," her father said incessantly.

She bathed first while David stirred the gently simmering oatmeal, put water on for tea, sliced bread, and placed the slices on the stove to warm them.

After David bathed, they ate in silence. He started to help with cleanup but she insisted he begin sewing again.

Their fingers once again nimbly guided needle and thread, as they talked about family.

"Family is everything," he said. "I know in my heart I would do whatever it took to protect them."

I have already shown what I was willing to do for my family but William and Ciaran died anyway.

"If it's not too painful, tell me about the brother and sister you lost."

"I love to talk about them. It keeps their memory alive. William was five when he died and Ciaran three. One time, when William was around three"—Myra smiled and looked into the distance as her memory visualized what she was about to tell David—"a little boy put his hand on Ciaran in an unkind way. She was but a baby. William pulled the offending hand off Ciaran and I swear he tried to unscrew it from the boy's wrist. The boy howled in pain while Will yelled to leave his sister alone."

"A fine brother to watch out for his sister."

"His bones were wide and he probably would have grown up to be wide and strong but not tall, just like my dad. When my father went out to work in the fields, no one could get more done in a day than him." Myra laughed and shook her head. "He also made short work of tossing those who drank too much out of the local public house. William also laughed like my dad and made us laugh at his antics. Of the four of us, Mother said William was the smartest. Ciaran laughed often as well but her laughter sounded more like glass chimes and her behavior was of a child who only wanted to please. She didn't have William's independent streak."

"Independent streak?"

"If you wanted him to do something, you'd show him how and get out of his way. Ciaran always wanted to do whatever the rest of us were doing … more like a team, not by herself."

"I think I'm more like William."

"I can see from the way you work."

They seemed to find reasons to touch each other in simple ways while they labored. Myra found it curiously reassuring when he put his hand on her shoulder or arm when they talked.

"How do you know when you're in love with someone?" he asked while they were cleaning up after dinner.

"I have no idea. I've been wondering for years."

David thought for a while. "My mother said it happens when you realize there's no one else you'd rather spend your life with."

"People are selfish. I think they just marry to have a family and, if they're lucky, they fall in love."

"Mom said she knew Dad was the one for her the first time she talked to him."

"Romantic nonsense, I'd say. People like to think those things but life consists of more practicality than romance. Tell me about your family and why they left Ireland."

"We were lucky. We left a couple years before the Potato Famine. There were weeks of heated arguments at Sunday dinner, the only meal we ate as a family due to my father's work schedule. I'm still amazed that he agreed to come over here. Possibly, he gave in to end the arguments."

***

"You'll work for my brother and he'll train you to become a foreman," David's mother, Hannah, told his father, Dillon, at Sunday dinner, many weeks prior to their voyage to America. "He's promised me you'll receive a good wage the minute we arrive in Philadelphia, America."

"I've never been a foreman and don't know how. I have a steady job at the ironmonger's here in Cork."

"Yes, but your family lives in one tiny room with one tiny window. David and Sarah deserve a better life."

"Hannah, it's a whole new country. I've heard they don't even speak English like we do. How do we know I can provide for my family when we get there? We don't know what to expect!"

"I expect just what my brother told us in his letter. He'll send money to pay our way. He's even promised to pay our rent for three months if we sail over there."

"Leaving what we know for what we don't know is foolishness, woman. My family has lived in Ireland for near one-hundred-years."

"Yes, and this country still doesn't recognize a Jewish marriage."

"I don't like this, Hannah. I'm a simple man who can't be twisted into something he's not. Nor am I someone who can suddenly change everything in his life."

***

Twelve-year-old Sarah and her two-years-older brother, David, enjoyed the trip across the ocean and their new home in Philadelphia.

With disdain in her expression she viewed her reflection in the full length mirror in her mother's sewing room.

"What's wrong, Sarah?" David said, looking up from the book he was reading.

"I'm big boned and tall. Maybe the Lord actually intended me to be a boy. I'm already taller than you and have as many curves as a ship's mast. I'm muscular and taller than all the boys my age."

Her mother stopped her sewing long enough to say, "You're a nice looking girl other than being a bit tall but don't worry. Plenty of boys will notice you."

"Lots of the boys are paying attention to the other girls but not one boy pays attention to me. The girls who were my friends don't want me around because the boys don't like me."

***

The following summer, Sarah watched her one-year-older neighbor, Kevin, play baseball numerous times.

David noticed her athletic skill and she desperately wanted to play the game but he heard the boys her age say, "It's not a girl's game and no one wants a girl on their team."

On the way home from school with David, she found a broken broom handle which was just under three-feet in length. She took a swing with it like the boys did when they played baseball. Throwing a rock into the air, she swung at it and missed. She missed a few more times and, finally, solidly hit it. It only went ten-feet in front of her and bounced across the ground.

Her shoulders drooped.

"You're not chopping wood, lassie," a nearby construction worker called out. "You need to get under it and swing up at it."

After a few more tries, she squarely hit a rock which traveled halfway down the block.

"Wow," David said.

"Solid hit there, lassie," the construction worker called again. "Now if you want it to go left, hit on the end of the bat and to hit right, strike closer to your hands."

Her brother saw Sarah practice with her 'bat' a few times a week and just as often play catch with Kevin.

"You have a powerful and accurate throw, Sarah," David said. "Kevin, how about giving her a chance to play baseball?"

Kevin put his head down, then smiled and said, "Come by the park Sunday afternoon and we'll see."

That evening, David saw their mother throw out a pair of her father's work pants. They were torn in a few places. He gave them to Sarah.

"You may want to prepare these for under the skirt, baseball use."

She grinned and briefly embraced him. "Thank you, big brother."

***

At fifteen years of age, David found a part time job at a supply store where, with his mathematical prowess, he quickly became involved in inventory management, purchasing, pricing, and bookkeeping.

"Look at your son," brooding Dillon said to his wife at the end of a Sunday dinner while grabbing one of David's hands. "Soft hands. He's working at a job where he sits most of the day."

"Pa, I'm helping the bookkeeper. I keep track of the inventory, do the purchasing, some accounting, and help total up orders. I'm paid an excellent wage and it doesn't interfere with school or my plans for college."

Dillon stood up, leaned toward and glared at David. "The lads I supervise at the forge, mostly married men, are breaking their backs for long hours every day for less hourly wage than you." He hoisted his glass of whiskey and noisily gulped down the last of it. "It's not fair."

"This is America," Hannah said quietly. "They pay according to how much thinking you use in your job."

"And if pay for thinking isn't crazy, I surely don't know what is. He's not married. He doesn't have children. Why should David get such a grand wage?"

"Because Mr. Mandel pays him what he's worth to their business," Hannah said in a pleading voice. "You should be proud of your son."

He ignored her remark and turned his icy stare to Sarah. "And you, little lady. Parading around here as if you're royalty; but on warm Sundays, you went out and ran around like a boy."

Sarah stared at her dinner plate while her mother asked, "What are you talking about? She and Kevin went for walks on Sunday afternoons."

"Yes and quite a walk it was. She and Kevin walked right out to a field on the other side of town to play baseball; a game which is the product of the devil like nothing else I've ever seen or heard of. Your daughter throws a ball like a boy, runs and uses a bat like a boy, and even slides on the ground like a boy. In fact, one of the lads at the forge told me she's better than all the boys her age."

Sarah squirmed in her chair.

"Sarah, is this true?" Hannah asked.

Before she could answer, her father's voice became louder as he raged. "And she wears britches under her skirt. I know. I've seen them. And don't be asking her to confirm what I'm saying. You're her mother. You should know about this, not me."

He pulled on a long coat, walked over to a cabinet, and took out a partially filled whiskey bottle. He shook it to see how much it held, took a long swig out of it, wiped his mouth on his coat sleeve and shoved the bottle into his coat pocket.

Turning back and glaring at his wife, he said in a sarcastic tone, "Ask your little queen about the fight she got into after school last week with Ray Black."

They all turned to Sarah.

"Ray and another boy started a fight with Kevin," she said. "He's the smallest boy his age. The other two were huge. I stepped in to help him."

"Sarah Kaplan, you were fighting? What in God's name were you thinking?"

"Mother, they were going to beat him up for defending me when they made fun because I'm so big."

"Tell your mother what you said, little queen, when you walked up to them."

Sarah was silent.

"Well?" Hannah demanded.

Sarah turned to her mother, sat up straight while remembering the moment, and said proudly, "I told them to leave Kevin alone because they were outnumbered."

"Next, according to the the lads I work with, I hear my charming and delicate flower of a daughter took on the likeness of a trained boxer. They said Sarah rained powerful blows on one of those fellows like the big hammer at the forge. I was told every time he swung at you, you knocked his arm aside and slammed a fist into him."

"I would have stopped but he kept getting up and trying to hit me."

"Apparently, he and Kevin wailed the tar out of them," Dillon said.

"Where did you learn to fight?" Hannah asked.

"One of the boys at school taught me."

"Tell the complete truth," David said.

"David taught me."

In a voice dripping with sarcasm, Dillon said, "Isn't he the fine brother?"

Sarah said, "Sometimes there are bullies on the way to school and he wanted me to be able to protect myself. He taught me how to block and count when I throw combinations."

Sarah leaned back and smiled, reliving the memory of Kevin and her teaching the bullies a lesson they wouldn't soon forget. "You should have seen Kevin, Ma. Once one of the boys turned on me, he wriggled lose from the other and lit into him. His arms and fists were flying as fast as a hummingbird's wings. He beat the other fellow groggy."

"Listen to this will you?" Dillon raged with eyes wide and fury in his expression. "She's proud of what she's done. To make things worse, the poor kid got another beating. After you finished with him his father learned what happened and blistered the boy's butt for fighting with a girl. He and his son found me on the way home from work where, after a cuff to the back of his head, his son apologized to me for fighting with my daughter."

Dillon leaned over and spoke in Sarah's ear. "One of the lad's eyes was blackened and puffy, nearly swollen shut, and there was tape across his broken nose. He could barely speak through his swollen lips. To think my own daughter beat and bloodied someone sickens me."

Sarah pleaded, "I was defending myself and helping my friend Kevin."

Dillon looked contemptuously at his daughter. "I'm going out."

"Please don't, Dillon. It's freezing outside."

"Anything is better than staying in a house full of crazy people."

He stormed across the kitchen to the back door, glared over his shoulder at his children, and angrily spat out, "I never should have come to this God forsaken country. You two are just like your mother and nothing like me. You'll cause nothing but pain to whoever the hell you marry."

Dillon tramped out of the house, slamming the back door shut. Hannah broke into tears as she left the table and hurried to her bedroom.

David slowly turned toward his sister.

"Are you really better at baseball than the boys?"

She smiled and said proudly, "All but two of them. And yes, during games I do wear the britches you gave me so I can slide and not show my legs. Playing ball is about my favorite thing to do but I knew our folks wouldn't approve so I kept it a secret."

While they cleaned up the table and kitchen, David shook his head, and shrugged his shoulders. "He's my father and I want him to be proud of me, but he's right. We're not like him."

"You may be right."

"So how are things at school?"

"My friend, Shayna Liechtenstein, quit school today. She, her mom, and her little sister Abbey are moving to Boston to live with her grandfather. I guess it's been rough on them since her father died last year. I liked her. You used to get together with her to study all the time."

"We were in the same grade so we studied together when we first moved here but I spent very little time with her the last year or so."

"David, there's a rumor at school which says Shayna became pregnant not long after we moved here."

"Not true," he said angrily as his cheeks turned red. "All the time I spent with her I would know. Shayna's a great student and a good person. You shouldn't spread gossip."

"Why are you angry?"

"Let me be. I have to study."

Chapter Four: Weekend Visit Continued

"Thanks for telling me about your family. I think I'd like to get to know Sarah," Myra said.

Saturday evening, Myra experienced the same rapture from David's lovemaking as Friday. She wrapped herself around him and momentarily imagined having this hard working, intelligent, and gentle man as her husband.

Wouldn't I love to have his arms around me for all my days, but he's from a different world having mostly grown up in America and being one of those awful Jews; being college educated, not having firsthand knowledge of the Famine, and younger than I. It would never work.

They completed their sewing tasks late Sunday afternoon. David said, "It's been a delightful weekend. I wouldn't mind seeing you again."

"If I have more work, I'll let you know."

"More work? I found it so easy to talk to you. Couldn't we just, you know, get together?"

"Surely we enjoyed this weekend but you're a Jew; a nice Jew I have to admit, but quite different from me. I've certainly enjoyed your company but things between us end now."

David's shoulders drooped and he stared at the floor as he put his coat on.

"David, you're off to your second year of college shortly and that's where your future lies … not with an uneducated Irish seamstress."

"May I write you a note when I'm back at school?"

"Sure. Why not? Study hard," she said as she pushed him out the door. "Goodbye, David."

She pulled a window curtain back slightly and watched him walk down the street. Myra saw him look back over his shoulder. He appeared deeply saddened.

***

A month later and, as usual, Colin woke Myra to prepare his breakfast and midday meal. Upon sitting up, her head wasn't clear like it usually was and she suddenly felt nauseous. Running to the sink, her stomach muscles contracted violently as she vomited.

"Myra, I need to eat before I go to work."

"I don't feel too good. Would you mind making your own breakfast and preparing your own midday meal?"

"I'm not a woman. You're the woman around here so get busy."

"I go to work just like you do."

"I'll be furious if I have to go without eating."

"You better make yourself something. The thought of food is making me sicker."

He angrily stormed out of the apartment as she vomited again. Myra dressed and gathered her things for work.

***

She still felt nauseous when she arrived and told Anna Lombardi how she was feeling.

"Myra, are you pregnant? My ma was feeling sick to her stomach nigh every morning when she was with child."

"He did it!" Myra said and would have been overjoyed if she hadn't felt so much nausea.

"Someone certainly did it if you're pregnant," Anna said as her skilled fingers rapidly hemmed a skirt. "When are you going to marry the father?"

"He doesn't know."

"When will you tell him?"

"Actually, I hadn't planned on telling him."

Anna's expression turned to fright as she stared over Myra's shoulder. Myra turned and saw Mrs. Lombardi, hands on hips, glaring at her.

"If you don't plan to marry the father, you're a bad influence on the other girls and must leave immediately."

"I need this job." Myra trembled. "It helps pay our rent."

Mrs. Lombardi scowled at Myra without responding.

"Please don't fire me."

"If you don't intend to have a father help raise your child, you will work from home starting this instant. I'll send work there until your baby arrives but afterward you stay home and take care of your child. Anna, you don't tell anyone about her situation. If anyone asks, we'll say she quit."

"Yes, Ma."

"Thank you, Mrs. Lombardi."

***

"Who did this to you? I need to know so I can make sure he marries you," Colin screamed during breakfast. Myra was no longer able to hide her six-month swollen belly. He slammed his fist on the kitchen table, rattling the dishes and tableware.

In a meek voice she said, "I'm not having the father involved in raising my child."

"So he'll be a bastard." He slammed a fist on the table again which made Myra jump.

"Colin, please…"

He raged at her through gritted teeth. "No bastard will be raised in my house." He stood up.

"I thought it was our house," she said quietly.

"Not any longer." He stood up. "Our parents would die of shame if they knew."

"I'll be naming the baby after William or Ciaran."

"Naming your bastard after my sweet brother or sister?" He began pacing with a pained expression. "The hell you will."

"Stop calling my child a bastard."

"I have an idea. Name the little bastard after his father."

"Colin, stop it!"

"When I find the Irishman who did this, I'll teach him a lesson he'll never forget."

"He's not Irish."

"What? Not Irish?" He stopped pacing and said, "Are you out whorin'? Have you lost all respect for yourself by lying with a foreigner?"

"He's an American."

"Let me have his name and I'll teach him an Irish lesson which will be legendary."

"I won't."

"Get out. You've shamed me, our sainted brother and sister, as well as the rest of the family."

"I have no place else to go. Please, please, let me stay until the baby arrives."

Once I have the baby, my kind brother wouldn't throw us out.

Chapter Five: William

Colin quit talking to her. She was in her last week of pregnancy and it was getting progressively more difficult to work.

William decided to arrive on a cool and rainy Friday morning after a painful and exhausting twelve-hour labor attended by a midwife.

Colin looked in on them.

"Would you like to hold your nephew?"

"You and the bastard leave."

"Colin…"

"I'm staying with a friend for the next three days. When I return, I expect you and the kid to have cleared out."

She trembled as a sense of abandonment overwhelmed her. Myra heard the door slam. Little William slept peacefully in his mother's arms, nestled against her breast while tears welled up.

"We've nowhere to go and no one to take us in." She felt exhausted, physically and emotionally.

"We'll rest today and tomorrow," she told her newborn son as she leaned her head back on the pillow, "before we get our things together to go … Heaven knows where."

Around noon the third day following William's birth, she placed everything she owned into one small bag. She dressed in heavy clothing as it was a cool day. Looking out a window she saw leaves emerging on an oak tree.

"There's what I need, William, a fresh new start to my life."

Wiping a tear away, she headed out the door and proceeded to a few of the shops with signs which said they wanted to hire seamstresses.

"You'll work from ten to fourteen hours depending on how much there is to get finished. I pay twelve cents-a-day. You'll have to find someone to take care of your child, we don't allow children in here."

"I'm still nursing him."

"Your concern; not mine. Plenty of you girls have kids you can't afford and they end up at the orphanage."

"You don't pay much. I could hardly feed us let alone pay for an apartment."

"If you don't want the job, there are plenty just off the boat who will."

"I have experience."

"So will they when they've been here a few weeks. I don't have time to argue with you. Do you want the job or not?"

"No thank you."

After visiting several more shops and hearing the same story, teary-eyed Myra sat on a bench and nursed William. The wind picked up. She just reached in her bag for an extra blanket to cover him when she spied a folded envelope.

"This is the letter your father sent me, William." Myra was startled to hear David's voice before unfolding it.

'Family is everything. I know in my heart I would do whatever it took to protect them."

She glanced around as if she expected to see him.

"William, your father sent me a letter last fall. It has his address on it. He may be our only hope to have a roof over our heads. I know he's a Jew and may be promised to someone but all we need is a small space so I can take care of you and begin sewing again. Lord willing, he'll let us have a corner."

She placed thoroughly bundled William in one arm and hoisted their bag with the other. Myra trudged to the train station through the beginning of a late spring snowfall.

***

"Two dollars for you and nothing for the little one," the train conductor said.

"Two dollars is a lot of money," Myra complained, knowing the price would seriously deplete the money she managed to save.

"If you wish to take the train to Boston, it's two dollars, ma'am."

The carriages rocked, bumped, and jolted their occupants. William seemed to enjoy the motion as he mostly slept during the journey; as long as his mother held him. A couple of older women and one man tried to hold him so Myra could sleep but the minute he left his mother's arms he cried.

"Some babies," the woman said, "don't feel secure in strangers' arms."

"Thank you for trying."

***

Arriving in Boston, scared and filled with apprehension, she plodded along according to the directions a man at the train station indicated.

What if he's moved? What if he's not in college and they don't know where he's gone? What if he's taken a wife? What if the Jew doesn't want anything to do with a Catholic? Maybe he's angry for the way I ended things last summer.

Her chest tightened and she trembled as she approached the address. Myra's legs were leaden as she trudged up the front steps, entered the building, and found the apartment. She stood as straight as she could, took a deep breath, and knocked on the door. Her heart pounded as loud as her knocking.

The door swung open. "Myra…"

"Hello David."

He just stood there with a blank expression for a moment then slowly smiled.

"Please come in."

She entered his tiny and messy one-room apartment which contained one bed, a table with two chairs, a small bureau, a small desk, and a tiny kitchen area. Rather oddly, the place smelled of hazelnuts.

"When did you arrive in Boston?"

"About an hour ago."

"What brings you here?"

"I'm here to see a friend."

"Is your husband with you?"

"Yes, William's father is here in Boston."

"You named him after your brother. I remember you said you planned on naming your child after William or Ciaran. Such a fine thing to do. Please let me help you with your coat. How old is William?"

"Three-days."

"A newborn… He's so tiny. I can make tea if you like."

"Tea would be nice."

"I baked *mandlebrot* with roasted hazelnuts this morning."

Myra wasn't sure if the *mandlebrot* were as flavorful as they tasted or she was so hungry anything would have been delicious. She was sitting on one of the chairs at the small table and suddenly felt exhaustion overwhelming her. Her lack of sleep on the train, not eating since she left Philadelphia, and the strength-draining mental tension from not knowing if she could find David was catching up to her. She kept yawning as she sipped her tea.

"Myra, you're tired."

"It's rude of me but would you mind if I lay down? I couldn't sleep on the train and I'm exhausted."

"Of course. Let me hold William while you sleep. He can study with me."

"I'm sorry but William doesn't like anyone else to hold…"

David took William from his mother and cradled him in his left arm. He walked across the room to the tiny desk.

Once seated, he held William against his chest and gently patted him. "Your mom's going to sleep, William. You can work math problems over here with me."

Myra was shocked. Unlike the strangers on the train, William seemed perfectly at ease nestled against his father's chest with his forehead against David's neck.

"Go ahead. Lie down, Myra. William and I have lots to study."

She was so exhausted, her fingers fumbled with her laces while trying to untie her shoes. Myra fell asleep listening to David's quiet chatter as he described infinitesimal calculus problem solving to their son.

When she woke, a number of hours later, she felt refreshed but was alone in the apartment which startled her. She read a note left on the kitchen table which made her laugh. "Mom—I'm taking David shopping. Love, William."

David arrived home a few minutes later with William in one arm, a grocery bag in the other, and an ear to ear smile.

"Sleep well?"

"I did. I'll make dinner."

"Certainly not. You just gave birth to a baby and completed a long journey. You take William. He's probably hungry after all our shopping. Besides, now I get the chance to show off one of the few dishes I can prepare."

Myra nursed William. Meanwhile, David stuffed cabbage leaves with chopped boiled beef seasoned with garlic and black pepper, finely diced onion, chopped flat parsley and cooked rice. Next he chopped tomatoes and put them into a pot with dried oregano, fresh basil, and sliced garlic. Placing the cabbage rolls in a Dutch oven, he covered them with the tomato and herb mixture before closing the oven with a heavy lid. He sliced a small French loaf and put it on the table, along with place settings for each of them. Within twenty-minutes, the apartment was redolent with the scent of garlic, basil and oregano.

"It smells wonderful in here. Where did you learn to cook?"

"At home. When my ma realized I saved enough money to get my own place this year, she and my grandmother taught me how to shop for food and prepare meals. I've learned to be the king of sandwiches. I don't often cook but with company, I thought I would."

There was a loud knock on the door. David rushed to open it. "Here it is, Mr. Kaplan," a young teen said as he handed him a rocking cradle. "And here you are," David said, handing the teen a few coins.

"William, when you're done with dinner, you can try out your new cradle."

"David, you didn't have to…"

"I thought you might need it when William, you, and your husband visit me."

"I see."

He sat on a chair opposite her. "When will William's father be joining you?"

She didn't reply.

"Myra, I said when…"

"He already has." She dropped her eyes to William who was contentedly nursing.

"I don't understand."

"You are his father, David."

David's smile evaporated. His gaze left Myra's eyes and slowly lowered to stare at William.

"My son…"

"David, I'm here because my brother threw us out and we have nowhere else to go."

With a look of astonishment, David said, "Myra—this is my son? William is *our* son?"

"I'm sorry to surprise you like this but all we need is a roof over our heads. I'll start sewing to support William and me. I'll cook for you, clean for you, and we won't be a bother. I give you my word."

"My son." David's eyes were still riveted on William. A slight smile returned to his lips. "Is he intelligent?"

"I don't know yet. He's only a few days old."

"If he's my son he must be." His smile broadened. "No wonder he was paying close attention while I explained how to solve the infinitesimal calculus problems."

"David, please listen to me. We need a place to live. Nothing else. Can we stay with you?"

"This is certainly a surprise; in fact, a bit of a shock. I need some time to think about how this is going to change my life."

"I'm not here to change your life."

David's expression slowly changed from joy to fright, "I must consider my new responsibilities." He stood up. "This could change everything; my school, my future. I'll have to get a full time job to support my family."

"David, please listen to me."

He slowly retreated to a far corner of the apartment as fright etched his face.

"A son … a wife … no time to prepare or plan."

"David, calm down."

"Myra, you've had nine months to prepare for a family. I can't just suddenly become his father."

"I'm not asking you to change anything. I'll take care of William and me. We just need a corner…"

"Privacy. You're a woman. You'll need privacy. We'll have to do something about that."

Myra took William off her breast. He cried as she placed him in the cradle. She stood in front of David. His eyes remained riveted on William.

"David, nothing will change. I'll see to it."

He seemed in a daze.

"But your son … our son."

She used her hands to lift his face. "Look at me." He was trembling and short of breath but shifted his gaze. "David, put your arms around me. I need you to hold me." He slowly complied. She embraced him and he felt his body relax.

"You will continue with college. I'm going to take in some sewing."

"Sewing. I can help with sewing."

"You help by studying. I'll take care of sewing and I'll take care of William."

"But I'm his father. I have to help you take care of him."

"As long as it doesn't get in the way of your studies."

"Myra, you said sewing to make money. I know about business. I can help you."

"That's fine, David. Are you alright now?"

He kissed her cheek. "Is it okay I, you know, kiss you and hold you? We're a family now, right?"

"First, let's see if we can live together to determine if we're a family." She hesitated and added, "And yes you can hold me."

"I'm overwhelmed by all this."

"I see. Perhaps you'd like to go for a walk or something until you pull yourself together."

"A walk might be good."

He still seemed in a daze as he headed out the door.

***

An hour later the apartment door opened. Myra was straightening things in the apartment while William slept in his cradle.

"David, we just need a corner."

Confidence had returned to his demeanor. "I promise I'll learn as fast as I can how to be a proper husband and father."

"Remember what I said… I only need a place to start sewing. I can support William and me. I have some sketches to show people what I can do."

"My parents send money every month to help support me and pay for my college. I tutor the kids at school. Our family will manage just fine until you start your sewing business."

"We're not a family yet."

"We're both responsible for bringing this amazing little man into the world."

"David…"

He placed his hands on either side of her face and his lips on hers.

After a long kiss which made Myra's heart pound, he said, "Yes, we're a family now. We take care of each other. Don't worry, Myra. I'm a responsible man. We'll learn to be a family as a team, you and me. I'll increase the hours I tutor students."

"No, no, no." She stamped her foot. "David Kaplan, listen to me. You will continue in school as if nothing has happened..." David leaned toward her and kissed her again.

After another long kiss, Myra felt her knees getting weak. She pushed him away; she didn't want a life with this Jew, but his kiss was unnerving. "Now you've calmed down so we have to talk. I didn't come here to disrupt your life."

"Last summer, you told me you didn't love me. You also told me people get together to have a family and sometimes fall in love. Our family is in his cradle and I've loved you since our weekend together."

"But David, I don't love you."

"I'll take such good care of you and William that you'll have to love me. And I *will* spend more hours working."

"No! Absolutely not. You must continue at college."

"I can take some odd jobs."

"As long as it doesn't interfere with your school work."

"If I get behind in my classes, Master William, the future scientist, will help me."

What did he say? My son a scientist...

She collapsed into a chair, staring at David.

Of course... He'll go to college like his father. My son will be the first in our family to attend college. David will teach him how to study and become an educated man. No back breaking labor for my son! Should I stay with him? Spend my life with a Jew? Impossible!

"Perhaps I should begin speaking to him in Yiddish so he can learn the language of his ancestors as well." William cooed as if in agreement.

"What? Yiddish?" *Raise William as a Jew? Never!*

Perplexed, Myra said, "David, we'll talk more about this later. You've prepared a lovely meal. Let's eat."

He jumped up and put dinner on the table for them.

"This is delightful," she said, as they finished.

"Grandma Kaplan's recipe."

They ended dinner with more hazelnut *mandlebrot* and tea.

"You have to teach me how to make these."

"I'd love to. They're easy actually."

She smiled at him. "I'll clean up. You study."

He looked at the pile of books on his desk. "Thank you, Myra. I have much to study tonight. If we're a family, shouldn't I help you?"

"Your responsibility is school. Get busy with that. I'll bake a pasty for your midday meal."

"Pasty? I've never heard of a pasty."

"Hear what he said, William? Poor lad has so much schooling but no knowledge of a pasty. We'll have to educate him about them."

After an eventful first day together they got into bed. "I've just given birth and don't want to become pregnant but I can still take care of you with my hands." David started to object but instead moaned as she stroked him.

William's cries woke them around one A.M. "He's probably hungry," Myra said, starting to get up.

David jumped out of bed. "Stay here, I'll get him."

He leaned over and kissed Myra while handing over his son. She nursed William while David quickly fell asleep again.

William, I thought we would come here and I would be taking care of your father so we might have a roof over our heads. It seems like he intends to take care of us as well. I wonder if I should tell him I have no intention of ever marrying him and nine-months ago only wanted his body.

***

Putting his coat on to attend classes the next morning, David said, "My parents are coming to visit in a few weeks. It's Friday so I'll be home around four this afternoon."

"Here's your pasty. You begin eating the end away from your initials."

"Initials?"

"I put your initials on one end; it's the last part you eat because the filling on the initialed end is sweet."

He turned toward the door but quickly spun around.

"Oh, I almost forgot. One of my college mates who graduated last year moved to Independence, Missouri. He sent me a letter asking me to join him and his brother to help run a supply store. I used to work for his father, who financed the Independence store. It's good money and he even offered me part ownership."

"Are you considering it?"

"No, but I thought you might want to know I'm capable of earning a good wage even without a college degree."

He walked over and kissed Myra and William. He paused again at the door. "Don't forget to stop by the print shop and have them make up the advertising flyers I designed. They should help get your sewing business going."

"If they get them done today, William and I will be visiting the neighborhoods you mapped out for us."

***

Myra talked to William as she walked and handed out flyers on a sunny but cool day. "Your father's signs read as if I owned my own dress shop. I'm just a seamstress for hire. I'd be happy to repair torn rags just to earn some coin for us."

William made some cute sounds and wiggled his arms against his blanket.

"I know. Your father has grandiose plans. Truthfully, William, I don't think I know enough to write a simple flyer like this."

Chapter Six: A *Shabbat* Surprise

David arrived home Friday afternoon carrying a bag of groceries. He avoided eye contact with Myra when he greeted her.

"Anything wrong?" She asked?

Still avoiding her gaze, he said, "No. Not a thing. Not a thing's wrong. Why would anything be wrong? I have to get ready for *Shabbat*."

"I put the chicken soup together like you asked; I think it's ready as is the *challah*."

He rushed around the kitchen preparing borscht, and slicing gefilte fish and an apple strudel.

"William is still asleep. What can I do to help?"

"I'll take care of things."

"I can at least set the table. Are you feeling ill? You seem on edge."

"I'm fine."

An hour later they heard a quiet knock.

The color drained from his face.

"David, what's wrong?"

He stood at the kitchen counter, unmoving.

"David..."

"Please answer the door, Myra," he said as he returned to slicing an onion.

A petite, bright eyed little girl with curly blonde hair stood there.

"Hi, I'm Abbey. I'm here to do *Shabbat* with Mr. Kaplan."

"Please come in, Abbey. I'm… Myra."

She bounced into the room carrying a small cloth bag which she placed next to David's desk, took off her coat and placed it on a chair. Her familiarity with the apartment indicated this wasn't her first visit.

"Hi, Mr. Kaplan."

"Hi Abbey," he responded without looking at her.

She sniffed the air. "It smells great in here." Abbey turned to Myra. "Are you going to do *Shabbat* with us?"

"Yes, I guess I am."

Abbey spotted the cradle and ran over. She looked up at Myra. "Is this your baby?"

"Yes. His name is William."

"He's beautiful. Can I hold him?"

"Time to light candles," David said before Myra could answer.

Abbey ran to his side and stood on a chair placed in front of the two *Shabbat* candlesticks. He took a third candle and lit its wick at the wood stove. David handed it to Abbey who used it to light the first candle. She turned and offered the candle to Myra.

"No, you go ahead."

"But every lady is supposed to light a candle," Abbey said. "You just have to hold it so you don't get burned."

Myra smiled as she lit the second candle.

Abbey put her hands over her eyes and recited the blessing with David.

"Good *Shabbos*," Abbey said, opening her arms to David who hugged her firmly. She turned to Myra. "Good *Shabbos*," she repeated, opening her arms to Myra who leaned toward Abbey and hugged her.

David poured glasses of wine for him and Myra. He recited the blessing and sipped the wine.

"How often do you drink?" Myra asked.

"Only on Friday nights and only one glass of wine. My father drank every night and was often drunk on weekends. I decided long ago to minimize my drinking."

David was uncharacteristically quiet during dinner. Abbey told Myra, "My mom and I used to do *Shabbat* but, since she got sick, Mr. Kaplan does *Shabbat* with me; we study together and go for a walk on Saturday morning before he takes me home."

"Is your mom still sick?"

"She died when I was three but I'm five now."

"I'm sorry about your mother. Do you live with your father?"

"I live with my grandfather. He said my father didn't want to be my dad. Mr. Kaplan, do we have a *Parsha* for tonight?"

"Here it is," he said, opening a book.

"A what?" Myra asked.

"Bible reading," David said.

"This *Parsha* says God counted His people. Why would He do that?"

Abbey stared at her lap; deep in thought. She said slowly, "Counting His people…"

"Abbey, do you have something you count?" David asked.

"I have some shells from the ocean. I like to count them."

"Why?"

"Because I like them… That's why God counted His people. He likes them."

"Perfect analysis, Abbey."

Myra smiled. "Excellent lesson, Mr. Kaplan." In a quiet tone she said to David with a nod in Abbey's direction. "Her dad didn't want her…"

"Anyone ready for dessert?" David interrupted.

"Me," yelled Abbey.

***

Following dinner, David played letter and word games with Abbey. *He easily keeps her entertained. She adores him … but why is he still on edge?*

Abbey whispered something to David.

"Myra, would you show Abbey how to hold William?"

"Of course."

Abbey ran to her, sitting on a chair at her side.

"Now, William doesn't always like strangers to hold him so don't feel bad if he doesn't. That's just the way some babies react."

She handed William to Abbey, showing her how to cradle his head in her arm.

He started fussing and crying.

Myra was about to take him back when Abbey, unperturbed by his tears, rocked him and began singing an old Hebrew song about King David but substituted William's name for King David's.

"William, *Melech Yisrael, Chai, chai, vikayom;* William, *Melech Yisrael Chai, chai chai vikayom.*"

The tiny one quieted and his expression brightened. He stared up at Abbey who continued singing and talking to him. She interspersed stories with more songs.

Myra smiled at David who raised his eyebrows. *Look at them... Abbey is entertaining William and holding him so gently.*

Half an hour went by when the little one started to yawn.

"I think he's tired, Abbey," Myra said.

"Thanks for letting me hold him."

"Let's put him to bed."

Abbey carefully slid off the chair and placed him in the cradle, gently tucking a blanket around him. He started to fuss so she started singing again while rocking his cradle. He relaxed and was soon asleep.

After Abbey was put to sleep, Myra sat on the couch next to David. "How well did you know her mother?"

"We grew up near each other."

"I would think she'd want Abbey to spend *Shabbat* with her grandfather."

"He's not religious, I guess."

Myra thought for a while, cuddled close to David, and said, "Thoughtful of you to spend *Shabbat* with her. Abbey's a bright little girl. I'm enjoying having her here, as is William."

He pulled her tight against him. "Her visits mean a lot to me."

He kissed her cheek and said, "There's something concerning Abbey which I need to tell you but I'm not sure how."

"David, I'm so tired. Can it wait?"

He breathed a sigh of relief. "Certainly."

Chapter Seven: Getting Started

After two weeks of passing out her name and address, a few people arrived at the apartment to see Myra's dress designs.

"I'm relieved but still worried as I haven't earned any money since I arrived in Boston and don't know how much longer we can keep living on the money your parents send. Besides, the money they send is supposed to be used for your college expenses."

"When your business grows, we can pay them back. What will you charge for the dresses?"

"Between five and seven-dollars per design. It depends on how complicated the dress is."

A well coifed, but *zaftig*, woman in an expensive looking dress sat down at their kitchen table and looked through

Myra's drawings and the small figures she dressed in doll sized wedding dresses. Myra's hands trembled as she turned the pages of the design book. David noticed the woman arrived in an expensive carriage with driver and attendant.

"These dress designs look sophisticated and elegant. I think my daughter would love one of them. How much money are we talking about?"

"Well..."

David interrupted. "If you wish to have my wife create a custom dress for your daughter it will cost fourteen dollars."

"Fine," the woman said as she paged up and back among Myra's designs.

"How many bridesmaids will she be having?" he asked.

"What?" The woman appeared confused; Myra as well.

"We need to know how many bridesmaids," David continued. "Surely you want the bridesmaids dresses coordinated with the bride's dress."

"Uh ... yes ... yes, of course I do. There will be five bridesmaids."

"Their dresses will be seven dollars each. We'll add a flower girl dress, coordinated with the bridesmaid dresses for three dollars. What type of custom design were you thinking of for yourself?"

"I hadn't thought about it yet."

"Please let us know. My wife feels the mother-of-the-bride dress should be breathtaking without detracting from the bride and her court."

The new client smiled and nodded.

"Depending on the design you prefer, the mother-of-the-bride dress will cost around ten dollars. You can return tomorrow with your daughter to review some designs for each of you as well as the bridesmaids. If you wish to reserve the next seven weeks of my wife's time we'll need ten dollars today. We have other customers coming later this afternoon who may want her time but you've arrived first."

"Ten dollars... Certainly." She dug in her purse and eagerly handed the money to Myra.

"We'll need half the money for the dresses when you settle on the designs."

"Tomorrow at one o'clock again?"

"Perfect. We'll be looking forward to seeing you and meeting your daughter, Mrs. Blumenthal."

David showed Mrs. Blumenthal out and Myra collapsed into a chair.

"I was so nervous I could hardly turn the pages of my design book. How did you know she would be willing to pay so much? Is it because you're a Jew?"

David stared at Myra. Any trace of his previous smile and cheerful humor evaporated. He sat down with furrowed brow, folding his arms against his chest.

Myra said, "Everyone knows Jews are good with money."

"If you think your words are a compliment they're not. We're people just like any other."

"I heard lots of stories when I lived in Ireland."

"But you never met any Jews until you came here."

"I knew one in Ireland."

"Wasn't it my family who paid part of your passage over here?"

"Yes."

"Not to mention the Rabbi's fund for the needy."

"You heard?"

"Word gets around. Just like the unkind words you and your brother said about Jews shortly after you arrived."

"David, I'm sorry."

"Have I ever treated you in an unkind manner?"

"No."

"I remember; you laughed and joked with me our entire weekend together. You also seemed to love being in bed with me."

She closed her eyes and smiled, remembering the weekend. "The entire time we were together you made me feel glad … well … glad I'm a woman."

"And always remember, Myra; your son is half Jewish. When you say bad things about Jews, you're talking about William, not to mention the man who is working hard to take care of you both."

His last remarks hurt and made her eyes damp. "I'm sorry, David. You're so different from what I expected."

"You mean different from what you expected a Jew to be?"

"I said I'm sorry."

"Don't forget to apologize to William."

She pleaded, "Please forgive me for what I said David ... and William. You've been nothing but kind and welcoming."

She wiped away a tear and said, "Can we change the subject and talk about the dresses?"

David again crossed his arms over his chest and nodded without smiling, so she continued, "I'm worried. It will be too much work to complete in seven weeks."

"You'll get it done."

"I'm the one who has to do the work and I say it can't be done."

"You need some help and I know where to get it. I know business and I'll take care of it."

He stood up. "I believe it's been eight days since William's birth. I'd like to take him for a walk."

"A walk with his father. How thoughtful. I'll get him ready."

***

The following morning, David got out of bed before Myra awakened and was at the harbor where immigrants were disembarking from their ships. He held a sign which read, "Seamstresses needed."

He gave his address to a number of women who were standing in line to check through customs and told them to be at his apartment the following morning.

A woman who appeared to be in her early thirties approached him. She used a crutch under her arm, taking long steps with her good leg and shorter, halting steps with the other.

"Excuse me, sir. I'm a seamstress and I design fashionable dresses as well."

David saw she was wearing a simple but stylish dress.

"I have a book with my designs." She removed it from a cloth bag.

"Let me see." David turned a few pages. This woman's designs were at least as fine as Myra's and may even have been better.

"I can make any woman's body look attractive in one of my dresses. It's a matter of the right shape and details which attract the eye."

"Your designs aren't necessarily symmetric."

"I can make them symmetric if you like, sir."

"Not necessary. These are most fetching. I would never imagine lines like this… My wife needs your talent in her business. I'm David Kaplan. What brings you to America?"

"I thought I might have a better chance to get hired as a dress designer. Where I come from, no one wanted to hire a cripple. People are ignorant and think having a cripple around will bring them bad luck. I've heard things are different here."

"Where are you staying?"

"I don't know yet, Mr. Kaplan."

"I live in the university district. There are plenty of rooms available. When you're done here, I'll get a driver to take us there so you can meet my wife. We'll help you find a room."

"You are most kind, sir."

An officious looking little man in a dark uniform with shiny brass buttons approached them.

He sneered at the crippled woman. "I'm sorry miss. We can't afford to support more crippled indigents in our country. You'll have to get back on the ship and they'll take you back where you came from."

The woman appeared as if she had just been given a death sentence. Her head drooped, her brow furrowed above tearing eyes and a trembling chin; she slowly turned to drag herself back to the ship.

"A cripple? Indigent?" David said, forcefully and rapidly, in a voice tinged with anger. The woman and the uniformed man turned in his direction. "Are you mad, sir? How dare you call her indigent? Don't you recognize one of France's finest dress designers, Miss Marie-Louise Moreau?"

"Dress designer? France? I didn't know… Sorry, sir."

"Don't apologize to me, my good man. Tell *her*."

"My deepest apology, Miss Moreau," he said as he removed his hat revealing a shiny bald head which he briefly nodded in her direction. "I didn't know who you were. Please come this way, ma'am. This is a shorter line for the first class passengers. You don't have to stand in a long line with them other folk."

"Thank you kindly," she said, regaining her composure.

"When you're finished registering, if you would be so kind madam, point out your trunk, and I'll have it brought over for you."

David stood next to her while she waited.

"A kind gesture, Mr. Kaplan. Thank you," she said, wiping her eyes while standing as tall as her crooked body would allow.

"My father taught me the only cripples in the world were people who couldn't see past someone's physical disabilities. My mother walked with a limp all her life but it never slowed her down."

"My slow walk won't get in the way of designing dresses you'll be proud to sell."

David saw her sadness was now replaced with strength as she most likely contemplated the possibilities a future in America might bring. With a sparkle in her eyes and in a playful voice, she asked, "Does your help mean I have to change my name to Marie-Louise Moreau?"

"What's your real name?"

"Margarita TelleMontaine-De-La-Campana."

"If you wish to have your children correctly spell their last name before adulthood, maybe you should."

***

After reviewing Margarita's designs, Myra was thoroughly impressed but staring daggers at David which he went out of his way to ignore. Before she could communicate the source of her anger, the client and her daughter arrived.

"My daughter is afraid she doesn't have enough curves to make a dress look attractive."

Margarita used the table to push herself up to a standing position. "Do you like the way this dress looks on me?"

"It is certainly stylish," the bride-to-be said.

"I have a body which has all the curves of a fence post; but the design causes your eye to see form. The dress Myra is recommending will be perfect for your figure. With her permission, I recommend a few small changes."

Myra nodded. Margarita leaned over the table and, with a few pen strokes, added details which awed the two clients.

"And for the bridesmaid and flower girl dresses?"

Sitting down again, Margarita grabbed two sheets of paper and, while referencing Myra's bridal design, quickly sketched complimentary dresses.

Myra and Margarita measured the two broadly smiling clients.

"Here is the advance money we discussed."

"We'll need the bridesmaids and flower girl for measurement."

"I'll have them stop by this week."

***

"Here is payment for your help today," David said to Margarita who then asked about finding a room.

"I think you should take this one."

"What are you talking about?" Myra queried.

"Come with me, Myra."

He walked down the hall and fished a key out of his pocket. Opening the door to an apartment with two bedrooms, a spacious living room and a separate kitchen at the back, he said, "This is available and I think we should take it. You'll have enough room for your dress making business, we'd have our own bedroom, and we can use the second bedroom for a study space for William and me. We might let you use part of it for doing designs and running your business, but I'll have to check with our son first."

"Why do we need all this space?"

"For the new workers. They'll be starting tomorrow."

"New workers?"

"Ten women will be here tomorrow. You need to interview them and decide how many you want to hire."

She silently stared at him for a long time.

"Myra, what's wrong?"

"Every time I have what seems like an insurmountable problem are you going to solve it?"

"No! Definitely not… Sometimes William will provide a solution. We're both engineers and engineers are problem solvers."

"I thought he was going to be a scientist."

"He can't make up his mind so I told him if he learned enough mathematics he could learn to engage in both…"

Myra reached up and put her hand over his mouth, shaking her head.

"David, you're making me dizzy. You and I are completely different. The only reason William and I came here was to have a roof over our heads. Nothing more."

She let her hand drop to her side and moved back a couple steps.

"This apartment has a roof to cover your heads. It just has more space underneath it. You'll need it for your business."

"My business? I don't know the first thing about running a business. I'm just an ignorant seamstress who only learned the basics of reading."

"I know business so I'll take care of that. Meanwhile, you can start reading my history books. I'll give you a dictionary to learn new words. You'll be learning history and increasing your vocabulary so you won't be ignorant and your reading will improve."

Myra shouted, "David, stop problem solving!"

She turned away from him, stiffened her arms, and stamped the floor. He gave her a few moments before putting his hands on her shoulders and gently messaging them.

Myra enjoyed the massage for a minute without talking.

"Thank you, David. It's so relaxing but… Oh nice… Listen; if I hire people I'll have to pay them… I'm uneducated. I can hardly do sums. How will I pay them?"

"I'll teach you. When I'm not around, William will check your sums to make sure they're correct."

Chapter Eight: Confrontations

Myra giggled but turned to face him. Her eyes were sending daggers his way again. She spoke slowly and without smiling. "I'm not a good person. Lord knows I've done terrible things… But what you've done to William makes us more than even. What you did was cruel and marks him for life. Anyone who sees he's been circumcised…"

"You knew I was and it didn't seem to get in your way."

"I'm talking about something else."

"No, Myra. After a brief weekend of getting to know me, you came here believing I would take you in. You were correct. It frightened me at first but, with your help, I'm learning a husband and father's responsibilities. I'm willing to put up with your not loving me hoping one day you will… But you need to know when it comes to William or any other children we have, I'll do what I think best for them; I will do what's necessary to raise my children to be their best at whatever they decide to do."

"Even if it angers me?"

"I will *always* carefully consider your thoughts but have no doubt; any children will come first."

She turned sideways away from him and crossed her arms.

I should take William and leave. How could he have the nerve to put a lifetime brand on William? Who does he think he is?

She briefly glanced at him and looked away.

He's William's father. But my son is not to be raised as a Jew. I won't allow it. Jews are hated all over the world. What would my family think? What would my departed brother and sister think?

She looked over her shoulder at David a second time.

Look at him standing there. Surely he loves me and takes good care of me. William takes to him… But what kind of life will my son have when raised as a Jew? Ending up like David? Might not be too bad. NO! I can't do this. So what if William turns into a man like David. Raising him as a Jew would betray my family… Still…

She turned to face him, putting her hands on her hips. "I should take William and leave." After a long pause she continued, "But if we stay… Will he become educated like you?"

"Of course."

"Will he love and respect his uneducated mother?"

"He will be taught to love and respect her as much as I do."

"Accomplished how?"

"By word, example, and consequence."

"Consequence?"

"When I was a young boy, I made some foolish remark to my father about my mother's lack of knowledge. I was about ten and should have known better. The back of my head hurt for a week."

She smiled briefly before becoming serious again. "You don't dare lay a hand on William."

"Then pray he's not like me and, when young, prone to saying something without thinking. We'll raise him with good values but if he ever disrespects you… Believe me. It won't happen more than once."

Myra stared at him.

What more could I want … other than his not being a Jew.

Miss Campana entered the open apartment door. "Excuse me but your son is crying."

"Thank you, Miss Campana."

"David, I have a lot of anger in me. We haven't even discussed what religion William should follow, which will be one bruising fight, I guarantee."

"We don't have to decide today."

"You don't really know me even a little bit. I can be a terrible person when I need to."

"William and I think you're the best. In fact, this morning he told me he wanted to go with me to the docks to help me look for workers but didn't want to get too far from his next meal."

She didn't react for a moment; then laughed.

Myra became serious again. "Why are you doing all this? I'm never going to marry you."

He took a deep breath. "I'm doing it for someone I love and because William needs to see an example of a good father and husband. Maybe … just maybe … you'll find you love me one day and we *will* get married."

Myra sighed and glanced around the apartment. "I think we should take this place." She walked back to the smaller apartment with David following.

She picked up William, sat on a rocking chair, and prepared to nurse him.

"It will be a nice place to receive your parents. Has William seen our new home?"

"For Heaven's sake, Myra; it was his idea."

Myra laughed, shaking her head.

***

Two months later, Myra's conscience was tormenting her for not telling David how she used him the previous summer. If he noticed how uncomfortable she was, he gave no indication as his nose was buried in his school books.

"David, I have some things I want to tell you. When you can take a break, please join me on the couch."

"Something wrong?"

She patted the cushion next to her. When she spoke her voice quivered and she couldn't look directly at him.

"I was sewing with Anna Lombardi last summer, the day you picked up some shirts. She told me about you. Anna mentioned your intelligence and good nature. Those things and your good looks impressed me. I planned my work week so I would have an excuse to invite you to our apartment. I knew ahead of time Colin would be staying with friends."

David tilted his head slightly.

"My intention was to take advantage of your young age so you would get me pregnant. I was desperate to bring children into the world to replace William and Ciaran. The time you and I spent together was the best time I'd ever experienced until I moved in with you; and I'm not just talking about your gentleness in bed. I enjoyed our conversations and your hard work. However, after the first weekend, I did not intend to see you again."

He folded his arms across his chest and leaned away from her.

"You chose me like a farmer chooses a bull to breed?"

"I chose you with the reasons most woman use."

"Except love and a desire to raise the child with his father?"

Still not able to look at him, she said, "Like I told you; I'm not a good person. After the Famine, I was obsessed with a desire to replace Ciaran and William."

"When you want another child will you go looking for a different bull to service you?"

Myra stared at him. Every bit of joy which usually illuminated his expression was gone; having been replaced with a dark, icy look which could have chilled an exploding volcano.

"David, you're not being fair. Having one child without being married has caused me enough grief."

"I'm only good enough to give you what you wanted to have a child but not good enough to marry?"

"Please, David. Try to understand how desperate I was to become pregnant. I'm a product of the Famine. You don't know what it was like and how it affected people."

"I'm going out." He stood up and reached for his jacket.

"David, I'll do everything I can to make you happy."

"Except, of course, marry a Jew or consider raising our son as a Jew?"

She stared at the floor.

He put his hands on his hips, leaned near her face, and shouted, "Answer me, Myra. You'd do anything to make me happy except those things?"

The weight of his anger was crushing her. She said weakly, "You're a good man; but—"

He interrupted, shouting again, "Good enough to father your child. Good enough to take you in when your own brother threw you out. Good enough to help you with your dress business, committed to taking care of you and helping you raise William… But still, I'm *not* good enough to marry?"

He stormed out of the apartment as Myra dissolved into sobs.

***

"William," she said as she cradled the little one in her arms, "your father is furious with me and deservedly so. The way I used him during our first weekend was cruel. Your mother is a terrible person."

She stopped talking to sob for a bit. Myra ran her finger down William's cheek.

"But what if you *are* as intelligent as your father? It would certainly be best to have him around to help raise you. Unlike me, he would know what books you should read to educate you and prepare you for college. Being raised by an educated man would be so good for you." She put his head on her shoulder and began patting him. "Honestly, having an educated man in my life is proving to be good for me as well."

She wiped her tears away.

"I pray he'll let us stay. Certainly, I couldn't run the dress business without him. Somehow I need to do something important, something he values, to keep him happy so he lets us stay here. I'm not sure how. I have to think hard… Certainly, I won't marry him."

***

Two hours later, David returned to the apartment, his face still dark.

"I apologize for shouting. It was uncalled for but you really hurt me, Myra."

She stood up. "David—"

"—Let me finish. You are the mother of my child and I care about both of you."

"David, I want to make you happy but I came here looking for nothing but a tiny corner for William and me. It's become so much more. Our lives have intertwined in a way I could never have imagined."

She firmly gripped his shoulders.

Looking in his eyes, she continued, "I could have ended up on the street and having to give our blessed son to an orphanage. Instead of trying to scratch out a meager existence, we've never been hungry, and you take care of the dress business. You make sure I always have coins in my purse … not to mention providing a loving home for William and me. Despite your having branded our son as a

Jew without discussing it with me and how terrible you make me feel when you're angry with me…"

She paused and stared at the floor. "I've been thinking."

Her throat tightened and she closed her eyes. Choking on the words, she said, "I'm willing to help you raise William as a Jew."

"Are you certain?"

She nodded.

David leaned toward her, kissed her forehead, and briefly embraced her before walking over to the kettle they kept on the stove.

"Myra, would you like a cup of tea?"

"Yes." She collapsed into a chair at the kitchen table like a deflated balloon. *I've just betrayed my upbringing.* Myra eyed him . *You'll never know how painful this is, Mr. Kaplan.*

There was a loud knock at the door.

David said, "My parents."

***

"Mom and Dad, you remember Myra?"

"Myra, how are you dear?"

"Fine thank you, Mrs. Kaplan."

Hannah glanced around the apartment.

"You're keeping your apartment neat and tidy, David."

"Thank you, Mother. Please join us for tea at the kitchen table."

After Myra poured tea for everyone, Dillon Kaplan said, "Myra, your child has lovely features. I heard you had a baby…"

Silence enveloped the room. First his mother's expression went blank, followed by his father's before they slowly shifted to obvious discomfort as they gazed from William to their son.

David ended the awkward silence. "He's *our* son."

Hannah Kaplan's jaw dropped. "I'm sorry. You said?"

"Myra is holding our son, William."

Mrs. Kaplan, visibly shaken, said, "David, no." She began to tremble.

"Calm down, Mother."

Dillon Kaplan grabbed his wife's upper arm to steady her as her face went ashen. "Are you sure it's yours?"

"Of course. Look at him, Father. He looks just like me."

After another long and awkward silence, Dillon asked, "Are you married?"

"Not yet."

Hannah appeared relieved. "Good, you don't have to stay with her."

Myra felt a knot in her stomach.

David said, "Leave the mother of my child? I was raised with better values than to abandon them."

"She's not Jewish so the child's not Jewish," Hannah said.

"He's half Jewish Mother, and we'll be raising him as a Jew. What was good enough for Abraham and Sarah is good enough for me."

Standing up and stepping toward Myra, Dillon shook a fist in her face. "You God-damned whore! You're ruining my son's life."

David's expression turned grim; clenching his fists and stepping in front of his father, he growled, "One more disparaging word about Myra and I'll throw you out of here … bodily if necessary."

"David, calm down," Myra whispered putting a hand on his shoulder. His dark expression and fierce tone frightened her.

His father put his hands up in a gesture of surrender, but he maintained an expression of fury.

Hannah said, "I'm trying to remain calm but it's difficult. Don't be a fool, David. Michal is waiting at the hotel with Sarah. Her father owns a factory in town here. You marry her and you'll go to work for him after college. We planned to bring you back to the hotel with us to have a chance to get to know her."

Dillon said, "Her parents and your parents have made an agreement. Surely you wouldn't embarrass us like this. We have a Jewish girl for you to marry so you can begin a Jewish family. Within the next year or so, we're moving here as well to expand your uncle's factory."

David put his arm around Myra. "Give my apology to Michal but this is my family. If you want to be part of it, you'll accept us."

His father rapidly shook his head from side to side, put his hands up and waved them in front of his face as if trying to ward off an evil presence. He turned away. "No! Never! She must have tricked you."

"Do you honestly believe you raised a son so ignorant he did it with a girl and didn't realize she might become pregnant? I took a chance because as soon as I met her I knew Myra was the right person for me. I couldn't imagine a better mother for my children."

Myra was immediately proud. She stood straighter as she regarded David.

"Hannah, we've raised a son who's twisted our values and used them to father a child with a *goy*. Let's get out of here."

"Dillon, we need to talk. We shouldn't leave on angry terms."

His father's voice increased in volume. "He's decided to leave our family and ignore our heritage. He's made his choice. He's dead to us. We'll sit *Shiva* for him."

Dillon, red-faced with anger, and Hannah, in tears, stormed out of the apartment.

Myra's eyes were wet. "What is *Shiva?*"

"It's the Jewish mourning ritual which takes place when a family member dies."

Myra's shoulder's drooped. "Oh, David... I appreciate what you said about me but I've cost you your family."

He turned to Myra, putting his hands on either side of her face. "I was part of this. I didn't have to do it with you. No one forced me; besides, you brought me my son."

She shook her head. "And now I've brought sorrow."

"It was their choice."

"My coming here poisoned your family against you." She placed William in his cradle.

"Myra, did you ever stop to consider that the Lord may have put us together for a good reason that we won't even know about until sometime in our future.?"

"David, you're talking nonsense."

"Why should I get pleasure out of your mere presence? You enter the room and it lights up. Why can I recall every moment of our first weekend together? Even now … your smile … the sound of your laughter … thrills me. Why has it been so easy for me to adjust to becoming a father, having a newborn and his mother in my life? We don't know but, in time, I'm certain the Lord will show us why He put us together. For now, blessed Myra, you make my life worth living."

She shook her head. "I'm not blessed anything and we'll be punished for what we did. Of that I'm certain."

He wrapped his arms around her and held her tight. She rested her head on his shoulder.

"Is this how love begins?" he said.

"Forget love. We need to figure out how we'll pay for your college if they stop giving you school money."

"Perhaps we should take the Mandel brothers' suggestion and move to Independence."

***

Sarah appeared at their door later the same day.

"Hello Myra. Hello David. I'm supposed to give you this letter and leave immediately but I'd like to visit."

"Please come in," Myra said as Sarah handed the letter to David.

He quickly read it and ripped it in half. "They're cutting me off. No more school money."

"William's awake," Sarah said. "Can I hold him?"

Myra nodded so she picked him up.

"He's so precious." She slowly twisted her body side to side as she cradled William in her arms while gazing into his shiny eyes. "He has David's eyes and Myra's warm smile."

William cooed as if he understood her.

"Hi William, I'm your Aunt Sarah."

"We were about to fix something to eat. Would you like to stay awhile?" Myra asked.

"I'd love to," she said, not taking her eyes off William.

On their way to the kitchen, Myra whispered to David, "Your sister acts as though she has Heaven in her arms."

He watched as Sarah started singing to William while swaying to and fro. "She *is* holding Heaven in her arms."

"I can hold him so you can eat," Myra said as she put dinner on the table.

She replied rapidly, "No. No. I'm fine. William and I can manage."

His parents exchanged a smile.

After dinner, Sarah put William in his cradle and helped Myra with cleanup. He started to cry so David picked him up. The tiny one quieted while his father talked to him and rocked him.

Myra smiled broadly. "Since the moment we arrived, David has had a calming effect on William. You should be proud of your brother. He takes such good care of us."

"We're moving to Boston for Father's new job in a year or so. Can I come and visit?"

"Your parents may try to stop you."

"When needed, I can be tough like my big brother and do what I think best instead of what others think."

"We'd be honored to have you visit. I'm going to bathe William. Would you like to help?"

"Of course."

Chapter Nine: More about Abbey

The week following his parents' visit, during David's Saturday morning walk with Abbey, he discovered an artist and invited him back to their apartment.

"I've asked Mr. Donovan to create a portrait of Abbey and William."

"Lovely," Myra said.

Donovan said, "If you'll place them near each other, I can draw the portrait so it will appear as if Abbey is holding William."

"Fine," David said as Myra nodded agreement and placed the two next to each other. Abbey flattened her dress and smoothed her top while Myra brushed her hair. David buried himself in his studies.

After an hour of work, the artist said, "You have handsome children, ma'am, although I have to say they both favor their father."

Myra stood behind him to examine his work. Her jaw dropped. She glanced from the artist's work to the children and then David.

Why didn't I see it sooner? Abbey's features are a clear copy of David's. It couldn't be. He'd have to have been around thirteen.

"When were you going to tell me?" Myra said in an anger-tinged voice after David returned from taking Abbey back to her grandfather.

"Tell you what?"

"About your daughter."

The color drained from David's face as he slumped onto their couch. "Since the first *Shabbat* you and I shared, I've been trying to think of a way to tell you."

Hands on hips, Myra said, "How about 'Myra, I have a daughter'?"

"I didn't know how you'd react. I was afraid if I told you, I would destroy what we've started."

"For Heaven's sake David, isn't it obvious how much I love children?"

"It's obvious how much you love our child and how well you treat Abbey."

Myra sat on the couch, body stiffened, and folding her arms across her chest. "David, I see how you act around William and Abbey. There's little difference and they both adore you. Abbey is always looking for your approval."

David stared at the floor. She continued, "Any other children I should know about?"

He shook his head.

"Since our first weekend, I was in pain with guilt for taking advantage of your youth but it turns out you experienced the bedroom with someone before me. I foolishly believed your story about learning from a married cousin. Abbey's mother told you what she liked, I suppose."

"She did."

"How did it happen?"

"We were playmates almost as soon as my family came over from Ireland. Abbey's grandmother worked seven days a week to make ends meet. Running around in the rain one day, I tripped and fell into a mud puddle the size of a bath tub. Abbey's mom, Shayna, tried to grab me but instead fell in as well. We went back to her apartment and decided to bathe each other and wash our clothes. We used soapy cloths on each other; discovering our bodies were sufficiently developed to cause wonderful sensations. Within a few weeks, touching turned to sex."

"Do your parents know?"

"No. When her mother realized she was pregnant, Shayna was kept hidden until Abbey arrived. Someone in their family worked with asbestos when Shayna was young. Her mother and she died from it."

"Asbestos?"

"It's been a well-known cause of sickness since Roman times when being sentenced to the asbestos mines was used as a form of capital punishment. I learned about it in a history class."

"I see."

"When Abbey's mother realized she wasn't long for the world, she and her grandfather found me here in Boston. She started dropping off Abbey every Friday night so our daughter would be comfortable around me."

"David, did you love Shayna?"

"We were kids. I loved how she made my body feel."

"Does Abbey know you're her father?"

"No."

"Did you ever consider taking her in, once her mother died?"

"Shayna's family hated me. They didn't want me anywhere near Abbey."

"You didn't answer my question."

"I would have loved to take her in but it never became an issue."

"When I think of all the agony I went through, plus the guilt I endured because of the secrets I kept from you; while you neglected to tell me about a living, breathing, five-year-old secret."

"Myra…"

"David, whether she knows it or not, you will continue to treat Abbey as your daughter."

"Of course."

Myra sat up straight. "One day … one day soon … you'll tell precious Abbey who her father is and why he hasn't been part of her life. You need to start contemplating how you'll discuss it."

"I will, Myra." He smiled at her. "Your vocabulary is improving. Contemplating is a good word."

She held her nose high and said, "My son the scientist has been teaching me language skills."

***

A few months later, David opened the door to the apartment on a Friday morning. Abbey stood there while an old man with snow white hair and beard stood just behind her. He coughed violently into a bloodstained handkerchief. Abbey held a large cloth bag in one hand and a letter in the other. Her cheeks were tear streaked.

"Abbey, what's the matter, sweetness?" She reached out so David picked her up. She buried her face in his shoulder and cried.

"Morning, David. I'm sorry to have to do this, but I'm dying of bleeding lungs. Abbey's all yours now. Please take care of her. She's been the jewel of my life."

"Please come in, Mr. Liechtenstein." The old man shook his head, briefly touched Abbey and walked away.

David picked up her bag and carried Abbey to the couch, placing her on his lap. Her body quaked with sobs while her arms were tight around David.

"Calm down and tell me what's going on."

"Grandfather said this is for you. He said goodbye to me and said he was sick and I wouldn't see him again."

David opened the letter.

"David, time to be a man and take care of your daughter. My lungs are going bad and the doctor says I won't live much longer. With Abbey's blessed mother gone since she was three, you're all she has left. Please do the right thing and make her part of your life."

"Grandfather said if you and Myra don't want me, I have to go to an orphanage."

"No! Never. Mark my words, Abbey. As long as I have a breath in my body, you will never see the inside of an orphanage. Erase any such thoughts from your mind. This is your home now."

Abbey wiped away a tear. "Are you sure?"

"Abbey, I'm your father. This is your home now."

Abbey's expression went momentarily blank. She slowly smiled and said, "One time I had a happy dream that you and Myra were my mom and dad."

"No more dreaming."

"But I thought you didn't want me."

"When you're older I'll tell you what happened but I love you and certainly want you living with us. And so did your mother. That's why she wanted you here every *Shabbat.* She wanted us to get to know each other so if anything happened to your grandfather, I'd take care of you."

Abbey didn't seem reassured.

"Sweetness, see the room over there? A minute ago it was my study but now it's your bedroom."

"Really? You think Myra will want me here?"

"She's delivering dresses now but I know she will... She adores you. It's *Shabbat* this evening. Would you like to go shopping for our *Shabbat* meal?"

Abbey nodded.

"Miss Campana, Abbey and I are going out. Please keep an eye on the girls and William for me."

***

Myra arrived home, surprised to find Abbey was already in the apartment.

"You're here early."

"I went shopping. We bought food and …" She turned to David and whispered, "What are those smelly, leafy things called?"

"Herbs."

"Yes, those herbs. He said you could teach me to make cottage pie."

"Certainly. David, why are your study materials on the kitchen table."

"I'll be working there until I can make a space in our bedroom."

He gave the letter to Myra who sat on their couch to read it.

Abbey said, "You should see my new bed."

"New bed?"

"Dad bought it for me when we were out. A nice man delivered it."

"Dad?"

"I told her."

Myra grinned. "Welcome home, Abbey." She picked up Abbey and put her on her lap. "I know William's needs and I have a routine with him. You'll have to tell me what a big girl like you needs. Will you help me with that?"

"Sure."

***

David returned from his Friday afternoon class.

"Dad," Abbey said excitedly, "we're eating cottage pie for dinner. I washed the carrots and potatoes and mushrooms. I tried to peel the onions but they made me cry. Myra said I'm a real good potato masher and garlic smasher."

"You worked hard today, Abbey," Myra said. "I'm sure David—Dad will find an extra fun activity for tonight because you helped me so."

***

After putting the children to bed, Myra, across the couch from David, sat stiffly with arms folded across her chest. "I'm a nervous wreck just thinking about becoming Abbey's mom."

"Does she belong here?"

"Of course. I'm not worried about her. I'm worried about me. What if she asks me a question I can't answer? What if I make a mistake?"

"You will make mistakes. We'll both make them but she'll know it doesn't mean we don't love her any less. Think of all the fun you two experienced on *Shabbat* for the last few months."

"You're right. I have to calm down."

"You'll be fine."

"That precious girl deserves better than fine."

"How did it go while I was in class?"

"I got teary at one point because her laughter and sparkling eyes reminded me so much of Ciaran." Myra tucked a handful of hair behind her ear. "I told her I was teary from peeling onions."

"This will be a tremendous extra burden on you."

"I know."

"Shall we talk about it?"

"Certainly. We'll discuss how she'll be made a part of our family; whether she'll stay with us is not a subject for discussion."

"We have so much to do some days."

"*You* insisted, the children come first. One thing happened today which you need to improve."

"Tell me."

"When Abbey tells you she helped me with sewing, preparing dinner, or anything else, you go out of your way to let her know how much you appreciate her effort."

"I will Myra… I need to get my new office space organized."

"David! You're not listening to me. Why do you think she told you what she'd accomplished the minute you walked in tonight?"

"I don't know. Maybe she wanted me to know she was busy."

"Wrong. She told you because she wants you to be proud of her. You ignored her."

David stared at the floor. "Oh my God… I did."

"That will not happen again. She's your—our daughter and deserves better."

"Okay. I'll tell her at breakfast. Now, about my office…"

"You're Mr. Problem Solver. Figure it out. I didn't mention it before but I'm appalled your own daughter needed a place to live after her mother died and you didn't provide it."

"Until Shayna found out she was dying, she and her family wanted nothing to do with me. Until you arrived, my time with Abbey was the highlight of my life." David grinned broadly. "And now blessed Myra will be her mother." He leaned into her and kissed her.

"Are you arguing because of me?" Abbey stood in the doorway to her bedroom; she frowned and her lower lip quivered.

"Come over here, sweetness," Myra said. When she was close enough, Myra picked her up and placed Abbey on her lap, keeping an arm around the five-year-old.

"We're just making some plans on how we're going to be living together as a happy family."

"With me?"

"Of course. In fact, seeing as he bought you a new bed today, I think Dad should take you shopping for a dresser to keep your clothing neat."

"I don't think I ever had one of those." She leaned her head on Myra's chest briefly, sat up, and said, "I have a question. When you're at work, where will I stay? Some babysitters are mean."

"I work here in the apartment. You and William will be with me all day long except when you're in school."

"Okay, but if I don't feel good, who's going to hold me?"

"One of us will hold you for as long as you want. Do you agree, Mr. Problem Solver?"

"As long as she wants."

Abbey said, "What should I do to make a happy family?"

"You can help me around the apartment and"—Myra looked at David—"you can be a big sister to William."

"His big sister?"

"David's your dad and William's dad. That makes you a sister."

"David's my dad and William's my brother; so you'll be my mom?"

Myra tightened her embrace around her and nodded.

Abbey stared at William's cradle, then asked, "Mom, will you teach me how to be a big sister?"

"Of course."

"Dad, what can we do to make a happy family?"

"We'll continue to study together, go for walks, and when I arrive home from school you need to tell me all about what you did that day."

A tear ran down Myra's cheek.

"Mom, why are you crying?"

"This is happy crying. No one ever called me mom before. Let's get you back in bed and I'll tell you a story about a wonderful little girl named Ciaran."

Myra leaned over and kissed David's cheek. "Excuse me but my daughter needs me."

Chapter Ten: Myra's Parents

Late the following summer, an Irish couple, recently arrived in Boston, were aware their daughter and her child lived in the university district.

"John, there she is. She's holding hands with a little boy and girl."

"She's walking up the block, Darcy. We better hurry if we're going to talk to her."

When the threesome disappeared into a building; the couple ran to catch up.

"Darcy, read the sign in the window."

"Myra's Frocks and Dresses. She must have her own business."

Myra was shocked to find them standing on her doorstep. She reached out and hugged her parents. William and Abbey stood on either side just behind her.

"This is Abbey and this is William. Children, these are my parents. Please come in and sit down. How did you find me?" Myra sat on a chair while the children sat on the floor at her side.

"You sent a letter to Colin letting him know you were safe."

Darcy said, "You look well."

"Thank you, Mother."

"Colin told us you refused to have the father involved in raising your son."

"His father is with us now. He's out on an errand."

"Have you married him?"

Myra sat back in her chair and crossed her arms across her chest. "Abbey, please take William to your room and close the door. We have some adult things to talk about."

"Yes, Mom."

"She called you mom," Darcy said.

"William's father is also her father and I've agreed to be her mother."

Darcy's eyebrows went up. "Raise someone else's child?"

"I love children. Abbey and I are as close as if I was her birth mother. She's nearly the same age Ciaran would have been. What brings you here?"

John said, "We wanted to see you and talk some sense into you and William's father."

Myra shook her head. "You wouldn't like him."

"Why not?" her father said.

"There are a number of reasons."

Darcy leaned toward Myra. "If he's any kind of a man, he could at least marry you and make an honest woman out of you."

"He's Jewish."

Her parents recoiled in horror.

Twisting his face as if his mouth was filled with something bitter, her father said, "You did it with a Jew?"

Myra nodded.

"Does his family know?"

"Yes. And except for his sister, they've rejected us and stopped paying for David's college."

David arrived and was introduced to Myra's angry-faced parents. John crossed his arms when David offered to shake his hand.

In a voice dripping with sarcasm, he said, "So you got two women with child. My daughter is taking care of both but you don't respect her enough to marry her?"

"We may not be married yet but we're still a family," David said. "I take care of them just like any husband and father would. We have sufficient income from my tutoring and Myra's dress business so I'm still completing college. I'll be able to secure a well-paying job when I graduate. Even now, Myra, Abbey, and William don't lack for anything."

"Well, clever Jew with all the answers, if you're a family, why don't you at least take the little bastards over to church to have them baptized?"

"Father, stop it." She could see David's clenched fists and dark expression; how he was about to lose control.

"It's the least you could do for my daughter."

"We've decided to raise the children as Jews," Myra said.

Silence enveloped the room.

Finally Darcy said, "Myra… No."

John turned his icy gaze to Myra. "So you continue to be a whore. Did you tell your Jew you were a whore back in Ireland?"

The blood in Myra's veins turned cold and her heart felt like it was in her throat. Terrified, she spun her head in David's direction. His scowl changed to a smile as he put his arm around her, pulled her close, and calmly replied, "I know everything about her and still love her. Thank you for visiting but it's time you left."

At the front door, Darcy asked, "Myra, may I come by to see you before I go shopping this Saturday?"

She eyed her suspiciously but said, "Yes, Ma."

***

Myra closed the door behind her parents. "Why didn't you tell them it's my fault we're not married?"

"They don't need to know who or why."

"Abbey, you and William can come in here now. Please play with your brother while Dad and I talk."

"I'm teaching him the alphabet," Abbey said as she started stacking his wood blocks, each of which was carved with a letter on its side.

David and Myra flopped onto their couch. Myra whispered, "David, Father was correct about what I did in Ireland. I'm pure evil. A friend and I used our bodies to get food for our families."

David's jaw dropped. He took a deep breath. "I have no concept of what horrors the Famine caused … what it drove people to do." He put an arm around her shoulders. "Your mother is an astounding person, Abbey and William. She is truly an angel. Both of you come over here and give her a hug." The two little ones ran over and did as he asked.

William went back to his blocks but looked up long enough to say, "Angel. My mommy angel."

"David, I used my body—"

"—A powerful angel," David interrupted as he wrapped both arms around her. "She would do anything to make sure her family was cared for. William, Abbey, and I have God's own angel to love."

He tightened his embrace. "I'm so proud of you."

"David—" Her speech was cut off by a long kiss.

"I don't know if I would have the strength to do what you did." He put his lips on hers again. "Yes, truly an angel you are."

With another kiss, she held him tightly. "I dreaded the day you might find out. Now it's come and you still love me."

"More than ever."

"My hands are shaking from my parents' visit but I'm going to make dinner. What would you like?"

Before David could answer, William interrupted, "Colcannon, please Mommy Angel."

His father said, "I think a strong suggestion has been made."

"And I suppose you want barley pudding for dessert, young man?"

He got to his feet and jumped in a circle while repeating, "Yes please."

"I'll bring the barley to a boil but you'll have to mix in the sugar and spices."

He looked up at David with sparkling eyes and a huge grin, "I make barley pudding."

Myra said, "Abbey and William, go wash your hands. Abbey, please get me four nice potatoes from the sack."

"Yes Mom, wash hands and four potatoes."

William ran to the sink, alternating pumping his little fists in the air and yelling, "I make barley pudding."

David started to move toward his desk but Myra grabbed his arm, pulled him toward her and embraced him. She briefly kissed his lips and said, "Thank you."

***

When her mother arrived Saturday morning, Myra put on a jacket and headed out the door.

"What about the children?" Darcy asked.

"You and I need to talk. David will take care of them. Let's sit down on the bench in the park across the street."

"Isn't William too young to be left without his mother?"

"Since he was a few days old, David has shared taking care of him."

Darcy appeared shocked. She cleared her throat and composed herself anew as they seated themselves. "I have something important we should discuss. Colin is living with us now. He has a friend your age who would be a good husband."

"Tell me about him. For instance, is he an educated man?"

"He has a good job working as an apprentice woodworker."

"So he's not educated. Does he earn enough to support me?"

"Perhaps not yet, but you could continue your sewing business."

"Does he earn enough to live on his own?"

"He lives with his parents for now, but I hear they're nice folk."

"Is he smart?"

"Smart enough."

"Does he drink?"

"Not more than most men."

"Will he accept William as his own?"

"Talk to him and you can ask."

"Will he accept me when I tell him I was a whore?"

"You don't have to tell him."

"When David learned, he said only an angel would put herself through what I did to feed her family."

"What?" her suddenly wide eyed mother said while leaning away as if distance would change Myra's words.

"He said his love for me increased because of what I did."

"I don't believe you… You're making this up… No man would…" She looked away, shaking her head.

Slowly turning back to Myra, she asked, "He actually said those words?"

She grabbed her mother by the shoulders. "Consider carefully who I am, Mother. My involvement in the Famine caused me to make some ghastly decisions. But don't you *ever* forget; when Colin threw your grandson and me out, we didn't know where to go or where we'd find our next meal. It was David who, thank the good Lord, took in an uneducated peasant and her child. He not only put a roof over our heads but we've never experienced a hungry day. Not one." Myra let her hands drop.

Darcy folded hers, pushing them into her lap. "Any good man would take care of his family." She twisted anxiously.

"Who do you think takes care of the money for my dress business and figures out how much material and supplies to buy? Who figures out how much to charge and how much to pay the girls? Do you think I know how to do those things?"

"You could learn. You're smart."

"And while I was learning, my business would fail and we'd be on the street and hungry."

Darcy turned away again.

"Mother, I'm sure you've been here long enough to know the other Irish girls are sewing for pennies a day. I have good coin in my purse because, besides going to college, David runs the business for me. All I have to do is supervise the girls, make designs, and share taking care of William and Abbey. And it was David who knew where to find workers at a moment's notice."

"Well he's a Jew. They all know about business."

"Ma… The four days I was sick with the chills, he told me to stay in bed. He cooked for us; made special meals for me so I could get my strength back, and took care of

William and Abbey. He read to me from a poetry book the first evening I was ill and the next day Abbey followed his example and read me a story from her school book. She thinks the world of him … and me."

"You're making this up."

"Except for a glass of wine on Friday night, he doesn't drink. He helps occasionally with cleanup after meals and does the grocery shopping when I'm busy with sewing."

"No."

"He even helps bathe and dress William and Abbey. He plays silly little games with them which fill the house with the children's laughter. Every day, no matter how tired, the minute he arrives from his classes, he listens carefully to Abbey's details of what she did during the day. He helps her with her school work. Whenever he learns of Abbey or William helping me, he praises them."

"You're making him out to be a saint."

"No. A saint he's not. We certainly don't always agree. When he gets angry he gets a fearful dark look on his face and yells which cuts me to the bone." Myra shuddered thinking about it. She hesitated and lowered her voice. "He had William circumcised without telling me."

"What? How hideous."

"I was furious with him but let's not forget; I was mean and kept terrible secrets from him."

Myra took her mother's hand in both of hers and leaned towards her. "All my children will be college educated. He'll see to it. How many girls I grew up with can say such a thing?" She smiled. "You should hear David talking to William about mathematics, becoming an engineer, and what fun they'll have learning about subjects I may never understand."

"An engineer in the family…"

"He even thinks girls should attend college. Abbey is already telling people she's going to college to learn science."

"Why would girls need so much education?"

"If, God forbid, David died tomorrow, I couldn't run my own business. A girl with an education could."

"Well… Really… I guess I never considered why."

"And my children will grow up watching a father who respects his wife and considers her counsel. My girls will grow up watching how he treats me and look for a husband who does the same for them. We spent a few days at the ocean. David spent hours and hours patiently playing water games with William plus teaching Abbey and me to swim."

"Such activities are fine but his parents rejected you."

"My entire family rejected him."

"He could join the church."

"If the values he learned in his home taught him to take care of us like he does, I'd be a fool to ask."

"No Myra. You remember Goldman. Jews are evil…"

"Goldman was evil. That does not make all Jews evil."

Her mom became silent and pensive. She slowly hunched forward and stared at her lap.

"Myra's children … my grandchildren … all college educated." She sat up straight, smiling. "Even the girls... Wouldn't I have loved to go to college and learn about so many things… In my wildest dreams, I never imagined I might live to see my grandchildren in college."

"David's made such a reputation for himself at school and at a part time job, one of the graduates, who started a supply store in Independence, Missouri, has twice written him. He's having trouble with the business. We've been offered partial ownership of the store if we go out there and help him."

"Will you go?"

"We haven't decided. He'd be earning more than enough to take care of us even without my dress business. They've offered to let us live in a three bedroom apartment over the store until we have enough money to buy our own property and build our own house."

"Your own house on property you owned; no one could throw you off your own property…" Her smile evaporated. "But it was a Jew who threw our neighbors off the land they worked, extorted painful rent, and seized our crops." She leaned away from Myra. "Jews are taught to be evil."

"Do you think I'm teaching my children to be evil? Come spend time with Abbey and see how evil she is."

"You'll destroy your children and doom them to hell by raising them as Jews."

"Was I destroying precious Ciaran and William while they lived? I'm raising Abbey and William the same way I taught my blessed brother and sister."

"If he treats you so well, why won't he marry you?"

"He would. It was my decision not to marry him."

"What foolishness would stop you from marrying the man who takes such good care of you and the children?"

"A number of things which I will not discuss."

"Myra, let the Lord bless you with the sacrament of marriage."

"The same Lord who cruelly destroyed Ciaran and William?"

Her mother stood up and said in a bitter voice, "I've tried to offer you a life away from David because we thought he wouldn't marry you—it turns out you are the one who desires to live in sin. There's nothing more to say."

Chapter Eleven: Tense Times

"Nearly home, William. Only two more blocks."

On a cool late fall day, Myra was walking home from a last minute shopping trip. Eighteen-month-old William was nearly asleep as she carried him in her left arm. A bag with vegetables and meat weighed heavily in her right hand. It was late in the day and stars were becoming visible.

She thought she heard footsteps running up behind her. Just as she turned to look, someone pulled a bag over her head, shoulders, and arms. She felt someone ripping William away from her, someone's arms restraining her before feeling a rope being tied around her, pinning her arms. She screamed and strained against her bonds. Something hit the side of her face. She became dizzy, dropped to her knees, and tried to yell; the side of her jaw ached when she tried.

"Quiet you. Don't worry; we'll take him to a home which will raise him proper."

"Ow!" she heard.

"What happened?"

"The little bugger bit me."

"Hey. Don't. She's not to be hurt."

"Up yours."

Myra felt a blow to her head and lost consciousness.

***

"Miss, are you alright?" A policeman was standing over her.

"My child. Where's William?"

"No child here, miss."

"He's been stolen. You have to find him."

"Let me help you up and you tell me what happened."

In between tear-filled sobs she relayed as much information as she could remember.

David came running up to them. "I was worried you were taking so long to come home. What happened?"

She burst into deep sobs. "Someone's kidnapped William. Where's Abbey?"

"I left her with Miss Campana."

"We'll look into it, miss," the policeman said. "Why don't you take her home, sir? We'll contact you when we know something."

They walked home. David kept an arm around Myra who had difficulty walking.

"The Lord is finally punishing us. We'll never find him."

"The Lord didn't steal our child and I don't believe He'd punish us by hurting William. We need to stay calm and think about this. Tell me what happened."

"Calm? Our son's been stolen and I should be calm?"

He repeated in a stern tone, "Tell me what happened."

"They put a bag over me, pinned and tied my arms."

"Did they say anything?"

"I started to scream but someone must have slugged me. My jaw aches like hell. One of them said I wasn't to be hurt; just before they knocked me out."

"Was the policeman hopeful?"

"Not really." She shook her head. "An odd thing about our conversation; he said he didn't know why anyone would commit a crime to steal a child when the orphanages are full of unwanted children."

Myra stopped. "Oh no!"

"What?"

"One of the kidnappers said I shouldn't worry as he'll get a proper home."

"One of our parents?"

"They wouldn't."

"My sister said my folks were still livid but pleased you and I would raise William as a Jew."

"Mother said Dad is still angry but satisfied you're taking good care of William and me."

"Then who?"

They looked at each other in disbelief. Myra said, "It couldn't be. He wouldn't…"

They simultaneously pronounced, "Colin."

They ran four blocks to Myra's parents' home, where they described William's disappearance to her mother who was alone at the time.

"Ma, did Colin know about our raising William as a Jew?"

"He and your father…" She started trembling.

"What's wrong, Ma?"

"They had a big fight a few days ago. We tried to explain to Colin how David's taking such good care of you and William. He wouldn't listen."

Myra asked, "Did you tell him we're raising him as a Jew?"

She looked down while wringing her hands. "That's when the screaming started."

"Do you know where he lives, Mrs. McCormick?"

"He's always been a good son."

"Ma, we have to talk to him."

David said, "How angry was he?"

"Myra, your brother wouldn't."

"Ma, tell us. How angry was he?"

"I pushed him out of the apartment because I thought he and your father would come to blows."

Myra shook her mother's shoulders. "You have to tell us where he lives."

***

They ran to the address.

Colin opened his door. He was taller than David, generally bigger, and he immediately smirked at them. "Well, if it isn't my sister and, I suppose, the devil's spawn who made her pregnant and refuses to marry her."

"Colin, someone kidnapped William."

"How sad. I wouldn't worry. He's probably with a family who will raise him right."

David stepped into the apartment and swung a half-hearted punch which glanced off the side of Colin's head.

Colin grinned. "So you need to be taught a lesson. You've come to the right place." He delivered a mighty blow to David's face which caused him to feel momentarily dizzy. Myra screamed at Colin to stop as he landed a second painful blow to his jaw. David staggered backwards into the hallway with Colin moving toward him. The side of his face was on fire. Now his belly hurt as Colin repeatedly slammed his fists into it. He was absorbing terrible punishment. He knew he couldn't take it much longer.

David's face turned dark as anger and fury welled up inside him realizing this man could prevent him from finding his son. His body filled with adrenaline and ignoring his pain, he brought both of his fists up like he'd taught Sarah. He set his lips in a grim line.

"You want more?" Colin yelled while he smirked.

David's demeanor changed. Colin swung a rapid right followed by a left, both of which David easily deflected. Just as he'd practiced with his sister, David brought his left arm up to push the next blow aside, rotating his body, and using the motion to help propel his right hand, with all his body weight behind it, into Colin's jaw which snapped his opponent's head back. He retreated a step as David advanced toward him, his body bent slightly forward. He delivered two vicious body blows, each of which were accented by a grunt from Colin; followed by a wicked uppercut into his opponent's chin which, along with the body blows, clearly removed the smirk from Colin's face.

Colin, his belly aching, the room beginning to spin, staggered backwards, having difficulty maintaining his balance. He shook his head to clear it, and regained his balance. Fury and pain entered his eyes.

"Where's my son?" David screamed.

Colin sent another powerful fist at David. He skillfully blocked it and threw a combination to Colin's head which opened a cut over his eye and split his lip. David hesitated for a moment giving his opponent an opportunity to land a blow which made his ribs ache. They exchanged punches until David fired a withering set of fast combinations which wearied his opponent's head and body. It knocked the fight out of Colin who tried to ward off the painful assault. His strength was depleted so he put his arms up with elbows and wrists together to block the ferocious onslaught. David continued with combinations. Colin tried to back up to get away but tripped over a chair and fell, his head thudding against the wooden floor. David kicked his belly and screamed again, "Where's my son?"

"Fuck you."

"No, fuck you."

David got on top of him and pummeled his face. His right fist came up and down like a jackhammer. Blood spurted from Colin's nose; he was no longer capable of protecting himself.

Myra screamed, "David stop. You're killing him. Colin, tell us where our son is."

Colin put a blood covered hand up in a gesture of surrender. He took a few deep breaths and spat blood out of his mouth. "Bell. His name is Bell. I paid a man named Bell."

"Where does he live?"

"Northwest corner of this block; his place is on the left as you enter."

David stood up, panting. His adrenaline charged body vibrated.

He looked next to the stove at the basket of firewood. David walked over and picked up a hand ax.

"David no!" Myra implored, running to stand between the two.

While menacing Colin with the ax, David said, "If you ever come near my family again, they'll send you back to Ireland in pieces. Little ones! Understand?"

Exhausted and bloodied, Colin nodded.

***

"David, let's get out of here," Myra said pushing him out the door. Running down the street, she took David's hand which was sticky from her brother's blood. They passed under a street lamp. She saw his face and shirt were flecked with blood as well. Myra tasted bile as she remembered David's sickening cruelty. Flashes of what he'd done to Colin flooded her mind but she pushed the thoughts away as best she could to concentrate on finding William.

Myra's heart beat in time to their footfalls which slapped an anxious rhythm on the rain dampened street as they ran to their next destination.

***

David pounded on Bell's apartment door and yelled. "Mr. Bell, the building's on fire. You need to get out." They heard footsteps running to the door. It swung open. David, who must have seemed like a terrifying apparition with bloody hands and a blood spattered shirt and face, translated all his weight and fury into his fist which smashed into the small man's jaw. All of his motion to run out the door was reversed by David's aggression; he staggered backward two steps on wobbling legs and slumped to the floor, unconscious. David moved him to a chair and used a clothes line to tie his chest, wrists, and ankles.

Throwing a bowl of water into Bell's face, he yelled, "Wake up you filth. Where's my son?"

"Go to Hell," Bell yelled as he coughed and struggled against his bonds.

"You tell me or I will be destroying you one part at a time."

"You wouldn't. Think you're the devil or something? Do anything to me and I'll get the coppers on your ass."

"I'm much more dangerous than the devil, Mr. Bell. I'm a father with a missing son who doesn't give a damn about coppers. Now where is he?"

"If I tell you he'll kill me."

David lifted the ax above his head. Bell screamed, "NO!" just before the flat face of the ax slammed into his wrist. He wailed in pain, his body trembling, and he began to weep. Blood ran onto the arm of the chair.

"You won't have to worry about someone else killing you. If you don't speak up, I'll kill you. Where's my son?"

"I can't. He'll destroy me."

David brought the ax down on his other wrist. Bell howled a second time.

"Myra, how many bones do you think I can destroy by slamming this ax into his knee?" he looked at her but she already turned away from the bloody sight. "Perhaps I should just cut his leg off a piece at a time."

"No, please." Bell was in terrible agony. His lower arms and wrists must have felt like they were burning. The slightest movement obviously caused intense pain.

David raised the ax. "Perhaps you'd prefer I chop off a more personal part?"

"No, No, please."

"Not the right answer."

"Grayson."

"Who?"

"Durant Grayson. He paid me for the kid."

"Where does he live?"

Bell couldn't hold his head up, spoke through rapidly swelling, torn lips while bits of blood and spittle came out as he spoke. "North on Main. Number 17. He's in the front flat on the first floor — east side."

They were about to leave when Myra said, "Shouldn't we at least cut him loose?"

He walked back to the constrained man whose body was wracked with sobs.

David used the sharp side of the ax to sever the bonds.

Out of breath, they arrived at the next address.

David pounded on the door.

A neighbor peaked out. "What's all the racket?"

"Looking for Grayson."

"You missed him by five minutes. He's headed to the train station. His wife and he said they're moving to New York."

Myra let out a little scream. "Oh Lord no. We'll never find him if he leaves Boston."

They started running again.

A block before the train station, they approached a large man dragging a trunk and a woman carrying a small child.

David said politely, "Mr. Grayson?"

"I'm Grayson."

"Going somewhere?"

"My wife and I are traveling … which is none of your damn business."

David recognized William, "I'm here about the fine young boy you have. He's my son."

William screamed, "Daddy!"

Grayson's eyes grew large. He released the trunk and drew back a fist the size of a ham. David ducked the blow, feeling the edge of Grayson's fist grazing his hair. Gripping the ax with both hands, David propelled its flat between Grayson's legs. The large man's angular face turned purple and he toppled like an oak with both hands on his severely injured crotch.

William clamped his teeth onto the woman's cheek. She screamed and released him. "Here, take the little devil." He ran to David and wrapped his arms around his father's leg. Myra picked him up, firmly surrounding him with her arms.

"See my face?" The woman pointed to the red marks on her cheek. "The little bastard kept biting me, even after I'd slap him."

David stepped to her side. He grabbed a handful of hair at the back of her head.

"You slapped him? You shouldn't have."

Using all his strength, he smashed her face into a street lamp. Myra cringed at the crunching sound as it struck. The woman lifted her head. Myra covered William's eyes and turned away as blood spurted out of the woman's nose and mouth. Her right cheek bone had sunk and her jaw was twisted. She collapsed in a heap.

David walked over to Grayson who remained clutching his crotch and moaning. "I suggest you stay out of the kidnapping business."

Grayson nodded and mumbled an unintelligible response.

They walked away. William yelled triumphantly through his tears, "YOU BAD. I TELL YOU! MY ANGRY DADDY COME. FIND WILLIAM. I TELL YOU, YOU BE SORRY! NOW YOU SORRY."

***

Back at their apartment, Myra, after putting William to bed, tried to embrace David but his body was too sore. The adrenaline wore off and the pain of the beating he sustained while defeating Colin surfaced.

"My elbows, shoulders, and wrists are killing me. Hell, my whole body aches." Angry purple welts covered his face and upper body. Myra chipped some ice and put it in a cloth so he could dull the ache from his numerous contusions and sore joints. She gently washed his blood and sweat soaked body.

"I'm exhausted. I'm going to bed."

David and William slept soundly.

Myra didn't sleep as something deep within caused her to recoil in dread. Was she sleeping next to a monster? She kept reliving David's fury as he brutally beat her brother, tortured Bell, and smashed Mrs. Grayson's face. Those memories terrified her.

David was always so gentle. Where did the sudden cruelty come from? What if he becomes infuriated with William or me? Surely a cruel beast surfaced tonight. Do I spend a lifetime worrying about the monster inside him?

The following afternoon, William seemed to be having a nightmare during his nap. He was tossing back and forth and spoke while still asleep. "Bim, Bam, my daddy come now. I tell you." She saw him bare his teeth.

Myra shook his shoulder. "William, wake up, you're having a bad dream." She pointed to David. "Look. Daddy's here with us." She picked him up. "You're safe now." Instead of returning him to his bed, she held him.

Does William have a monster inside him? Should I be frightened of William as well? No! I'm his mother and will explain to him when violence is justified.

***

The sheriff who interviewed Myra at the scene of the kidnapping appeared in their doorway the following day.

"I'm glad you found your son, but you should have contacted us to find the kidnappers."

"There was no time," David said. "We nearly missed them taking William to New York. We'd have lost him."

"Mr. Kaplan, you've put two men and a woman in the hospital. One may never use his hands again, one won't have kids, and the woman has enough broken bones in her face she'll never look the same."

"They'd stolen my child."

"I have a daughter your son's age. No telling what I would have done in your situation." The policeman shrugged and took deep breath. "The problem is we're a civilized town now. We can't have vigilante justice. I'm sorry to do this but you must leave town before the end of the week. I'm the one what's in charge of the investigation. When I complete my work this coming Friday, I'll have to interview and probably arrest the person I think took justice into his own hands. If he's gone … faraway gone … a long ways out of the state gone … I won't be able to complete my investigation; get the other side of the story so to speak, and no charges will be filed."

David pleaded. "We can't leave town. We have a business here and I'm finishing college."

"You can't run a business or attend college from jail. Good day to you both."

He abruptly turned and walked away.

"David, what are we going to do?" Myra said despondently.

"Let's think about what to do. But we'll pack while we're thinking. Maybe I should send a letter to the Mandel Brothers?"

***

A large man, whose crotch was severely injured, sat at the bedside of a woman with a half crushed face. Her breathing was difficult since the injury and an infection was attacking her which was draining the last of her strength. In two weeks the man would be limping to her graveside.

"If I find the bastard who did this, I'll destroy his family and then destroy him."

Chapter Twelve: Train Ride to the Mississippi River

The train's shrill steam whistle cut through the air indicating it was nearly time to leave.

"Let's get on board," David said.

Myra bowed her head and prayed, "May the Lord bless us during our travel to Independence."

They scrambled onto the train and found a place to sit on the inward facing seats.

The train picked up speed. A teary-eyed Myra said, "We've lost our last chance to have family around us and I'm frightened for our future."

He put an arm around her as she continued, "I know we'll do our best to build a good life. We know nothing about the town we're going to, what kind of people we'll meet… It all worries me… We have to work hard for William and Abbey's sake."

"Mommy, don't cry. William work hard."

"I know you will." She leaned over and kissed her son who put his small arms around her, giving Myra his best hug.

"Will we be a happy family just like before?" Abbey said.

"We'll do our best," Myra said, wiping away a tear and cuddling Abbey against her side.

The train moved a sedate ten to fifteen miles-an-hour but carried many more passengers than could be accommodated by horse drawn carriages. There were many gaps between railroads where passengers disembarked and, depending on their objective, separated in numerous directions, riding on a combination of horse drawn coaches and/or the next railroad to their final destination. At various stops they were able to buy food and consume it on the conveyance of the moment.

During their trip, the foursome changed trains four times before they reached the Mississippi. This mode of travel made them physically sore and exhausted. None of the steam or horse drawn coaches provided sleeping accommodations. While the speed was sedate, the ride was anything but. Due to the uneven road bed they were jostled, bumped, and thrown around. This made sleeping nearly impossible. In the middle of Ohio, the train the Kaplans expected to take them on the next part of their journey broke down, so they stayed overnight at a hotel.

Myra stared at the bed.

William didn't waste time staring. He walked over, pulled himself onto the end and immediately fell asleep. His sister joined him.

"A bed at last," Myra said while placing a blanket over them. "A simple thing but a blessing the way my body is worn and bruised from bouncing around on those awful hard wood seats."

"We're making good progress; we may be halfway there by now. Are you still frightened, Myra?"

"Certainly. I trust you'll do the best for us but who knows what the future holds? Our recent past has shown how frightening life can be."

"I've been praying the job in Independence is as promised."

"I'll pray about that as well. David, please hold me."

He wrapped his arms around her.

"This helps," she said.

"It does indeed."

He lifted her chin and kissed her.

After a lengthy kiss, Myra said, "The children have been angels although William seemed restless."

"He's not the type to just sit."

"Will you please look away while I put on my night shirt and get in bed?" she asked.

"I will. I'm going to sleep in my undershirt and drawers."

Myra changed and slid under the quilted blanket. David followed, reached over to the little table next to the bed and turned down the wick of the oil lamp.

They didn't touch for a while. Myra rolled so she could lie on her side against him with her head on his chest. He kissed her cheek, put his arm around her and she put one arm across his body. The bone-weary travelers fell fast asleep.

***

The same day, a letter from Myra and David arrived at his parents' Philadelphia home addressed to Sarah. It told of their move to Independence. Based on the date, she knew her brother and his family were already far from Boston.

She was inconsolable. In-between sobs, Sarah railed at her parents. "You've pushed them away and they've gone out west. Are you proud of what you've done? Their children will be raised without knowing any of us. I'm sick and ashamed you allowed this to happen."

Chapter Thirteen: Travel on the Mississippi River

After a few more days of sleepless rail and horse drawn travel from Ohio, it was a huge relief when the Kaplans were assigned a cabin on the steamboat which was to take them down the Mississippi River from Davenport, Iowa to St. Louis, Missouri with many stops in-between. Exhausted, they slept soundly. The steamboat's ride was smooth; a far cry from the discomfort of the train. It was also relatively quiet. The whooshing sound of the steam engine plus the splashing of the paddle wheel, was rhythmic and sufficiently quiet to lull them to sleep; until the captain decided to use the steam whistle. Its shrill cry startled everyone on board.

Around noon, the captain was yelling instructions into a megaphone to direct his crew while they were preparing to dock at Burlington, Iowa.

Fifty-yards from shore, the boat ran aground on one of the constantly shifting Mississippi River sandbars. The sudden stop threw David and Myra to their cabin's floor. They grabbed William and Abbey, ran on deck, and heard the steam engine straining to power the boat off the sandbar, but to no avail.

They heard yelling from the back of the boat. Standing at the rail, halfway down the side of the ship, a few people ran toward the bow. A crewman walked swiftly by them. He was covered in sweat and appeared to have difficulty maintaining his composure.

***

"What's going on?" David asked.

The crewman stopped, leaned toward them and with a quivering voice said, "The sudden stop caused a fire in the boiler room. They can't control it and the boiler might blow. If it does, there'll be nothing left of the boat or the folks still on board. I don't want to start a panic but you need to get to the bow of the ship, swim to shore, and run as far away from the boat as you can."

"This can't be happening," Myra said.

They heard splashes as passengers at the front of the boat jumped into the river. Thick black smoke billowed out of the back and people were starting to scream.

"I can hardly swim," Myra said, terrified.

"Can you?" the crewman asked David.

"I can," he replied.

"Take your children. Get them to the shore as quickly as you can. I'll take your wife. Remember! You must get out of the water and as far from the boat as you can."

They ran to the bow. "Abbey, you're going to stay on my back with your arms around my neck while I swim just like we did at the ocean," David said.

"Should I help by kicking?"

"Yes but if we go under water, hold your breath like we practiced." He picked up William. "William, remember how to hold your nose if we go under water?" He nodded, eyes wide with fright.

David eased into the frigid springtime water with his two children. He used powerful strokes with one hand and forceful kicks to move them toward shore while the strong Mississippi current tugged at them. David could feel Abbey kicking hard and heard occasional coughing.

Myra's brief scream was cut short as she and the crewman plunged into the icy water. When they broke the surface, she began hacking and coughing the muddy Mississippi water out of her lungs. David scrambled up the shore and saw Myra in full panic mode while trying to climb on the crewman to get as far out of the water as she could. He struggled to tear loose from her grip so he could begin propelling them toward shore. The powerful current continuously pulled them downstream. Grabbing Myra's right arm with his right hand, the crewman viciously spun her around and came up behind her. She kept trying to turn toward him and grab at him.

"Myra, stop fighting him or you're both going to drown," David yelled while he walked along the shore as his wife and the crewman were inexorably dragged downstream by the current.

She coughed and sputtered with terror in her eyes, still fighting to turn towards the crewman.

"Mom," Abbey yelled. "Do what Dad says."

David thought he might lose Myra.

The crewman grabbed a handful of her hair, pulled her close, and screamed into her ear at the top of his lungs, "STOP MOVING!"

She froze and he proceeded to propel the two of them toward shore. Her panic subsided and Myra started helping by kicking and stroking with one arm. The screaming on the boat increased and they could hear the cracks and pops of the fire as it rapidly consumed the wooden structure of the boat.

Nearing the shore, Myra finally relaxed enough to swim on her own with the crewman swimming at her side. They crossed the sand bar, scrambling up the muddy bank. The crewman helped steady her and reminded them to run away from the boat. He swam back to rescue others. Just as he climbed on the boat, the boiler exploded.

David carried William and Myra ran holding Abbey's hand. They were a good distance from the river but even at seventy-five-yards, the pressure wave from the explosion knocked them to the ground. Shards of wood and metal whistled over their heads. Their ears were in pain as if slapped. David cradled terrified William as he lifted himself back to his feet. He saw the entire rear section of the boat disintegrated. The children cried from the pain in their ears. Most of the boat separated into a myriad of large and small pieces which flew through the air in all directions. David dragged Myra and Abbey to their feet and they took off running again. Boat parts and body parts rained down, mostly into the Mississippi but some reached the area of the shore where they ran.

Breathing hard after minutes of strenuous running, Myra said, "David, stop. I can't run any farther. My legs are killing me." She doubled over and grabbed David's arm for support.

He turned back towards the river. Only a dark cloud of smoke remained hanging in the air over the steamboat's previous position. A small section of the bow, marooned on the sand bar, was the only intact piece of the once proud ship. He saw numerous bodies, some struggling to keep their head above water, being dragged downstream by the river's current. Cries and screams from the injured reached their ears.

"We should go back and see if we can help anyone," David said. Myra was still bent forward at her waist, hands on knees trying to catch her breath.

After resting a minute longer, they started rapidly walking around debris to the river's edge. A number of bodies were twisted into grotesque shapes. David covered William's eyes as he and Myra did their best to ignore the various bodies and body parts thrown onto shore. She tried to cover Abbey's eyes but Abbey kept pulling her hand away. She seemed to examine each of the bodies with a cold detachment. Most evidence of the explosion was being erased as the Mississippi's strong current carried lifeless bodies and debris downstream. A few people were still in the water desperately trying to swim to safety. David handed William to Myra and waded into the water to help survivors get to their feet and onto shore.

"David, isn't he the man who warned us and helped us off the boat?"

She indicated a man, lying on his back on the shore, whose exposed skin was charred and sooty. He raised his hand towards them. Myra immediately covered her mouth, turned away, and bent over as if she was about to vomit. The right side of his face was crushed and his legs were torn off below his knees. The ends of his lower limbs were smoldering. Abbey walked up to him and took the man's remaining hand in hers.

"You saved my wife, our children, and me," David said, doing his best to ignore the wave of nausea coming over him. "God bless you, sir."

"Thank you for saving my mom," Abbey said.

The man attempted a smile with what was left of his face. He squeezed Abbey's hand. His remaining eye rolled back in his head and he was gone. Abbey gently lowered his hand.

They spotted a young teenager swimming toward shore, working desperately to fight the current while trying to keep a toddler's head above water. David again ran down the muddy bank and waded out a few yards; this time taking the crying toddler in one arm and wrapping the other around the teen to lift him to his feet. They walked out of the water and the few yards up the bank.

"David," Myra said, nodding at the teen's mid-section. He observed the short section of one-inch diameter pipe protruding from his stomach and back. The teen said, "This little guy's name is Eric. His brother handed him to me, because he couldn't swim. He just celebrated his third birthday."

"You saved him," David said.

"It was a long swim," the teen said.

The boy put his hand on the shoulder of the crying toddler, smiled briefly, and collapsed to his knees. He again glanced at Eric as he grimaced and moaned while putting his hands on either side of the pipe. The adrenaline which allowed him to ignore his pain was wearing off. He rolled onto his side, coughed up blood a few times, and stopped breathing.

Abbey was shivering but seemed unphased by the carnage.

"We need to get the children away from here. They're shivering," Myra said. "We've got to get them warmed up."

"I'll take William and Eric."

"I was scared in the water, Mom," Abbey said. "Sometimes it went over my head."

David told her, "I felt you kicking the whole time, Abbey. You helped me save your brother. You're a great big sister."

"I don't feel so great; just cold and wet." She began crying. Myra picked her up.

They walked toward town.

Abbey kept her arms wrapped tightly around Myra's neck. Shivering, Eric and William pulled their arms and legs in, nearly curling themselves into a tight ball. David did his best to hold them close, bundling his arms and hands around them.

People started arriving from town. A woman who appeared to be in her mid-fifties, wearing a plain white, long-sleeved blouse and gingham skirt approached them.

With a serious expression she said, "I'm Claire Watson. My home is one block away. Bring your children over and we'll get all of you dried off and warmed up."

"Thank you, Mrs. Watson," David said. "I'm David Kaplan and this is … my wife, Myra."

"A pleasure to meet you, Mr. and Mrs. Kaplan," Claire said while Myra glared at David.

They entered the living room of a compact home, containing a small kitchen and two bedrooms on the second floor.

"Come into the kitchen," Claire said. "I've been cooking so it's warmer in there."

Myra tried to have Abbey to begin drying her, but she yelled "No," and kept her arms tightly around Myra's neck.

"It's okay, Abbey. I'll hold you while I dry you off," she said in a gentle voice.

Keeping the little one in her left arm, Myra helped Abbey out of her wet clothing. She gently dried her while trying to keep as much of her still shivering body wrapped in the towel, all the while talking to her.

"You're going to be all dried off and nice and warm in a few minutes, pretty girl."

She wrapped a dry towel around Abbey and picked up a second towel to begin drying her hair.

"Do you feel better sweetness?" Myra asked.

Abbey nodded, wiping away a tear.

During this time, Mrs. Watson was drying off William and David was taking care of Eric, who was crying and seemed to be talking in nonsense words.

Mrs. Watson said, "I'll change William's under garment." She put a folded towel on the table as David placed him on his back.

"A little Jew," she said when she saw his circumcision.

"As am I," David stated. He dried Eric and noticed Eric was circumcised as well.

Mrs. Watson continued in a stern voice, "Let me have their clothes and I'll wash and hang them to dry. You can use my spare bedroom. I'll give you some things you can wear. See if the kids need a nap and by the time they wake I'll have dinner ready."

They proceeded to the bedroom which contained a bed, rocking chair, and small square table with chairs.

David placed sleepy William on the bed. Little Eric was yawning by the time David placed him next to William. He covered them with a blanket which he tucked around them.

They heard scraping noises in the hallway and moved to help Mrs. Watson push and pull a large copper tub into the bedroom.

"I'll have hot water ready in a few minutes so you two can get cleaned up. Here are my husband's and my clothes for you."

Myra, still holding Abbey, sat down in the rocking chair and, after rocking for a few minutes, realized her daughter was asleep. She gently placed her on the bed next to the boys, pulling a blanket over her.

After two buckets of cold water were poured into the tub, two large pots of boiling water were added.

"Here's a fresh bar of lye soap and a few more towels. If you need anything else just ask," Mrs. Watson said, closing the door as she left the room.

"You bathe first," David said.

Myra walked over to the tub while David turned the rocking chair he was seated in so he wouldn't see her while she bathed.

"Wait," he said. "Are you still dressed?"

"Yes."

He walked over and put his arms around her.

"Remember last summer? When you learned I knew how to swim, you insisted I start teaching the children swimming skills even though I thought they were too young. I'm certain those hours teaching them helped them do as they were told while in the water today. Look at the little angels now; safe and sound, asleep next to Eric."

He kissed her cheek. "You're a redheaded angel, you are."

"They did better than me. Instead of panicking like I did, they did what their father taught them." She tightened her arms around him and glanced at the sleeping children. "We need to find Eric's family. They must be sick with worry."

***

Returning to the rocking chair, David said, "I need to think about how we're going to continue our journey. What are your thoughts?" He turned towards Myra just in time to see her stepping into the tub.

"David! Turn around," she yelled.

He jammed his eyes shut and, blushing, quickly turned away from her.

"Myra I'm so sorry," he said quickly. "I forgot what you were doing for a moment and wanted to ask you something. Please forgive me."

She imagined what was probably riveted in his memory; her cream-colored skin, perky breasts with large nipples, shapely legs, and cute behind.

"I forgive you. We've always undressed in the dark so we've never really seen each other." His cheeks were turning deep red while her own were on fire. "Besides, you've already called me your wife."

"Do you mind?"

She didn't reply but relaxed in the tub and soaped her body. A smile came to her lips as she thought of David's embarrassment. "Did you get a good look?" she teased.

"Good enough to put backbone in my buggy whip."

Myra burst into laughter.

After thinking a moment she said, "I'm not sure I like you calling me your wife. I don't want to live a lie."

"I thought it would be easier. No one here knows or needs to know our past; besides, we've been living as a family since you arrived at my apartment. We've taken good care of each other. I'm sure it's how married folks must feel." He sat still for a bit, staring at the floor. "Considering my mom and dad's sometimes awful relationship, I should have said it's how couples who care about each other must feel."

When she was dressed, she changed places with David.

"You saw me so let me know when I can see you."

After a few moments he said, "Now would be good."

She turned to find him facing her wearing nothing but a smile below firmly shut eyelids. When he opened them, Myra was trying to soak up every detail of his body. Finally looking away, she said, "You have a well-muscled body. Thank you."

After bathing and dressing, he volunteered, "I can watch the kids if you want to see if Claire needs any help."

"I want to be here if any of them waken. I especially want Eric to know I'll be here for him until we find his folks."

David kissed her cheek and went to assist Mrs. Watson. He returned quickly.

"I was practically thrown out of her kitchen. Apparently men aren't allowed in there except to eat. She said you and I need to rest and she'll have a healthy meal ready for us in an hour. Instead of her stern expression, she was broadly smiling and was mumbling about the joy of having someone to cook for again. She gave me the kids' washed and dried clothing."

"David, we've lost everything we brought from Boston including our money. How will we continue our journey?"

David patted his belt. "I have gold coins in my belt. It's specially made for holding coins. We'll get some things in town and still have enough to get us to Independence."

Eric woke an hour later. He smiled at David and said in Yiddish, "*Good Morning.*"

David raised his eyebrows, and replied, "*Good Morning,* Eric."

The three-year-old frowned. "*Not Eric, I Nathan.*"

"I'm sorry," David replied. "*Good Morning*, Nathan,"

The little one continued, "*I want Aba v'Ema*."

"I know you want your *Aba* and *Ema*, Nathan."

While tears filled his bright blue eyes, Nathan asked, "*Where Aba v'Ema?*"

David animatedly shrugged his shoulders, shook his head, and with a sad expression said, "I'm sorry. I don't know where they are."

Nathan began crying. Myra picked him up.

"David, you know what he's saying?"

"Yes. He wasn't speaking nonsense words. He speaks Yiddish. He just told me his name is Nathan. Poor little guy, my conversational Yiddish is weak at best. How will we talk to him? Too bad my sister isn't here; she's fluent."

Myra was smiling warmly, patting Nathan while she held him. He briefly returned her smile. "Let me help you get dressed, little man."

Abbey rolled over and opened her eyes.

"Have you found his mommy and daddy?"

"No, we haven't … but your dress is nice and clean so you can put it on and we'll have some dinner."

Abbey stared at Nathan as she dressed.

"I'll bet he's sad because he doesn't have his mom and dad around. I know what that's like."

They walked into the fragrant kitchen.

"Mrs. Watson, this is lovely," Myra said while looking over bread rolls covered in salt and caraway seeds, strawberry jam, sliced beef in thick brown gravy, sauerkraut with caraway seeds and dried apple slices, stewed tomatoes, and broccoli.

"Please sit. I want you and your children to get your strength back after being in the cold river. A good dinner will help. I don't have milk for the children now but will have by our evening meal."

They gathered around the table.

Nathan immediately bowed his head.

"He's waiting for a prayer," Claire observed.

"Lord, please bless us and this food," Myra said. "We are grateful for all your blessings, the food we are about to eat"—she smiled at David while she continued—"and seeing to it we learned the water skills which allowed us to survive the terrible boat explosion."

Nathan picked up a roll, held it up, and glanced at David who nodded to him.

"*Barukh atah Adonai Eloheinu melekh ha'olam, ha'motzi lehem min ha-aretz*. Amen," Nathan intoned as he pronounced the Hebrew blessing for bread.

"Nice *Brucha*, Nathan," David told him with a pat on his head.

Smiling, Nathan enthusiastically bit off a piece of his roll.

Abbey was watching intently and said, "Amen" soon after Nathan did and took a bite out of her roll as did William.

"He said the same prayer like we do on *Shabbat*." She turned to Myra. "Why did you say the other things?" she asked.

"We want to thank the Lord for saving us and providing us a scrumptious dinner."

"Scrumptious dinner," William said after eating a bite of beef.

Abbey said, "Yes, a scrumptious dinner."

Nathan was watching them and said slowly, "Scrumptious dinner."

"Your children have healthy appetites," Claire said, "and William seems to love my sauerkraut."

"What's it made from?" Abbey asked.

"Pickled cabbage, dried apples, vinegar, and caraway seeds. I'll write down the recipe if you like."

"Thanks. We need to make this, Mom." Abbey said.

Myra smiled at the boys and said, "The way William and Nathan are inhaling it, I agree." She nodded toward Nathan. "Mrs. Watson, this little guy is not ours. A teen came out of the water and handed him to us after the steamboat exploded."

"I see."

"We'll walk into town after we eat and let the authorities know he's here," David said.

After dinner the six of them walked toward the river. Half a block away, Abbey stopped walking. "I don't want to be near the water."

"We'll stay here, Abbey," Myra told her.

Mrs. Watson called to the town mayor who was standing nearby.

She introduced them and Myra explained they were caring for someone else's child.

"Let me write your names down," he said. "We're putting together a list of survivors to place in the paper. It should be complete by tomorrow. Hopefully, the children's parents will recognize their names.

"This is our son William and daughter Abbey. We don't know two-year-old Nathan's last name. When we ask, he just replies Nathan."

"I'm sad to say this was a major tragedy. With the swiftly flowing river's temperature being so cold this time of year combined with the force of the explosion, only a small fraction of the travelers and crew survived."

The mayor perused the river, sighed, and continued.

"We don't have a passenger list. It went down with the steamboat. At this time, it looks like thirty people survived. On a typical day, there may have been as many as one-hundred-seventy on board plus crew."

"Are there any parents missing children?" Myra asked.

"I've talked to all the survivors we've found. None of them are missing children this young." The mayor shook his head and added, "Surely, the Lord was watching you. You may be the only intact family. How long will you be in town?"

"We haven't decided," Myra said. "We're on our way to Missouri."

"I'd appreciate if you could stay a few days and take care of the child while we get word out about the tragedy. If you need supplies or anything, come by my office."

"We could use an extra bed," Claire said, "plus milk for the little ones."

"I'll have those things sent over within the hour. Thanks for taking them in, Mrs. Watson."

***

The next day consisted of resting and eating. After they put the children to sleep, David saw tears well up in Myra's eyes.

"What's wrong?" he asked.

Myra embraced and kissed him. "I just remembered you sliding into the water with our children. You looked like a warrior going into battle; grim determination on your face. It's the second time you've rescued Abbey and the third time you've come to William's rescue. You're our hero."

"No hero. Just a lad whose father insisted he learned to become a proficient swimmer. What a hero the crewman was. He told us to get off the boat, saved you, and returned to help others."

"He paid for his heroism with his life and we don't even know his name."

"We should remember to tell his story to folks so at least his memory will live longer than he did."

David became pensive. He looked at Myra with a puzzled expression. "Three times I've come to William's rescue?"

"The steamboat, the kidnapping, and when you took us in."

"Two times with Abbey?"

"When you agreed to take her in and the steamboat."

"Oh. Still not a hero. I can swim, I learned to fight, and it didn't take any hero to give William and Abbey a place to live."

In bed, Myra cuddled tight against him.

You are my hero, Mr. Kaplan. Thank you Lord for putting him in our lives; and seeing to it he learned the skills necessary to protect our blessed Abbey and William.

"David, I want you tonight."

"You think we can manage another child?"

"We'll be fine." She kissed his cheek. "I know we'll manage."

Late the same night, Abbey started whimpering. Myra saw her twisting up and back in the moonlight illuminated room and then her whole body jumped. She sobbed. On hearing this, Nathan started crying as well. William awoke briefly, turned over and returned to sleep.

"David, light the lamp." The lone oil lamp illuminated their movements and drew long shadows on the walls of the small room they shared.

Myra picked up Abbey and held her while David cradled Nathan.

"I was dreaming I was getting covered by the water," Abbey said. "I couldn't breathe."

"You lay down next to me. Dad's going to lie down with William and Nathan in the other bed. We'll be right here if either of you get scared again."

Abbey whimpered for a while, and then slept but Nathan kept crying. David moved to the rocking chair holding Nathan while he sobbed and kept asking for his mother and father.

***

The following day dawned bright and sunny.

"Let's take the children for a picnic to get their minds off the tragedy," Claire suggested during breakfast. "We'll stop by the blacksmith's and rent a buggy and horse. There's a beautiful point of land just north of town. It's on a high bluff overlooking the river, which allows one to see many miles upriver."

"Sound's lovely," Myra said.

"It is," Claire continued, "there's talk of making it into a city park. It's lovely now but in the fall there's so many mosquitoes up there my neighbor said it should be called Mosquito Point. We experienced a hard freeze two weeks ago so it shouldn't be too buggy now."

They walked the short distance to the livery where they secured a horse and buckboard.

They climbed on; David looked at Claire and said, "I've never handled one of these."

"Grab the reins. It's time you learned."

Their buggy slowly climbed the narrow road to the bluff. David asked, "Mrs. Watson, do you have children of your own?"

"Yes, I do. They live on farms in western Iowa and Minnesota. My husband and I raised them on a farm just west of Mt. Pleasant. He died not long after we moved back to town. We planned to start a boarding house. I've been alone for the last year."

"Thank you for taking us in," Myra said.

"Don't mention it, dear. I love the sounds of people living in my house and I adore cooking for someone besides myself."

"We were on our way to my husband's new job in Independence, Missouri. He's going to be part owner of a supply store. We need to begin traveling again fairly soon."

Upon arrival at Mosquito Point they found themselves at the top of a tall bluff, looking out on a magnificent and distant view of the Mississippi River. Just north of their location, the river widened to such an extent it looked like a lake with a few heavily wooded islands.

"There's a keg with water tied to the buckboard. Pour some in the bucket and let the horse have a drink," Claire instructed David. Afterward they sat on a large blanket while Abbey, William, and Nathan played together.

Myra observed, "Abbey's been trying to teach Nathan the names of things in English."

"The only thing more astounding than her teaching him is how quickly he learns and remembers the words," David said. "Listen carefully and I think you'll see Abbey and William are picking up words in Yiddish as well."

They watched the little ones running around, laughing and playing. At one point Nathan tripped and bumped his head. Abbey and William helped him up while he cried. He was holding his head as they walked him over to Myra.

"He hit his head on a rock," Abbey explained.

"Poor Nathan," Myra said putting her hand on his shoulder.

"No," Abbey said. "You have to kiss him where it hurts, like you do for us." She turned to Mrs. Watson and explained, "Mommy kisses make little kids feel better."

Myra leaned towards him and kissed his forehead.

Abbey asked in a motherly voice, "Do you feel better, Nathan?"

Nathan smiled and hugged Myra. The three children joined hands and when they'd walked a few steps, Abbey looked back over her shoulder. "See? Mommy kisses always work."

"You need to think about something," Claire said. "What will you do if his parents can't be found?"

"My favorite thing in life is being a mother," Myra said. "But I know having another child will be a lot more work. It would be a blessing to have more family around."

Claire sighed. "Life can be so cruel, we never know what obstacles may be thrown in our path … especially with no family around … and we don't always know why things happen. I talked to the folks in town last night. Everyone agrees you should take Nathan with you if his parents can't be located. No one here knows anything about raising a little Jew."

Claire watched the children for a while. "I adored how Abbey asked you to make Nathan feel better with mommy kisses. She certainly sees you as a strong mother … and Nathan felt better after you kissed him."

"Speaking of Abbey," Myra said. "I was reflecting on the tragedy last night. Walking along the shore, I didn't want Abbey viewing the torn and broken bodies. I put my hand over her eyes but she pulled it away. She seemed unmoved by the bloody sights which made me sick to my stomach."

"That's strange," Claire said.

"We found the man who rescued me. His body and face were so severely injured that I couldn't look at him but Abbey held his remaining hand and smiled at him." Myra turned to David. "Do you think I should be concerned about her behavior?"

"Not now. We have too many other things to worry about. I adore Nathan but I'm not ready to be a father to three. I'll have so much to do when we arrive in Independence; it takes all my extra energy to be a father to William and Abbey."

He was sitting cross legged while leaning back on one elbow. Abbey whispered something to the boys. The threesome ran towards David with Nathan and William following Abbey as quickly as their short legs could carry them.

"We're going to tickle you," she screamed with delight.

He rolled onto his back as she leaned into him and tickled his belly.

"No," he said. "Ah, oo, ah, Abbey you're tickling me. Oh stop! Please stop. William, Nathan, you're making me laugh."

David noisily carried on and on. The four of them rolled around the grass laughing and screaming.

"We're good ticklers!" out of breath Abbey declared.

"Yes, good ticklers," William said.

"Ticklers," Nathan added with a huge grin.

Claire stated quietly to Myra, "Who's not ready to be a father to three? The children's faces are radiant around him. It seems daunting but listen to them, love them, and demonstrate good values and I'm sure you'll be fine."

On the ride home, Nathan sobbed as he asked for his missing parents. Myra held him while Abbey patted him, doing their best to console him. Meanwhile, David tried to explain to William the cause of Nathan's tears.

***

"We need to start traveling again," David said two days later as they put the children to bed.

"And Nathan?

"Myra, I love him dearly. You can't imagine how my heart soars when Nathan calls me *Aba* David. I absolutely melt when he smiles at me or laughs at my silliness; but I'll be so tied up with the store I'll have little time for our own, let alone Nathan."

"So we'll leave him and hope someone will take good care of him?"

She put her arms around his neck and kissed his lips for a long time.

Leaning away, she said, "I've been thinking of nothing else but how to make him part of our lives. The responsibility of raising children still frightens me to death but I think we have an obligation to continue taking care of him."

"What if his parents show up?"

"We'll take pride in how we've loved him while he lived with us. The rest we'll deal with when it happens. Maybe we'll have more of our own children by then."

"It seems he comes from a strong religious background."

"So I have some learning to do. The town has our names and where we're going. It may be he came out of the water just when we would be there to care for him. I'll manage; you don't have to worry."

He kissed her forehead. "It's me I'm worried about. What if I don't have time for the children once we're in Independence? It means more pressure on you."

"David, when we started living together, we became a family. The children come first. You've already demonstrated they will be the priority. The Lord has put three amazing children in our lives. They regularly fill the air with their laughter. We should consider ourselves blessed."

"I've felt blessed since our first weekend together."

"I feel blessed you will be their father. You take such good care of us … and now Nathan. We may have a rugged road ahead but I have confidence in you. I love you dearly and so do the children."

"It's the first time you've said you loved me."

"I should have said it the first moment you opened the door to William and me. You took us into your home and more importantly your heart. I feared a tragic existence after Colin threw us out but the moment we moved in… Like you said, we've been a family. I know we struggled at first, argued at times, and we don't always agree, but I guess it happens in some families. I care deeply for you."

"Enough to marry me?"

"Let's get settled in Independence and we'll talk." She sighed. "At times you frighten me."

"Frighten you?"

"We need to talk about something which has bothered me for a while. Let's sit on the porch."

Outside, Myra continued, "From the time you beat Colin bloody, to the time we took William from Grayson, your expression was… I've never seen the devil but if I ever do, I'm sure he'll have a grim and cruel expression like you did. I get shivers just remembering the fury in your eyes." Myra shuddered. "In the bible, there's the story about Jonah being swallowed by the whale. If it was you instead of Jonah in the belly of the whale, I'd fear for the safety of the whale. It's as if you have the ability to command a monster out of your soul."

David laughed. "Myra, you're talking nonsense. I'm no monster."

"I don't believe it would have bothered you in the least to have killed any or all of the people involved in the kidnapping."

"If destroying them would have helped me rescue William, I'd have done it without hesitation."

"Would you have been concerned about their deaths?"

"I'm not sure; perhaps afterward."

"That's what frightens me. What if you became infuriated at the children or me? Would you summon your monster?"

"Never."

She looked in his eyes and pleaded, "How can I be sure?"

"If you think my willingness to put my life on the line for my family is wrong; may I suggest I have already demonstrated nothing is more important to me. I would certainly give my life to make sure they were safe… If that meant taking someone else's life, so be it."

"You're strong as an ox; physically and mentally. You can do those things but you've a partner who most likely couldn't. Does my inability to help in a confrontation bother you?"

"I pray you'll never be in a situation where you need to fight; but if you do, as a last resort, remember you've got teeth. William made a lasting impression on his kidnappers with his teeth."

She smiled.

"Also, if you do have to fight, look for something to even the odds. I doubt I could have defeated Grayson without the help of the ax."

He sighed and held her tighter. "I have to admit ... it's only been a week but I feel so close to Nathan."

Myra kissed his cheek. "When we were in Boston, you said the Lord may have put us together for a reason; perhaps to include Nathan and Abbey in our lives?"

"Possibly."

"So we take Nathan with us?"

"Other than his parents showing up, I couldn't leave without him."

***

"We're leaving tomorrow, Abbey."

The day was hot and humid.

Abbey sat up straight and asked, "If we leave, how will Nathan's mommy and daddy find him?"

"We've told Mrs. Watson where we're going so she can tell his parents when they come looking for him." Seated in a rocking chair on the small porch, Abbey sat on Myra's lap while they tried to stay cool with a shared iced tea.

Abbey stared up at Myra and asked, "Will you be his mommy until his real mommy comes?"

"Of course I will," she said wrapping both arms around her and kissing the top of her head.

While she leaned her head against Myra's shoulder, Abbey watched the boys playing at Myra's feet. Myra oscillated in the old rocking chair whose white paint was peeling. The boards of the porch creaked as the chair swayed. "Nathan and William are like brothers. This is the first time I've had two brothers. "

"I'm proud you're being such a good big sister."

Abbey sighed. "We're still a happy family, aren't we?"

"Yes we are, precious girl."

"Do you love me?"

"Of course I do."

Abbey squeezed her arms around Myra. "I know."

"I've been expecting your father to return with a wagon and team. I don't know what could be taking so long."

"I'm glad we're not going on one of those boats again."

Chapter Fourteen: David Learns about Horses

Four hours later, Myra saw David slowly walking up the street. His head was bandaged; he walked with a limp and kept his left arm across his body.

She ran to him. "David, what happened?"

"I didn't know you don't walk up to a horse from the rear so I got kicked in the head. I learned horses not only don't mind stepping on your foot, they don't mind crushing your body against a corral when you try to harness them. My ribs are killing me. I'm going to lie down."

"You have broken ribs?"

"The doctor said they're just bruised."

"Did you secure the horses and wagon for our journey?"

"The livery owner wouldn't sell them to me."

"Why not?"

"He's afraid the horses would kill me."

"What are we going to do?"

"Steamboat again. We'll have to prepare Abbey. At the moment, my head is throbbing and my ribs hurt so bad I can hardly think. I need to rest."

***

Dillon Kaplan came home after work with a newspaper under his arm, greeting Hannah and Sarah as he entered the kitchen.

"I want to show you something I read in the paper. It seems a steamboat blew up on the Mississippi a few days ago. They've printed a list of survivors."

"The children?" Hannah asked, frightened.

He opened the paper and read aloud, "Of the known survivors were, Mr. and Mrs. David Kaplan plus their children; one-year-old William, six-year-old Abbey, and two-year-old Nathan."

"They're safe?"

"Apparently."

Sarah said, "They're married and have a boy in between Abbey and William? It doesn't make sense."

"That's the way the paper reads."

"We should get word to Myra's parents."

"At work tomorrow I'll give the article to Colin."

***

Sitting and waiting for a barber to become available, a large man who walked with a limp read a newspaper report of a steamboat accident on the Mississippi. He raised his eyebrows and reacted with anger when he noticed one of the names.

"Kaplan survived … lucky bastard. When the day comes I find him he won't be so lucky." He turned to his friend. "He's the one what crushed my wife's face."

"Isn't that what killed her?"

"It was." He stared at the paper. "I'll bet someone in that river town knows where they settled."

Chapter Fifteen: Adventures in St. Louis

The steamboat trip to St. Louis was, thankfully, uneventful. Abbey was most relieved to disembark. They found a hotel for the night and David secured passage on a second steamboat which left for Independence in four days.

"I'm meeting with Jack Kaufman sometime tomorrow. He's the man who sells supplies to the store," David said the following morning.

The children were awake just after dawn, so Myra decided to take them for a walk and find a place to eat. David was still experiencing terrible headaches. He left them to find a doctor.

While the foursome proceeded up the bustling street, two slovenly, unshorn men on horseback, dressed in black drover's coats, approached. Four tired-looking, sweat covered, and frightened Negro men, dressed in scraps of torn clothing were chained together; their lines of chains were roped to one of the men's horses which led them up the street.

"Why are those men wearing chains?" Abbey asked.

"I suspect they're escaped slaves and the men on horses are called bounty hunters."

"What's a slave?" she asked.

"Some people believe it is acceptable to own another person to work for them. It's a cruel and dreadful practice." Myra purposely spoke in a voice which was loud enough for the bounty hunters to hear.

"You new around here?" one of the men asked as he dismounted.

"We arrived yesterday. We're headed to Independence."

"The bible allows slavery and it's legal in Missouri," the second bounty hunter called out while tying his horse to the hitching post."

"I am not a slave," the tallest of the men in chains said.

"Shut the fuck up," a bounty hunter said as he clubbed the man.

Myra shouted, "He's in chains. You don't need to hit him."

"Ain't none of your damn business, lady."

The tall man called out, "Madam; I thank you for your interference. I assure you I am an educated and free man. I have a home near Hannibal, Missouri with a wife and children awaiting my return."

"Maybe I should get the sheriff," Myra said.

"Go ahead," the bounty hunter said with a smirk. "Ain't you heard of the Fugitive Slave Law of 1850? It says I gots every damn right to take these niggers back to their rightful owners an' get paid for doin' so."

"How do you know you have the right men?"

"Them three got brands on 'em and I got this here drawing for the one with the big mouth." He took a page out of his pocket, uncrumpled it and held it up to Myra's face.

"He looks nothing like the drawing. Release him or I *will* find a sheriff."

She glanced around, spotted a man with broad shoulders wearing a badge on his barrel shaped chest. Myra called to him. He walked up. "Is there a problem, miss?"

Myra glared at the bounty hunters. "They're telling me the tall man is an escaped slave but he looks nothing like the picture they have.

"Let me see it." He was reluctantly handed the paper.

"He looks nothing like this."

"We don't want no trouble, copper," one of them said as they quickly removed tools from their saddle bags and released the man. One of them whispered to him. "Next time we're up here, we'll be looking for you, nigger."

"Thank you kindly, ma'am," the man said as he hurried away.

"You're welcome," Myra said. She nodded to the sheriff, "And thank you, sir." He tipped his hat in her direction before walking away.

She herded the children into a small eatery.

"You have an Irish accent," Myra commented to the waitress.

"St. Louis primarily consists of German and Irish immigrants," the waitress said.

"What brought them all the way out here?"

"The Germans were persuaded to immigrate by the writings of Bek and others. The area around town reminds them of home. Many of the Irish left their homeland due to the Potato Famine."

"Seems a bustling community," Myra said.

The waitress said proudly, "We've our own public schools and water system plus Catholic, Protestant, Methodist, and Jewish religious institutions, plus a university."

***

After eating, Myra decided to continue exploring the town.

Proceeding up the wood planked walkway which fronted the stores, someone yelled, "Stop hitting her." An average sized, scruffy and balding man accosted a woman, knocking her off the side walk and into the street.

"She's my woman and I'll do as I please." He cuffed her again. "How dare you spend money without my permission?"

Myra gasped in horror when she saw the woman's face. The woman raised her hands and arms to protect her head in a vain attempt to ward off another blow.

"Abbey, keep the boys with you."

She approached the man. "Keep your hands off her."

He looked at Myra out of the corner of his eye and backhanded her across the face. She saw stars and fell to her knees. William tried to move toward his mother but Abbey restrained him.

"Mom said to stay here, William."

The man slapped his wife across her face which knocked her to the ground. Myra struggled to her feet and grabbed his arm before he could hit the woman again. She suddenly remembered David's instruction concerning teeth; she clamped them on the side of the man's jaw. He howled in pain, pulled her off by the hair, and threw her to the ground.

William continued to struggle to get free of Abbey's grip. Finally, he tried to bite her hand which she quickly withdrew, allowing him to run toward Myra. On the way he picked up a rock and threw it at the man. Two more rocks flew past William as Nathan and Abbey did the same.

The man's attention momentarily focused on the children after one of their rocks painfully caught him in the temple. The distraction gave Myra the opportunity to grab a shovel out of his wagon. She swung it with all her might; catching him on the back of his head where it struck with a resounding clang. He tottered briefly then keeled over like a felled oak. The woman smiled at Myra who dropped the shovel and, panting heavily, helped her woozy childhood friend to her feet.

"The Lord bless you Myra," Kathleen Devlin said as they embraced. "You appeared just in the nick of time."

The same sheriff they'd spoken to earlier in the day ran up. After a brief discussion with Myra he dragged the women's nemesis to his feet. "Are you drunk and beating your wife again, Kessler?" He started to drag him away, but paused long enough to tell Myra, "You will find the folk in Missouri are good people and not like this contemptible man."

Abbey yelled to the sheriff. "Thanks for helping my mom."

"Yeah, thanks," Nathan called out.

"It was my pleasure. You should be proud of your mother. She has a good heart."

Myra dusted off and straightened her clothing.

"Children, I want you to meet my good friend, Kathleen Devlin. Kathleen, this is Abbey, Nathan, and William."

"Myra's family," Kathleen said smiling broadly. "They're gorgeous; and brave."

"When we get home, we'll have a talk about following what I tell them to do."

"William started it," Abbey said.

"Why am I not surprised?"

"My rock hit him first," Nathan said proudly.

"Are you okay?" Myra asked Kathleen.

"It would have been worse if you hadn't shown up."

"Does this happen often?"

"Only when he's drunk; so it happens a lot."

"Are you married?"

"No. He's a friend of a friend of my father and paid my passage from Ireland. I've been his housekeeper and whipping boy … while I pay off my passage."

"To hell with him," Myra said as she rubbed her sore jaw. "Any money you owe him has already come out of your hide. My family and I are on our way to Independence. I think you should leave the bastard behind and come with us."

"He'll be in jail for at least a day," Kathleen said. She looked around. "I've no future here."

"If you can drive this wagon, let's get your things."

"One thing I've learned here in America is how to drive horses. Let's get the kids on." They lifted the boys onto the back and Myra put Abbey on the seat between her and Kathleen.

"Motherhood suits you, Myra."

"It's been a trial at times but worth every moment."

"My insides ache to have a child," she said, looking over the children. "Your husband?"

"An educated man who's been offered part ownership in a business. That's why we're traveling."

"Educated? You're doing well."

"How long have you been here?"

"I left Ireland some months after you."

Nathan and William chatted away behind them.

"I don't understand what the boys are saying," Kathleen said.

"They speak their own combination of Yiddish and English."

"What? Yiddish?"

"My husband is Jewish and I'm raising them as Jews."

Her friend's jaw dropped.

"He's a good man and a wonderful father."

Kathleen sat silently for a while. "Myra, how are you getting your things to Independence?"

"We'll be taking a steamboat again."

"We have two large freight wagons on the farm. I bought one of them plus a team with my butter and egg money. We'll load my things and I'll hitch up the horses. We can get my belongings to the dock and sell the horses and wagon at the livery. That way I'll have some cash besides what I've saved. I've become knowledgeable about horses, cattle, and chickens in the years I've lived here." She laughed. "I wish my parents could see their daughter the cowboy."

They arrived at a modest cabin. Kathleen hitched a team of four horses to her freight wagon and moved it near the front door. Myra lined up items for her and the children to carry out to the wagon. She helped Kathleen load her trunk with items she'd brought from Ireland, some food, clothing, and a handful of kitchenware.

"When we're back to town, I'll buy another trunk for the loose items," Kathleen said. "It's delightful how your children follow what you ask. You're a good mother."

"Let's return to the hotel. You'll stay with us. We'll be a couple nights before we get on the steamboat to Independence."

***

After selling the wagon and horses, plus loading the balance of her things in a second trunk, Kathleen left instructions to have the trunks delivered to the hotel.

She helped Myra put the children to bed for a nap. David arrived and was introduced.

"A pleasure to meet you, sir."

Myra related how she discovered Kathleen.

"I've invited her to travel with us to Independence."

"I'm paying my own way," Kathleen said.

"We can always use another set of eyes to watch the children plus you'll have a chance at a new life," David said.

"I did my best to imitate your fury, David," Myra said.

"Did it help?"

"I'm not sure. I do know I put my anger into the metal end of a shovel. I used it to dent his head. That certainly slowed him down."

When the children awoke from their nap, she nodded to the three little ones. "Your children did their best to back me up."

"Abbey didn't want me to help," William said.

"He tried to bite me."

William put his little hands on his hips. "A bad man was hurting Mommy."

David gave William a stern look and a rapid swat on his butt. "You don't ever … ever … bite your sister. Is that clear?"

"Yes Dad."

"And you?" he asked Nathan who proudly replied, "My rock hit his head."

David turned to Myra. "Don't look at me," she said. "They attacked a grown man. I imagine you would have acted the same when you were their age."

"By the way, Mr. Kaufman invited us to dinner tonight."

***

The following day, David studied Myra and Kathleen as they reminisced about their childhood. They were similar in height and build; the big difference being Kathleen's raven black hair. Even their laughter sounded similar.

"You two look like sisters."

"Should I tell him?" Myra whispered to Kathleen.

"Why not?"

Myra said, "There were rumors around our village. Supposedly my dad was in bed with a woman other than my mom roughly a year after Colin was born."

Kathleen said, "The rumor says we have the same father."

"Is it true?"

"No one's certain," Kathleen said.

"Maybe having illegitimate children runs through all our families," Myra said laughing.

"My lady parts ache on a regular basis which lets me know they want a child," Kathleen said, then added with an impish grin, "Married or not."

David thought they did look and act like sisters. "Myra, is this the other angel?"

"She is."

"You get a hug." He warmly embraced her. She blushed. David wondered if Kathleen's lady parts were warming her.

"Myra, what's he talking about?"

"He knows about us."

"You mean…"

"Yes."

"It must have taken incredible strength of character," David said.

Kathleen shook her head. "Not really; just hunger… Plus the look on my little sister's face."

"Like I told Myra, I doubt I would have been strong enough to do what you great ladies did."

"Great ladies?" She turned to Myra who said, "That's what he thinks."

In a quiet voice, Kathleen said slowly, "Thank you, David."

Myra asked him, "What did the doctor say about your headaches?"

"He said they'd stop after a few days. He also said a blow like this can cause problems when I'm older.

Chapter Sixteen: Travel to Independence

The steamboat is a gentle way to travel," Kathleen said.

"Unless the boiler blows up." Myra detailed their misadventure and how they became parents to Nathan. Kathleen visibly shivered as she learned of their brush with death.

"It's lovely on deck," Myra said. "How about we sit outside? Abbey, would you like to join us?"

"Sure."

"David, will you keep an eye on the boys?"

"I think it's time for them to help me write a story."

Nathan enjoyed providing suggestions for stories where he and his brother were heroes, but William adored the activity. David quickly penned the two boys into a storyline where they were on horseback and raced to rescue a runaway train.

"Thank you, *Aba* David." Nathan gave David his best hug. "We make good stories."

"We're really heroes. My horse went super-fast," William said.

"I jumped from my horse to the train," Nathan added proudly.

***

"How did your family manage during the Famine, Kathleen?" Myra asked.

"I watched my father waste away to nothing. He was one of the strongest men in the village; second only to your father. He, two of my brothers and my older sister died before I left Ireland."

"Your younger sister Kaitlyn and your mom?"

"No idea. The last letter I received from her said they were leaving Ireland for America. I never heard from her again. One of my brothers was talking of going to Australia. She and Kaitlyn might have gone with him."

They sat quietly for a while and then Kathleen said, "I enjoyed meeting Mr. Kaufman. Do you think he'll ever visit Independence?"

"I believe David said he'll stop by every couple months or so."

On the third evening of the five day trip to Independence, the children asked about the Potato Famine.

Myra said, "It was a terrible time."

"Will you tell us about it?" Abbey asked her mother.

"I'm not feeling so well. The boat motion is bothering me. It would sadden me too much right now but one day I will."

"Come children. We'll let your mom rest," Kathleen said. "Let's go to the benches on the deck and I'll tell you what it was like."

The children sat on either side of her and paid close attention. "We were poor; farmers mostly. We didn't own the land our fathers' worked. Not even the land under the houses we built. There was generally enough to eat because we could depend on the potatoes which grew in the fields around our village. One day the potatoes became diseased and we couldn't eat them. People were so hungry they were in pain."

"I've never been so hungry I felt pain," Abbey said.

"Hunger every day; all day long. Young children like your Aunt Ciaran and Uncle William became sick and died, as well as many other people. It was a terrible time as we were constantly surrounded by sickness and death. I lost my father, two brothers and a sister. Sometimes entire families died. Your mother and I were lucky because someone paid our way to this blessed land of plenty."

Kathleen noted Abbey tearing up and Nathan seemed sad but William showed anger.

Through clenched teeth he said, "I going to be scientist. I fix potatoes."

Kathleen smiled at him. "Surely we could have used a wise scientist."

"You and Mom seem like sisters," Abbey said, resting her hand on Kathleen's arm.

"Why?"

"You sound the same when you laugh and have the same smile."

"And when I bad, you make face like Mom," William said.

William and Nathan engaged in a Yiddish-English conversation.

"I don't know what they're talking about," Abbey said, shrugging her shoulders. "How can they understand each other?"

"Some people have a gift for learning languages. I certainly don't."

"Me neither."

Nathan nodded to William and pointed at Kathleen. "You and *Ema* Myra. I think sister."

"We should call you Aunt Kathleen," Abbey said.

"Yeah," William said.

Nathan put his hand on her arm. "Aunt Kathleen… Yes… Aunt Kathleen."

"Is that okay?" Abbey asked.

"Children, it's fine with me but let's ask your parents."

***

After disembarking in Independence they arrived at a flat-fronted, two-story building with a sign on the front which read, 'Mandel-Kaplan Emporium'.

Al swung the front door open for them with a loud greeting.

"We're glad to be here," Myra said after introducing the children and Kathleen.

"Where's Joe?" David asked about the younger Mandel brother shortly after they arrived.

"He's not here," Al replied.

"When's he coming in?"

"He's not. Not now, not ever. Let's get your things upstairs and I'll tell you what happened."

"We'd been up here for a number of months which is when I wrote you the first letter. This woman comes in for some supplies. She'd been crying. Joe was all over her. Her husband just died and left a livery business down by the river. She has five little kids and no time to run it. He left to help her and hasn't been back since except to sign over his share of the store. You're now a half partner."

"Who's been doing the bookkeeping and inventory?"

"I've been trying but it's been an absolute parade of people coming in here day and night so I have time to order goods, take money to the bank but not much else. I think Jack Kaufman, the man we buy from, is cheating us. I hardly have any money left at the end of the month."

David's head felt dizzy. "You have three months bookkeeping to get caught up on?"

"Actually, I think it's closer to six."

"Oh no."

"You and Joe always did it. I figured when you got here you could get things organized. It's also why I decided you should have half the business."

***

The apartment consisted of a kitchen with a dining table, a small sitting area, and three bedrooms.

"Which bedroom do I use?" Abbey asked.

"This one is for your dad and me. You and Kathleen get to pick which one you want as she's going to be sharing with you."

"I don't have to sleep with the boys?"

"No. I think the girls should have their own room."

Abbey gleefully grabbed Kathleen's hand and they inspected the two bedrooms.

"I like this one," Kathleen said. "It has two windows so it's brighter. What do you think?"

"I never shared a bedroom with a girl."

"It will be lots of fun. We'll read to each other and tell stories… We can close the door when we need some privacy."

Myra entered. "Is this room suitable?"

Kathleen nodded. Abbey enthused, "Aunt Kathleen said we're going to have storytelling, reading, and privacy. Oh, and lots of light."

Myra raised her eyebrows when Abbey referred to Kathleen as Aunt.

"On the steamboat ride, I was telling the children a story about the Famine. They said we were alike so they decided I was their aunt. Do you mind?"

Myra smiled and shook her head.

"One thing troubles me, Myra; when I told the children how we suffered and lost family members, Nathan and Abbey were truly sad but William seemed angry. He gritted his teeth and said he would have fixed the potatoes."

"He's a problem solver. I gave birth to him but he's a true copy of his father."

***

While he inventoried the store the first night, David heard Nathan calling from the top of the stairs to the apartment, "*Aba* David! You come home. This house."

"Nathan, I have work to do."

Two minutes later Myra walked down to the store carrying Nathan whose eyes were filled with tears.

"One of your sons is asking for you."

"Myra, I have so much…"

"You played with him every night during our travel. He misses that."

She lowered Nathan to the floor. He ran to David and wrapped his arms around his leg.

David ruffled Nathan's hair. "C'mon buddy. You can help me work."

David counted aloud, putting a finger on each item. Nathan cheerfully imitated him. After an hour, Nathan yawned.

"Why don't you rest on this bag of coffee beans for a bit and then start helping me again?" In a few minutes, Nathan was fast asleep.

An hour later, David picked him up to carry him upstairs. He raised his head from his father's shoulder long enough to ask, "Was I a big helper, *Aba* David?"

"Yes you were!"

Nathan smiled briefly, put his head back on his father's shoulder, and promptly fell asleep.

Myra asked, "Is Jack Kaufman cheating the store?"

"Al has the markups all wrong. I'm getting it straightened out and we'll be fine. I suspect the store is making more than enough to support two families. We may even be able to put some savings away."

***

"Everyone, this is Carol," Al said, two months later one Friday night as he introduced his girlfriend and her family.

They enjoyed a pleasant *Shabbat* while getting to know Carol.

Al cornered David. "Her family owns a food importing business in New Orleans, Louisiana. I'm giving her a ring tonight and they've asked me to move down there to work in their business."

"You going?"

"I'd make more money than I possibly could here. I'll be leaving in two weeks."

"And your share of this business?"

"I'll sell it to you. Also you can buy the house I've been renting. It's for sale. It's only two blocks from the store."

Chapter Seventeen: Four Years in Independence

At breakfast, Myra made an announcement.

"In six weeks, we'll celebrate four years in Independence and I'm proud to announce I'm pregnant." She looked at the children. "I have a baby growing in my tummy."

"Congratulations, Myra," Kathleen said giving her a hug.

"Mom, will you have a boy or a girl?" Abbey asked.

"I won't know until the baby arrives."

"I need a sister so you should work on that." She turned to Kathleen. "If I have another sister, we can make room for her in our bedroom."

"Wouldn't I love that?" Kathleen said.

"How did the baby get in there?" William asked, looking at Myra.

"Well…"

Kathleen quickly said, "The Lord looks down from heaven and when he finds a great mother he puts a baby in her."

"Oh…" William said.

"Why doesn't he put a baby in the dad?" Nathan asked.

Everyone looked at Kathleen for an answer.

"Well… Because… Because men don't have breasts so babies can nurse." The children seemed satisfied with her answer and the three adults appeared relieved there weren't further questions.

When the children went out to play Myra said to David, "I'm pregnant again and I don't think it's a good idea to have your thing poking around inside me."

"I've never heard of it being a problem."

"My first pregnancy didn't have problems so I want things just as they were."

"Okay, Myra."

When Kathleen and Myra went shopping, Kathleen asked, "Why are you cutting him off? My folks did it until a couple of weeks before Ma delivered."

"And how many miscarriages did she have?"

"A number."

"I'm not taking any chances."

"He may want to get it from someone else."

"He'll have to manage."

"Men aren't like us. They can't just turn it off."

"He's a good man. He'll do as I ask."

Kathleen selected a few carrots from a vendor's cart. "You may be asking too much."

***

"Four years in Independence today," Kathleen said. "We should celebrate. I found cherries in the market and squeezed them into juice. We can use it to flavor the whiskey I bought."

After the children were asleep, Kathleen fixed them each a drink. Holding up her glass she toasted, "Here's to my Myra … who found and rescued me."

"Thank you, Kathleen, and here's to a continued successful business."

"*L'Chiam*," David said.

They chatted for a couple of hours before David went to bed.

Myra said, "Are you going to look for a husband?"

"Yes. I'm ready but I'm not looking forward to it after my miserable experience in St. Louis. I do want a family so I'll have to have a man in my life. For now, I enjoy working in the store and being close to your children. Since David taught me bookkeeping, I find I enjoy it. It's a challenge to keep all the accounts balanced."

"He tried to show me one time. I hated it so I'm glad you like it."

"Thinking about a man… I enjoy when Jack Kaufman visits. I think he likes me but he's so shy it's difficult to tell."

"He's a Jew."

"I know. Like you, I heard nothing but bad things about them; but I see how David treats you and the children. It makes me wonder. When did you decide to become a Jew?"

"I didn't."

"But you're raising the children as Jews."

"David and I had an ugly fight after I confessed something terrible about our first weekend together. I was terrified he would throw me and infant William out of his home so I said I would raise our children as Jews."

"Would he have thrown you out?"

Myra shook her head. "Never; but I didn't know back then. We were only together a handful of days. Months would pass before I realized the full extent of his devotion to us."

"Didn't you have to become Jewish to marry him?"

"We avoided the problem. We've never married."

"Myra, you're such a close family… I'd have never known. Is he sad you've never married?"

"I think so but he doesn't mention it anymore."

"May I ask why you didn't marry?"

"I couldn't marry a Jew. It doesn't seem so reasonable now, but I felt this deep seated emotion I would betray my family if I became or married a Jew."

"And if he asked you now?"

"If he asked me now, I'd say yes to the marriage and if he wanted, yes to becoming a Jew."

"You love him so much?"

"Besides being a wonderful father and husband, he's truly the family hero. I arrived in his life frightened nearly to death and loaded with bushels of problems. He attacked and knocked them aside just like he attacked and solved his school problems. That's why you'll sometimes hear me call him Mr. Problem Solver."

"I wondered why."

Myra took a deep breath and smiled looking into the distance. "Every time he solved a problem, it was like he took a load of bricks off my back."

She returned her gaze to Kathleen. "What if Jack Kaufman asked you to become a Jew?"

Kathleen looked around the apartment.

"To live like this, have children to adore like your three, and a husband who cherished me and my children like your David, I'd say yes."

Suddenly, Abbey came running out of her room crying. Myra picked her up and asked, "What's wrong?"

"I was having the dream about the water over my head."

"I'll spend the night with you and, if you have a bad dream, I'll be right next to you."

Myra nodded to Kathleen as she walked away. Kathleen collected the glasses and washed them. She checked on Abbey and Myra who were sound asleep.

All that day, her memory kept replaying the moment she saw David stepping out of his bath. Her insides throbbed every time she remembered. She poured herself another drink and quickly downed it.

***

David awoke to the sounds of his wife undressing in their darkened bedroom. He became excited by the outline of her body; minimally visible and dully backlit by the yellowish lunar light coming in the window. She slid under the covers and immediately reached between his legs.

"So… You've decided you want me, Myra."

He kissed and caressed her body then rolled on top of her. She moaned as he entered her. Even buzzed from the drinking, he still did everything he knew to excite her. He heard her moan again as he finished.

She let him rest for a while before gently moving her fingers on him until he wanted her again.

David rolled on top of her a second time and stroked her while stimulating her breasts.

Kathleen whispered, "This is so beautiful." He quit moving; partially withdrawing. She wrapped her legs around him and lifted her hips, taking him fully inside her again.

"Don't worry, David. This will be our secret."

He didn't move. "Finish, David. I'll help you." She reached between their bodies. It was David's turn to moan. He rapidly stroked her.

After he finished, she kissed his cheek. "Thank you." Kathleen picked up her clothing, and proceeded to her own bed.

***

Besides keeping track of inventory, Kathleen helped with sales in the store during the day. She kept an eye on David, who, after weeks of Myra's enforced celibacy, gave hungry smiles to the more shapely women who entered the store. At times he was downright flirting with them. When a freight wagon arrived, David requested it be parked at the back door so he could unload it after the store closed. Kathleen volunteered to help. All the new items went into the storage room at the back of the store until they could be entered into inventory. When the last item was put away, Kathleen closed the door to the store room from the inside.

"David, I want to talk about something. I know Myra won't do it with you while she's pregnant. I think it's a mistake but it's her decision."

She walked up to him and put her hands on either side of his face.

"If you need to do it with someone, please use me."

"I'm fine."

"While you were helping busty Miss Gladstone buy cloth, your pants were bulging like a beehive. Rather than do it with someone else, let me take care of you."

He pushed past her and walked to the front of the store to change the window display.

***

The following morning, Myra announced she was taking the children to Synagogue. David and Kathleen stayed behind as they would open the store.

The two of them alone, Kathleen purposely left the door to her room open as she dressed.

David saw her naked from the waist up.

"Kathleen…"

"Come here, David. Let me take care of your beehive."

"No," he said. "You tricked me before but it won't happen again."

***

The following day, David told Myra what happened after the four year anniversary celebration.

"I honestly thought it was you."

"No…"

I don't believe it; my childhood friend and my husband. How could they? Is David trying to have another child without me? What if she becomes pregnant? Is it my fault because I've refused David? Is it because we're not married?

"We'll talk about this later, David."

Making dinner, Myra said to Kathleen, "You were with my husband the night of the four year celebration."

"I was."

Myra slapped her. "How could you?"

Her hand on her cheek, Kathleen said, "I guess I deserve that… It was wrong of me but… You made it easy by denying him. The night we got drunk, I desperately needed a man so I took your place in bed. I don't think he even realized it was me until we were nearly finished. After you cut him off, I told him he could use me whenever he wanted as long as he didn't go looking for it in the street."

Hands on hips, Myra said, "I helped you out of a horrible life and this is the thanks I get?"

"You didn't want him but I did. He's a strong and healthy man with normal desires. What do you think he should have done? Would you rather he brings home a sickness from using street women?"

"He could have kept it in his trousers but now you may be pregnant by him."

"I'm not, but if you want me to be unhappy about becoming pregnant, you're out of your mind. Have you forgotten your burning desire to replace William and Ciaran? The same fire burns in me, Myra. You have three children. You don't know the river of tears I've cried, not having a child."

"If you were having David's child..."

"Don't act like you're a damn saint. He loves you, Myra. He's given you more than we ever dared dream about. Look at you; money in the bank, a business, and three well-mannered, intelligent, and cheerful children who adore their parents … plus another on the way. David's seed gave life to three of those heaven-sent bundles and, unless you tell them, no one would believe Nathan wasn't your own flesh and blood. Every girl we grew up with should be surrounded by the love and comfort David's put in your life."

"He's not a saint."

"None of us are saints. He's a man and has failings like most men. When a man's part becomes hard, it somehow blocks their brain. For certain their thing has no conscience. I'll never understand why the Lord designed men as such but we women have to deal with them as they are … not how we'd like them to be."

"You're my best friend."

Kathleen said in a subdued tone, "And sister."

"How do you know?"

"Just after Father died and Mother was quite ill, she said to seek out your father if she died. Mother assured me he would take me in."

"No wonder we've been so close."

"I know."

Myra returned to preparing dinner. "Did you enjoy having David?"

"He made my body do something I've never experienced. It was beautiful. I can't wait to have my own husband to do it with."

"How do we work this out?"

"You start taking care of him and I'll avoid him."

***

At the docks in Philadelphia, a large man stepped up to the pay window.

"Durant Grayson," he said.

The paymaster handed him an envelope.

He counted its contents and announced, "I'll be traveling west for a few weeks."

Grayson used part of the money he'd been saving to travel to Burlington, Iowa. He asked around town about the whereabouts of the survivors from the steamboat explosion.

A man told him, "You should talk to the mayor. He kept track of their names."

Finding the mayor, he said, "I was a close friend of a man named Kaplan. I was wondering if you knew where he lives or if he continued his journey."

"They continued their journey but I don't remember where. You might head over to Mrs. Watson's place. They stayed with her. She lives up on Third Street. I'll get her address for you."

***

Claire Watson opened her door to find a rather unkempt man asking about his good friends, the Kaplans. His appearance led her to question his voracity; he didn't look like a man who might be friends with the Kaplans.

"They went on to St. Louis," she said. She was about to tell him more but something about his grin made her skin crawl. "Yes, he and his wife Anabelle left for St. Louis."

"Were David and Anabelle staying there or going on somewhere else?"

"Sorry, I don't know. I'm doing some cooking so you'll have to excuse me."

"Certainly. I didn't mean to keep you."

The man turned and limped away.

***

"Myra, we need to talk about what happened between Kathleen and me."

They slipped into bed. "I feel someone's stabbing my heart every time I think about it."

Calming down somewhat, she said, "Part of this is my fault. I shouldn't have stopped us, but you should have talked to me."

"Would you have listened?"

She shook her head. "Probably not."

"Then how could I have gotten your attention?"

"I'm not sure. I asked the doctor today and he said it wouldn't affect my pregnancy." She put her head on his chest and one arm and a leg across him. "Sometimes I get so wrapped up with the children I forget I'm to take care of you as well. I'll try to do better."

He kissed her cheek and said, relieved, "I as well."

***

In St. Louis, a large man with a limp went from hotel to hotel asking about a couple and their three children.

"Name of Kaplan," he said.

Each hotelier reminded him hundreds of people came through each year. He nearly gave up his search when one owner said, "Kaplan. I remember a man came through here about three years ago who might have the name … with a family. He wore a big bandage on his head and was having terrible headaches. I told him where to find a doctor. Hurt his ribs as well when he was up river … in Burlington I believe."

"Any idea where they went?"

"No, sorry."

He thought he was at a dead end. On a lark he decided to interview doctors who might have treated a man with a bandaged head.

"Bandaged head? Hmmm … a few years ago … funny story about getting kicked by a horse … might have been named Kaplan. Traveling to Independence if I remember."

Chapter Eighteen: Jack Kaufman

One month before Thanksgiving, Myra entered the store and heard David cursing. She heard a panel of wood breaking and hurried into the back. He wore the dark look she hated. David was examining his skinned knuckles when she saw a hole in the store room door.

He pointed to the two freight wagons which carried goods recently unloaded from a steamboat. "None of this crap is what I ordered," he raged. "What the hell am I supposed to do with this shit?"

Fury was written into his body language as he paced up and back. Myra thought David's head would explode. "Please don't use those words. The children may hear you."

"Myra," he said, through clenched teeth, "I sent Jack Kaufman a fifty-percent down-payment on my order. I'll start running out of things before he can get me a correct shipment."

"I'm sure it's an honest mistake. He's never cheated you or caused you any problems before."

"A few weeks and it's Thanksgiving. Folks are already arriving to prepare for the springtime trip across the Oregon Trail. How will I supply them? If the river freezes, it will cost a fortune to have the goods brought over here by wagon. Look at this stuff. What the hell am I supposed to do with … four John Deere plows? Who would want a metal plow? Everyone makes their own out of wood. I'll bet it's expensive as well."

"Send him a letter."

"Do you know what letters cost?" he shouted.

"It's better than having you angry enough to kill someone."

Kathleen left the front counter when she heard David shouting.

"What's wrong?"

"Kaufman sent me the wrong goods. I'm worried I'll start running out before he can replace the order."

She looked over the material. "I'll inventory them and post a sign as to what we have. We might be able to sell some."

"I'm sure every family heading out on the Oregon Trail is going to want to carry a heavy metal plow with them."

David walked away in a huff.

"Where are you going?" Myra asked.

"Post office."

***

A concise reply arrived.

"My fault. Replacement shipment and myself leaving today on steamboat for Independence. Be there in five days. Jack K."

Abbey said, "I like Mr. Kaufman. He has funny stories for us when he visits."

"Be sure you and Nathan have your school work done so you can spend time with him."

"I enjoy his visits as well," Kathleen said. Myra raised her eyebrows to Kathleen who returned a smile.

The same day a father and his two grown sons spent some time reading the list Kathleen posted. They walked into the store and asked to see one of the plows.

"I've got four you can look at," David said sarcastically.

The father eyed it carefully and ran his hand over it. "My brother in Iowa said I should get one. Any chance we can try it?"

"Why not?"

Three hours later, the old man and one of his sons hurried back into the store.

"You still got them other plows?" the father asked anxiously.

"Yes."

They appeared relieved.

"How much for three?" the son said.

"Three?" David said.

"The one we got and two more."

"I don't have a price yet. They were sent here by mistake."

"Mistake my ass," the older man said. "That thing plowed through my field like shit through a goose. I'll give you five dollars for each one."

"I'm sorry but I don't know what to charge."

He looked at his son who nodded. "Okay. I'll give you seven for each one and sign a paper which says I'll settle up with you when you get the proper price."

David was shocked. "What's so special about this plow?"

"I plowed twelve furrows the length of a field and didn't have to stop to clean the moldboard."

David appeared confused. The farmer explained, "That's the part which reaches down and cuts into the soil. With my old wood plow, I have to stop and clean the moldboard a few times in every furrow because my soil is so sticky. This thing kept clean so I didn't have to stop. A clean plow was easier on the mules as well. That plow is gonna save me enough time to double or triple the acreage we plant."

His son nodded in agreement.

***

"Nathan and William!" Abbey called out when she saw their expected visitor arrive. "Mr. Kaufman is here."

The children greeted him with hugs and tittering voices. In the family's parlor, Abbey sat next to him and the boys sat on his lap.

"So children, tell me what adventures you've experienced since I was here two months ago."

"We don't really have adventures," William said, "just school."

"What have you learned in school?"

The children talked about their lessons and he entertained them with stories about his travels around the Midwest.

Jack brought the correct supplies and tons of apologies for the incorrect shipment. He reviewed pricing with David and Kathleen.

"Everything looks good," David declared, "and I want more of those John Deere plows."

"Whenever I can get more. They sell like—"

"—Shit through a goose?"

Jack laughed and the children giggled.

"David, no crude language in front of the children, please," Myra said.

"Sorry."

"Please join us for dinner," Myra said, noting how Kathleen's eyes shone when she gazed at Jack.

While walking into the kitchen, Myra whispered to Kathleen, "He's great with the children."

"I love watching their faces when he tells them stories. We could pull down the shades and we'd still have light coming from the children's smiles. He'll make a great father."

***

The following morning, Jack and Kathleen took the children for a walk along the river.

"Dad said you were a soldier," Abbey said.

"I was."

"What kind of soldier?" William asked.

"I was a scout."

"How do you scout?" Nathan asked.

"Usually you're on your own ahead of the other soldiers. You have to be quiet and try to move without making a sound and without being seen."

"You mean like invisible?" Abbey asked.

"Something like that."

Jack said, "We can play a game to see how quiet you can be. Aunt Kathleen will stand here on the trail facing the river. We'll walk out in this field and take turns trying to sneak up behind her. If she hears the person trying to sneak up on her, she'll raise her hand and that person has to start over."

"Wow, a sneaking game," William said, jumping up and down and applauding.

First Abbey then Nathan tried walking up behind her. They each moved halfway across the field before she heard them. Then it was quiet for so long that Kathleen wondered if they played a trick on her and weren't even trying. She jumped, however, when she felt a tap on her back and spun around to find a grinning William right behind her.

"I'm pretty sneaky," William said, grinning broadly as his brother and sister cheered.

"But you didn't make us invisible," Nathan complained.

Jack gazed around the field, spotting two bushes about fifteen-yards behind them. Each was five-feet-wide and three-feet-high.

"Abbey and William face the river. I'll make Nathan disappear. Kathleen, please watch them and make sure they don't peek."

He quickly cut a few branches off one of the bushes and showed Nathan how to kneel at the edge of the other bush while holding the branches in front of him at an angle to make it appear he was part of the bush.

Jack walked back to the other two.

"Okay, turn around and tell me where you see your brother."

They stared and stared.

"He's close enough, he could hit you with a rock," Jack said.

William finally spotted him when Nathan's arm got tired and one of the branches wiggled. "I don't believe it. He's right here."

"Where?" Abbey said.

"At the end of the bush," William told her while pointing.

Abbey finally saw him. "My brother is invisible!" she yelled.

Nathan came running up to them. "I'm a scout. Right, Mr. Kaufman?"

"Definitely," he said.

"What does a scout do if someone gets hurt?" Abbey asked.

"It depends. First you have to stay calm so the person who's hurt stays calm. If they're bleeding, you find a cloth and put pressure on the injury until the bleeding stops or a doctor comes along."

"I could do that," she said.

"Here, I have a handkerchief. Let me show you and we'll practice."

***

At dinner, Jack told the family, "I'm selling my supply business in St. Louis and opening a warehouse to store goods which I'll distribute to towns in the Northwest. I'm basing it in Portland, Oregon. It's near the ocean and has a good harbor. David, I'd like you to come in with me."

"We've only been here four years," David said. "Why would I give up a successful business?"

"You're making huge money now as the immigrants buy supplies but they've started building railroads which will take people west without wagon trains. The city of Portland will be a port for the next hundred years at least. Every time a ship unloads, the goods go into storage until they can be distributed. We'll rent space to the good's owners. They'll also pay us to load and unload the ships."

"What if they don't pay?"

"They sign a contract before we store anything which says we can sell their goods to recoup our money. I also think we can buy wagons and hire teamsters. That allows us to charge for delivery to final destinations as well. I can sell anything but I'm not skilled at running a business like you."

"How big an operation are you talking about?"

"I've purchased a large building and land at dockside; eventually we'll need maybe fifteen or twenty employees to staff the place." He opened a briefcase and pulled out a contract. "Go over this with a lawyer. If it's to your liking, sign it, give me five-hundred dollars and we're in business together; fifty-fifty partners. I've also looked at a couple of nice lots where we could build homes. We'd be neighbors."

David turned to Myra, "He's right about the railroads. It's been all over the paper lately. If I sell the store, it would be worth at least five hundred."

"We wouldn't have to spend our savings. We've been here long enough it feels like home. I dread the thought of moving again but maybe it's for a better future."

Jack smiled at Kathleen. "Miss Devlin, would you like to go for a walk so these folks can consider my offer?"

"Let me get my coat."

After they left, Myra said, "The thought of six-months living in a wagon while we crossed the Oregon Trail is not pleasant."

"When the railroads come through, there's no way the store will support us like it has."

"What kind of place is this Portland?"

"No idea. We'll head to the library this weekend and find out. If we decide to leave, we can travel with the wagon trains leaving this spring."

***

"I'm returning to St. Louis to sign paperwork to sell my business," Jack told Kathleen during their walk. "I'll be back here in two weeks with more goods for the store. By the end of December, I'll journey to Portland by ship to begin my new venture."

"What will you do if David doesn't agree to your terms?"

He briefly glanced at the star filled sky. "That would be sad. He has a flair for business and from what I know is honest."

Jack looked up at the new moon, and asked, "What are you doing with your life?"

She smiled. "Waiting for a husband."

"You're a good woman. I'm sure you'll find someone."

Kathleen said under her breath, "Not such a good woman."

They returned to the apartment. Myra removed an apple pie from the oven. Its rich, apple-cinnamon scent permeated the air.

"This is delicious," Jack said. "The business in Portland is going to be big enough I'm going to need an assistant."

"You can hire one when you get there," David said.

"I need someone I can trust."

"With all the folks heading west, surely you'll find someone," Myra said.

He turned to Kathleen and said in a nervous voice. "I need someone who I can love and loves me."

"What?" Kathleen said surprised, and blushing.

He stood up, kneeled at Kathleen's side, and took her hand in both of his. "Kathleen Devlin, I don't drink, I don't gamble, and I have a successful business but I'm as far from perfect as a man can get. Will you marry me?"

"Being far from perfect myself, we may have a chance but you hardly know me."

"Myra, David, and the children know you and all love you. That's good enough for me. We can get married when I return to Independence at the end of December. Then we'll head down the Mississippi and get on a sailing ship to take us to Panama. We cross Panama on a train to the Pacific Ocean where we take another sailing ship to Portland. It's an expensive way to travel as opposed to the Oregon Trail, but it's rapid. We'll have plenty of time to get to know each other on the journey."

Flustered, Kathleen said, "Who's going to marry us?"

"You work it out. I don't care. Whatever makes you happy, that's what we'll do."

"Portland is a long way from here. I won't know a soul."

Myra said, "Kathleen, David and I talked while you were out. We'll be in Portland with next spring's wagon train."

Kathleen put her hand on the cheek of the man kneeling in front of her and slowly nodded. "I'll marry you. I'd love to marry you." She leaned forward and slowly kissed him.

Chapter Nineteen: Trappers and Spears

"Trappers are gathering in town this week. You stay away from them. They look like ruffians," Myra told the children.

Despite their mother's warning, and perhaps because of it, William and Nathan went to see their encampment. They watched in amazement at ax, rifle, bow, and spear throwing competitions. When one of the contestants broke his spear, Nathan picked it up. He and William carefully examined it.

"You boys," one of the trappers yelled. "The blade is sharp. Don't touch it."

"How do you throw it?" Nathan asked.

"Let me clean the broken end first and I'll show you."

The boys watched with rapt attention as the man used a wide bladed knife to smoothly round the broken end of the shaft leaving the spear roughly four-feet long.

"You run a couple of steps, lean way back and use all your weight and strength to throw it as hard as you can. While you're running you aim with your other hand."

"Can I try?" Nathan asked.

"Aim for the big tree."

Nathan did his best and managed to knock some bark off the edge of the tree.

"How about me?" William asked.

"You might be too little."

"He's strong as me," Nathan said.

"Let's see," the trapper said. Nathan handed the spear to William.

He threw in the direction of the tree but it fell short.

"No, no, no," the trapper said. "You don't throw *at* the tree; you throw it like you want to send the spear *through* the tree. You must lean way back just before you launch it and use as much strength as possible."

Nathan tried again. The spear struck the side of the tree and bounced off.

"Better."

"Okay, little one, your turn. Run fast and throw hard. Just before you send it, lean back like you're going to fall over backwards then put all your strength into it... But this time pretend your brother is in danger and you have to save him with the spear."

William hoisted the spear over his head.

He accelerated five steps, leaned far back and transferred enough energy into the spear that his forward motion stopped. The spear embedded itself into the tree with a resounding thud.

"*Le peu de chose que l'on est puissant comme un ours*," the second trapper said.

"He said you are strong like a bear cub, little one. I agree. Stay a moment and I'll make one for you."

"Wow. Thanks Mister."

The boys watched intently as a second spear was fashioned for William.

"You must be careful. The blade is sharp and can cut deeply. This is not a toy."

The second trapper mumbled something in French and both men laughed.

"Here. We're going to give each of you a bag to cover the sharp edges. It has a leather string to pull it tight around the shaft."

"Thank you, sir," Nathan told each of the men as he shook their hands. William did the same.

"One more thing. Take this and keep it in your pocket. A bear tooth will bring you luck and keep you safe." He handed one to each of them.

"Thank you a lot, Mister," William said with a spear in one hand and bear tooth in the other. "This has been the greatest day ever."

***

The two brothers, spears in hand, were half a block from home when Myra spotted them. She sat on the front porch of their house, talking to Kathleen.

"What are those and where did you get them?"

"They're spears and we got 'em from some nice men. They made one for each of us," Nathan said.

"And a bear tooth," William said.

"Let me see," Myra said removing the cover which she handed to Kathleen.

"This is sharp as a razor. You will keep them covered and you are not allowed to use them unless your father or one of us is with you."

"Yes Mom," they replied in unison.

Kathleen giggled. She handed the cover back to Myra.

She tried to keep a straight face while telling Myra, "No seams except around the opening where it was doubled over to secure the string."

Nathan volunteered, "The man said it was a bull bag."

Myra held it between her thumb and forefinger. "Here, take it." She and Kathleen both laughed. "Keep them covered and leave them inside the back door."

Kathleen said, "Where do you think the spears came from?"

"I distinctly remember telling them not to go near the trappers, so I'll bet that's where they were."

"They're learning to be rebellious at a young age."

***

David took them for spear throwing practice when he arrived home most days.

"The boys are both good but William throws with a fluid motion which buries his spear further into the target. His aim is more consistent as well. I think he has Sarah's athleticism."

William was stretching his arm before their evening meal.

"William, maybe you should skip practice for a couple of days if your arm is sore."

"No Mom," he pleaded. "What if something happens? We have to be ready." William looked at Nathan who nodded in agreement.

***

"It's going to be a lovely day, children," Myra said.

"How about a picnic along the river?" Kathleen suggested.

"Perfect," Myra said. "We can take the leftover lamb roast and make sandwiches."

They placed a carving knife, dishes, and food in a wicker basket.

The boys insisted on taking their spears "just in case."

"Boys and their spears," Kathleen said.

She looked at Myra and the two laughed hysterically.

"That must be an old people's joke," Abbey explained to her brothers.

They followed a trail next to the Missouri River for a few miles and looked for a clearing.

Abbey absent-mindedly gazed back down the trail. She stopped walking and stared.

"There's a man following us," Abbey said as she pointed. "He's behind those big bushes over there."

"I don't see anyone," Kathleen said.

They scanned the area and saw a large man awkwardly running, before sliding behind a tree. Myra sucked in her breath. "Oh no!"

"Do you know him?" Kathleen asked.

"The man who tried to steal William. Let's try to circle around and head back to town."

William pulled the cover off his spear, tucking it in his belt. Nathan did the same. The five walked rapidly; continually looking over their shoulders.

"He's getting closer," Abbey said.

"Should we run?" Kathleen asked.

"What if he can outrun the children?" Myra said, beginning to tremble.

"What shall we do?" Kathleen said, terrified.

"Head back to town through the woods."

They moved about fifteen-yards when a large hand reached out from the cover of a huge oak tree and grabbed for Myra.

"Mom, watch out!" Abbey yelled.

She ducked but he still managed to grab her shirt collar. Myra twisted violently away, the collar ripping off in his hand. He threw it down and menaced her with a knife.

Myra yelled, "Children, run away."

Kathleen was petrified, her face turning pale, while the children's faces evidenced horror as they turned to run—except for William whose angry countenance was accompanied by action as he ran up behind Grayson and plunged his razor sharp spear into the big man's thigh.

Grayson, fury in his eyes and chest heaving, bellowed in pain while grasping at his leg. He turned and thrust his knife at William. The five-year-old ducked, dropped his spear and began running. Myra grabbed the carving knife from the picnic basket.

Grayson yelled, "After I kill your mother, I'll butcher you, you stinking pig."

He spun back toward Myra who was breathing hard and trembling.

Grayson grinned, "You think a carving knife will save you? Your husband isn't here this time. He killed my wife and now I'll kill his."

Accompanied by a grunt when he put weight on his injured leg, Grayson swung his knife at Myra's belly. He telegraphed the move so she jumped back just in time to avoid becoming disemboweled.

Even at the fighting distance separating them, she smelled his liquored breath. Another thrust opened a cut on Myra's forearm. She saw him grimace every time he put weight on his torn thigh. Blood was beginning to soak his trouser leg. Keeping a hand on his wound he staggered toward her.

"This is the end for you, bitch!"

Out of the corner of her eye, she saw William approaching with Nathan's spear. Nathan, appearing terrified, wasn't far behind holding a baseball sized rock. Abbey followed with the largest tree branch she could handle.

Grayson noticed Myra looking past him. He turned toward the children. William launched Nathan's spear. He jumped aside as it narrowly missed and bellowed as he landed on his torn thigh. Kathleen finally decided to get in the fight. She retrieved William's spear. Grayson lunged at her, slashing with his knife. This provided an opening for Myra. She was able to drive the carving knife into his throat. He staggered backwards a few steps with blood spurting from his neck. Nathan's baseball-sized rock bounced off his head, snapping it sideways. Grayson dropped his knife, briefly looked at the children, and stared at Myra in disbelief. He tried to say something but only a low gurgle came out. He toppled over like a felled tree.

"Mom, you're bleeding," Abbey yelled. She ran to the picnic basket and pulled out some napkins.

Myra looked at her waist. Grayson's knife opened a thin, six-inch long cut.

"I didn't think he cut me there," she said. Myra bent over as she felt pain at the wound site. Abbey placed a napkin on it. "Hold this, Mom."

William ran over, picked up his spear and brandished it at Grayson's lifeless body. "DAD'S NOT HERE BUT WILLIAM IS, YOU BASTARD."

"Try and stay still, Mom," Abbey said.

Abbey took another napkin and wrapped it around the cut on her mother's forearm. Kathleen cut a third napkin into strips.

"Nathan, keep pressure on this while I tie the strips," Abbey said.

Nathan was staring at Grayson's lifeless body whose eyes were still wide and even in death showed anger. He dropped to his knees. "We killed him."

"Of course we did," William said, still brandishing his spear.

"NATHAN," Abbey screamed. He rocked back on his feet and ran to Abbey's side.

Myra moaned as Abbey tied the strips on her arm.

Abbey said, "Sorry if that hurts, but we have to do this to stop the bleeding."

Myra nodded. She tried to talk through her clenched teeth but was in too much pain.

Abbey and Nathan completed duplicating Jack's lessons and helped their trembling mother to her feet.

"Come children," Kathleen said, "we've got to get your mother to a doctor."

***

William led. Still the scout, he angrily eyed the woods around them while carrying his and Nathan's spears. Abbey and Nathan were on either end of the picnic basket's handle and Kathleen supported Myra who felt dizzy from the pain and loss of blood.

A block from home, a prairie wagon passed them. The driver brought it to a halt and jumped off.

"What have we got here? I'm Dr. Beckham. Let me see those injuries." He checked her arm and belly. "Rivka, I'm going to have to sew the arm."

A tiny woman, not much taller than ten-year-old Abbey, said, "I'm his wife and medical assistant. We'll get you fixed up, dear."

"Sit down," the doctor said as he placed a chair and small table next to her. "Put your arm on the table." He laid out his medical instruments. "I'll wrap your belly but I've got to sew up the gash in your arm first." He turned to Kathleen. "You may not want the children to see this."

Kathleen tried to move them away but Abbey pushed past her and yelled, "I'm going to watch."

"Me too," Nathan yelled and ran to stand at his sister's side.

"I'll stay with Aunt Kathleen to make sure she's okay," William called out. He looked up at Kathleen. "I don't want to see any more blood."

"Me neither," she said.

Dr. Beckham observed the children after he put the first three of twenty stitches in Myra's arm. Despite her mother's obvious pain with each needle insertion, Abbey concentrated on mimicking his moves. Nathan seemed a little squeamish but watched intently.

"Why do you sew up wounds?" Abbey asked

"If it's deep, it may not heal without stiches to bring the tissue together. Closing it also keeps it clean and stops blood loss."

"How do you learn to do that?" Nathan asked.

"You begin by sewing the skin from oranges together. If your mother brings home a roast from a lamb or pig with skin on it, ask her to remove, slice, and split the skin. Practice sewing it back together." He eyed Myra. "If your mother agrees, I have a needle you can practice with but only under your parents' supervision."

Myra nodded.

"What else?" Abbey asked.

"If your mother or a neighbor cooks macaroni, you know, like little pasta tubes, ask for a few pieces and try sewing the ends together. It's difficult but simulates repairing blood vessels."

"What kind of knot is that?" she asked.

"It's called a surgeon's knot. We have to use one which won't come loose."

"Wow, just wow," Abbey said.

After ten more minutes of sewing, he said to Myra. "Rivka's going to cover the arm wound. The belly wound isn't too deep so a light dressing will do. I'd like to see you in a week or you can see your own doctor."

"We don't have one," Kathleen said.

"I'll be staying in town until the first wagon train leaves around April. Let me know where you live and I'll stop by."

Myra waved Kathleen over and whispered, "Dinner."

"We'd be pleased if you came to our house for dinner. We're just up the next street over, number 327."

He looked at his wife, who said, "We'd love to but we've got to get settled first. We're going to open a medical office until we leave. How about we visit a week from today?"

"We'll be looking forward to it."

The doctor stood up and took Myra and Kathleen aside. "I've seen tough as nails cowboys pass out when I sew up a wound like yours. You should think about a career in medicine for those two, especially the girl. The boy forced himself to watch, but not her. She's one tough cookie. She asked intelligent questions as well."

"Thanks for letting us know," Kathleen said.

"In eighteen-fifty, they started a medical school for women called the Female Medical College of Pennsylvania. It could be just right for her. Keep those wounds clean and I'll see you in a week."

***

They stopped at the front steps of the house. "Myra, if you can get inside without me, I'll go and tell the sheriff what happened and where to find the body."

Myra nodded. Once inside, she tried to tell the children how proud she was but momentarily choked up.

Finally, she whispered through her tears, "You saved me. You are the world's best children. I love you so much."

Nathan said, "Mom, don't cry. You're safe now."

"I speared him, Nathan hit him with a rock, and Abbey stopped your bleeding," William said.

"Just like Mr. Kaufman taught me," Abbey added.

Myra wrapped her arms around her children.

"Are you happy-crying?" Abbey asked.

Myra nodded, then whispered, "Abbey, please run to the store and get your father."

***

"Myra, Abbey said you've got bad cuts."

She lay in bed. "A doctor treated them. I'll be okay."

"She said it was Grayson and you killed him."

Myra nodded.

"How?"

"With your help." Myra's eyes filled with tears.

"I wasn't there."

She lifted herself onto her elbow. "Your son was. That wretched man initially focused his anger on me, so William snuck up behind him and jammed his spear into Grayson's thigh, slicing open a severe wound. It was difficult for him to move afterward. It caused a lot of bleeding which probably tired him. Things ended when he was forced to jump aside as William threw a spear at him which gave me the opening to slice his throat. The others helped but William…" Myra grinned, "Thank the Lord for William… His bravery helped save our lives. I couldn't have done it without him."

"Are you in a lot of pain?"

"Not so bad. I'm awfully tired. How's Kathleen?"

"Not sure."

"Please check on her."

She lay back on the pillow.

"Try to sleep, Myra. I'll be back shortly." He leaned over and kissed her.

***

"William, your mother told me what you did today."

"I was…" The five-year-old ran to his father, threw his arms around his legs, and cried.

David picked up teary eyed William and held him in a long embrace.

"I was really scared, Dad. My hands were shaking so bad I could hardly hold my spear."

He buried his face in his father's shoulder and sobbed.

"I wish you were there," he said.

"Let's sit outside for a bit."

The sat on a swing in their backyard.

"You could have been killed today."

"I know. I keep thinking about what I did… It might be wrong but I think I'd do the same thing if it happened again."

"I've considered what occurred. If you hadn't wounded him, he most likely would have killed your mom. I feel terrible you were all involved in so much danger."

"What would you have done?"

"I can guess but I wasn't there so I don't know."

"Did I do stuff right?"

"Your mom's alive, so yes you did."

"I hope you'll be around next time."

"Me too, although I hope there won't be a next time."

William nodded.

***

Just before her wedding, David noticed Kathleen fidgeting. "Are you nervous?"

"A little."

"I realize you still haven't spent much time together … but he's a good and honest man."

"If I can teach him to be as good in bed as you, I won't care about the rest."

She glanced over her shoulder and saw Myra nearby.

"Sorry Myra."

Myra smiled and shook her head.

After a joyous wedding for Jack and Kathleen, the Kaplan family accompanied the newlyweds to their steamboat.

"We'll miss you, Aunt Kathleen," Abbey said, hugging her.

"Yeah, we'll miss you," Nathan said.

"Thanks for teaching me to be a scout, Uncle Jack," William said.

"Stay healthy Kathleen," Myra said as she embraced her, "and we'll see you later in the year."

"We'll take on the Northwest as a team like we did here in Independence. God bless you for making me part of your family."

***

"David, our baby is arriving in a few weeks," Myra said the following weekend.

"Do you want me to stay home and not go on the fishing trip with the boys?"

"No, but we do have a decision to make."

"Morris or Ciaran," he said while laying out camping gear.

"What?"

"Morris if it's a boy, after my grandfather, and Ciaran if it's a girl after your sister."

"You've decided without our talking about it?"

He answered without looking up. "You picked the name of our first child so I pick the name of our second."

"Morris or Ciaran…" she said smiling. "Lovely names."

"David, I'm worried about Nathan. Since the incident with Grayson, he's been awfully quiet. See if you can find out what's bothering him."

Chapter Twenty: Camping

Out near the river, David, William, and Nathan were gathered around a campfire having just completed their evening meal. A large thunderclap echoed across the sky.

"Sounds like a thunderstorm, boys. Let's get in the tent and I'll tell you how to determine how far away the lightning is by its flash and when we hear the thunder."

After a brief discussion they wrapped themselves in their blankets.

William was asleep in a few minutes but David noticed Nathan staring at the ceiling.

"What's wrong, Nathan,"

"Nothing."

"Having trouble sleeping?"

"I do lots of nights."

"What do you think about when you can't sleep?"

"The man we killed."

"He was a terrible person."

"But he's dead."

"He would have killed your mom and the rest of you if he wasn't stopped."

"I know."

Nathan took a deep breath and slowly let it out. "William's happy we killed him."

"Are you?"

"I don't know… The night it happened, William fell asleep like nothing. I was awake all night… I still see the pain and anger in the man's face. I wish we didn't kill him."

"Sometimes killing is part of life. Like soldiers or sheriffs or when you have to defend your family."

"Am I wrong to be sad about him dying?"

"Any death is sad and shouldn't be an occasion for celebration. You're sad because you're a compassionate person."

"Compassionate?"

"It means you can feel another person's pain."

"Is compassion a good thing?"

"Definitely."

"Does William have compassion?"

"Not like you and your sister."

"Oh." He thought for a minute, and said, "*Aha*, do you have compassion?"

"I like to think so but I'm really more like William."

"Should I be more like you and William?"

"You're becoming a wonderful young man. You don't need to be more like anyone else."

"Ok."

"Have no doubt, Nathan, you did the right thing. You helped save your mother's life."

"Abbey and I wanted to stay hidden but William grabbed my spear and moved to attack. I thought if William isn't afraid I shouldn't be so I went with him."

"William told me he was scared as hell."

Nathan sighed and shook his head. "He didn't look scared. He looked angry; kind of like when you get upset. His face almost scared me. William led us and he's the youngest. I'm older so I should have known what to do and been the leader."

"Not everyone reacts to danger the same way."

Nathan pulled his blanket up to his neck. "Remember when Rabbi Rubin and his wife visited?"

"Yes. They were on their way to Idaho and they joined us for *Shabbat* dinner."

"He said in ancient times Rabbis were required to be doctors before they could be a Rabbi."

"I remember."

"Maybe if I grow up to be a doctor I could save someone's life."

"If you become a doctor, of course you will."

"Would saving a life make up for killing someone?"

"There's nothing to make up for. You, William, and Abbey saved your mom's life. We're Jews and we have a duty to defend ourselves. The *Talmud* says when someone is coming to kill you, go quickly and kill him first."

Nathan stared at him for a while and said, "Okay, *Aba*."

David ruffled his son's hair.

I wonder if Nathan's too young to understand what a great Rabbi he might be…

***

With David and the boys on their fishing trip and their evening meal just completed, Myra and Abbey were discussing the thunderstorm. The sound of its lightning strikes rattled the house.

Myra suddenly yelled, "Ouch! That hurt."

"What's wrong?" Abbey asked.

"Please, not on a stormy night like this."

"Mom…"

"Abbey, it feels like I'm having the baby tonight. We need to get some supplies into my room and get ready." She paused for a moment and stared at Abbey. *Is it fair to ask a ten-year-old to help her mother deliver a baby? Does she have enough of her father in her to view what may be gruesome sights and still do as I ask? Bloody sights never bothered her before and if I need help she's the only one here.* "Abbey, would you help me?"

"Sure I would. Should I run to our neighbors and tell Mrs. Johnson?"

The storm replied with a thunderclap which shook their house as rain pelted the windows.

"Definitely not. It's awful outside."

Myra gathered what she needed and put on a night shirt.

"Mom, look out the window. That white stuff is falling."

"Snow? This better be an easy delivery."

"How does the baby come out?" Abbey asked.

"Remember when we watched our neighbor's dog have puppies?"

"Oh yeah."

"Mommies have to work to push their babies out as well."

"Is the baby hungry when she comes out?"

"Yes, I expect Morris or Ciaran will be."

"Where does the baby come out?"

"Mommies have a special place where their legs come together."

"Wow, Mom. Lots of stuff comes out down there. Pee, poop, and babies… That's funny," she said, laughing.

Myra joined her laughter. "Oh, Oh. My robe's getting wet."

"Why?"

"That's the water which was surrounding the baby. He or she is going to be here tonight."

"What's wrong?" Abbey said, frightened.

Myra realized she must have been showing her fear.

I have to be smiling and happy. I can't let Abbey see how scared I am while I'm delivering the baby.

She forced a smile. "Abbey, Dad's not here so I'd prefer you stay with me if I need help."

"I will, Mom, just tell me what to do."

"When Mommy's face is covered in sweat you have to wipe away the sweat with the little towel and I may need a drink of water."

Myra reclined on her bed and pulled up her night shirt.

"You have lots of red hair down there, Mom!"

She giggled. "Yes, I do, Angel."

Abbey wiped her mom's brow after a few pushes. "Abbey you are such a great helper."

"You're doing great as well, Mom."

"Thank you, Princess. I love hearing you say that."

Abby gave Myra a little water and mopped her mother's brow again.

A number of hours later, Myra said, "Abbey, I'm trying hard to push the baby out and I might yell on the next push."

"Why?"

"Well … um … I'm hoping it'll hear me and come out sooner … because I can't wait to meet our new family member."

"Am I still doing great?"

"You are doing superb. How am I doing?"

"Great Mom. You're doing just great. This baby is lucky cuz you're going to be its mom."

"Thank you, Abbey. You're an angel to say that."

Myra reached between her legs.

"What are you doing?"

"I was checking to see if I can feel the baby's head. I can so it's almost out. I feel another push coming on."

She leaned forward, pushing hard, and yelled.

Myra leaned back and closed her eyes.

"Are you okay?"

"I'm okay sweetness … just getting tired. I hope the baby comes soon."

"I think he must be a boy because he's not listening to you even after you yelled."

Abbey wore a disapproving furrow on her brow while kneeling near her mother's head. She rocked back onto her feet, took a couple of steps, leaned over Myra's belly, took in a deep breath while putting her hands on either side of her mouth, and shouted in her loudest voice, "HEY BUSTER! YOU BETTER GET OUT HERE CUZ MOM IS GETTING TIRED. YOU DON'T DO WHAT SHE SAYS AND YOU'LL GET A SMACK ON YOUR BUTT."

Myra's laughter filled the room.

"Abbey, I need to push again. Get behind me and help lift my shoulders this time."

Myra strained and yelled. A head appeared. Abbey took two steps toward Myra's hips.

"Mom," she announced excitedly while pointing. "There's a baby head over here … but I can't tell if it's a boy head or a girl head."

Myra laughed briefly, reached down and gently delivered her daughter. She turned her upside down and slapped her bottom. Ciaran immediately started crying.

"I told you what would happen if you didn't listen," Abbey admonished.

She studied Ciaran intently while Myra dried her. "I can see her girl part and everything. Look at her tiny toes." Abbey noticed the umbilical cord. "I think she's still connected."

"I'm going to take care of that right now. There might be a little blood but it's normal."

Myra quickly tied off the cord and let Abbey cut through it.

The ten-year-old stared in wide-eyed amazement at her new sister as she helped her mother wrap the newborn in a blanket.

"Abbey we did it." Myra leaned over and kissed her older daughter.

Abbey's eyes were still wide as she reached out, touched her sister's face, and said slowly, "We did it … my new sister … I feel so happy… Why are you crying, Mom?"

"I'm happy Ciaran is here and her amazing big sister helped me on tonight's journey." She hugged Abbey whose attention was still riveted on Ciaran.

"She's looking right at me, Mom."

"I'm sure Ciaran is happy to see her big sister. Sweetness, I want you to lie down and lean against this pillow. I'm going to put Ciaran next to you. Please keep an eye on her for me because I have a little more work to do."

She placed Ciaran next to Abbey, who rolled onto her side away from her mom putting an arm across her sister; gently patting Ciaran's shoulder.

"She's so tiny. Look at her little bitty fingers. Too bad Dad and my brothers aren't here."

***

When David and the boys arrived from camping the following morning, Abbey ran downstairs and met them at the back door. "You have to be quiet because Ciaran is sleeping."

"Who?" David inquired.

"My new sister, Ciaran."

David, who held sleeping William in his left arm, launched himself across the room and up the stairs, taking them two at a time.

"Wow, I never saw Dad run so fast. C'mon Nathan, want to see our new sister?"

"Sure, I do."

They scrambled up the stairs and into their parents' bedroom.

***

"Are you okay?" David asked.

"I'm fine."

"Should I get the doctor?"

"David, I'm fine and so is Ciaran."

"You delivered her by yourself?"

"Not really. Abbey helped me the entire time. Nothing seemed to bother her. She kept telling me I was doing great and said the funniest things."

"I should have the doctor over to check on both of you just in case."

"Okay. But you haven't held your daughter yet."

He picked her up.

"She's beautiful. Ciaran looks like her mom."

"She has your eyes."

Abbey and Nathan ran into the room.

"My sister," Nathan's eyes widened as David bent over so he could see her. "My new sister…"

William smiled at her. "Hello Ciaran. I'm William. Now six in my family."

"Do you think Ciaran is going to be strong like William and me?" Nathan asked.

"We don't know yet. You and your brother are big boned the same as my sister Sarah. I wonder if you'll grow to have her shape. I'm told Mom's father was a strong man as well." David remembered how close he and Sarah were. "You would adore my sister. I hope things are going well for her."

Chapter Twenty-One: Sarah

A number of years after David and his family moved to Independence, his mother, Hannah, arrived home with news for his sister, Sarah.

"There's a man who's been coming to services lately who's looking for a wife."

"Mother…"

"Sarah, please listen."

"But—"

"—He's a business man from Chicago who comes to Boston to sell leather and leather goods. He's nice looking, religious, and dresses well."

"Mother, I'm not interested in taking a husband. I'm happy living at home for now."

They sat quietly for a while.

Sarah's shoulders drooped and she looked at the floor. "I was hoping for more than an arranged marriage. I was hoping to fall in love with someone." She shook her head. "Mom, while I visited David's family, anytime William started crying, David took him out of his cradle. When I saw the way Myra looked at David while he gently calmed William her demeanor told me there wasn't anywhere else on Earth she'd rather be than at his side. I want to feel the same way about the man I marry."

"Meanwhile there's a man who'd like to have a chance to get to know you."

After a long sigh, she said, "Okay, Mama. I'll meet him."

***

After Sarah met him at synagogue, Alvin Levin, a pleasant appearing, balding man who looked older than his claimed late twenties and was nearly a head shorter than her, was invited to Sunday dinner at the Kaplans' home.

"Have you been married before?" Sarah asked.

"No, I've spent my teen and young adult years building my business," he said, wiping his continuously runny nose. "Now I'm financially successful so I want to start a family.

"I'm surprised you've come all the way out here to find a wife," Dillon said.

"I travel a few months a year," he said. "I've heard wonderful things about Sarah so I thought I would see if we might develop an interest in each other."

After dinner, Sarah and Alvin sat by themselves in the living room.

"So Sarah, what vision do you have for your future?"

"I hope it will include a family. I love children and look forward to raising them."

"A homemaker! How wonderful. A family has always been a goal of mine."

"How do you think children should be raised?" Sarah asked.

"In a loving home, of course. Scholarship is certainly important, as well as character development. My parents taught me setting an example is more important than what we say to our children."

"I agree," Sarah said.

"I used to play baseball with the neighborhood boys, being a bit of an athletically-minded person."

"If we have a future together, you'll know what to do with children who may inherit your physical abilities."

After another hour of conversation, Alvin declared he needed to prepare some things for the following day's business meetings.

"Thank your parents for a lovely dinner and thank you for spending time with me. I hope I can see you again."

"We'll see each other again," Sarah said without any enthusiasm while shaking his hand.

She watched him walk down the street.

How can I tell if he is sincere? Am I to spend my life with a man who constantly sweats and wipes his nose? Is this the price I pay for being tall, muscular, and plain?

"What do you think of him?" Hannah asked after he left.

"I don't feel any attraction to him."

"We don't always have perfection in our lives. Not many men are asking about you."

"How did you feel when you married Dad?"

"Somewhat attracted, but Alvin is different. He has already built a business which will provide you with a comfortable living. He wants children the same as you do. What more do you want?"

"I want to find someone who fills me with such wonderment and joy my body aches to hold him."

Hannah shook her head and looked at the floor. "Few of us find such love in our lives. You need to decide quickly. He'll be returning to Chicago in little more than two weeks."

***

Dillon and Hannah were talking just before they went to sleep.

"There's something about him," he told her. "I don't know exactly what but something's wrong."

"Dillon, our daughter is bigger than most men and plain-looking. How many opportunities do you think she'll have?"

"She's kind and intelligent. She deserves better than him."

"Spoken like a father."

"He doesn't know how lucky he is to spend his life with Sarah."

"She's accepted him. We need to support her decision."

***

The day before the wedding, Hannah, Uncle Zeb and their friends gave Sarah money to help her start her married life in Chicago. She carefully put half the money deep into her trunk and decided to sew the balance into her clothing.

This will be my emergency money in case my trunk becomes lost or stolen.

Sarah and Alvin were married on a mild spring day with overcast skies.

Hannah, who appeared overjoyed, as every mother should be at her daughter's wedding, was convinced Sarah's smiles were artificial. She watched the newlyweds, but never saw her touch him nor do the little things people in love often do. No longing looks… Nothing but forced a smile when she looked him.

Dillon and Hannah were leaving for his new job in Boston immediately after the wedding, so there were lots of tears and sad goodbyes.

***

There was no romance on their wedding night. He got in bed, pushed her nightgown up, pinched and pulled on her nipples for a while, and forced his way inside her. It was painful and within a minute he made some grunting noises and rolled off. After a few minutes he repeated the unpleasant act.

When Sarah awoke the next morning, Alvin was not in the room. She saw his suitcase was still next to her trunk.

It was awful last night. With any luck, he'll travel a lot.

After lying in bed for a while, she decided to dress. When she opened her trunk, she noticed the clothing was not folded properly.

"Oh no," she said to the empty room as panic gripped her.

Her gift money was gone. She rapidly opened his suitcase and found it empty!

This can't be happening.

She hurriedly dressed and ran to the front desk.

"Have you seen my husband?"

"The night clerk said he left early this morning. He said you would be paying the bill when you checked out."

She felt the lining of her underskirt and discovered he hadn't found the money she secreted there.

Alone in the room, she cried. Why was this happening to her? Everyone was gone who might have comforted her. She was ashamed she accepted him so readily. Sarah felt empty and abandoned, but couldn't dwell on those thoughts. She needed to make some decisions. She couldn't stay at the hotel and didn't want to become a bother to her parents while they set up a new life in Boston. What would Myra and David think of her predicament? She tore open her skirt and was relieved to discover enough money to journey west. But what might her brother and his wife think when she suddenly appeared? Would they be happy to see her or feel she was imposing on them? She didn't want to be a burden to anyone.

I'll have to make my own life … but it would be so reassuring if they valued my presence. Perhaps Abbey, Nathan, and William would accept me as their aunt. Thinking of the children brought a smile to her lips. She engaged in a long sigh and prepared for her trip to Independence.

***

Two weeks after they arrived in Boston, the mail forwarded from Philadelphia, caught up with Hannah and Dillon. He arrived home and found his wife sobbing. Rushing into the kitchen he saw her sitting at the table with one hand over her mouth and a letter in the other. It appeared she had been crying for some time.

"You were correct!" She handed him the letter.

> Dear Mrs. Kaplan, I regret to inform you we have no knowledge of Alvin Levin. We do have knowledge of a man named Alvin Singer (NO RELATION!) who has been going around the country posing as an unmarried man looking for a wife but is in reality a crook who manages to marry, spend one or two nights with a woman, steal any money she has, and abandon her. I pray this message reaches you in time.
>
> Rabbi Meyer Singer, Chicago, Il.

Chapter Twenty-Two: Colin at work

"Colin," his supervisor said, "I need you to take the new kid and load the cart with those big iron castings. They need to get over to the building next door for finishing."

"Right away, sir." He pushed and pulled the empty cart, a reinforced buckboard, next to the pile of material.

"Timothy, I need some help. We load this here cart with them castings, and a couple of the other lads will help us push it next door for finishing. These are heavy so we lift them together."

The parts were piled to a height of three-feet above the bed of the cart. Colin called two other men over. One pulled on and guided the steering axle, Timothy and another man pushed the spokes of the tall rear wheels and Colin shoved from the rear.

After they'd move about twenty-feet, Timothy yelled, "Colin, this wheel's wobbling." They stopped pushing. Timothy dropped to his knees and leaned slightly under the cart to check the axle.

"Broke, I'd say." The wheel tilted as they heard wood splitting. Colin grabbed Timothy and shoved him away from the cart just as it tilted and the load slid toward them. The first casting off the cart landed on Colin's legs, knocking him down and trapping him. The balance of the load piled itself on top of him. Men shouted for help but by the time they removed the last of the hundreds of pounds of iron, Colin's breathing stopped and he was without a pulse.

Someone said, "Should we get a doctor?"

One of the men removed his hat. "Never mind a doctor. Only thing poor Colin needs is a coffin. Someone needs to tell his wife and parents."

***

A few days later, Colin's parents, wife, and one-year-old son buried his body on a snowy mid-January day.

"Myra is our only child now," John said. "We should write and tell her of Colin's passing. Maybe she'd let us visit."

"My heart aches to visit my grandchildren. Do you think David will allow us to see them?"

"We won't know until we ask."

A woman who appeared to be in her mid-forties and her daughter approached them.

"At confession yesterday, I heard Colin died while pushing someone out of danger. I'm sad to hear of his passing. He was a good boy."

"Anna Devlin and Kaitlyn, we didn't know you were in America."

"I came some time ago to look for my daughter Kathleen but I lost her address. She lives near a town called St. Louis. I thought it might be close enough to travel to but it's way out on the frontier. I'm saving to travel there."

"Myra is living on the frontier now as well. Some place called Independence."

"How is she?"

"She has a husband and three children."

"Lord be praised."

"This is Colin's widow, Kelly, and her son Leland. They're coming to live with us."

"I'm so sorry child."

Kelly nodded.

"Anna, we're headed home for dinner," Darcy said. "I'd be pleased if you'd join us."

***

Myra was deeply saddened. "David, I've just received a letter from my father."

"How's the family?"

"Colin was killed in an accident at work. He left a wife and child behind who are living with my folks."

"I'm sorry, Myra. You're their only child now. Not having a relationship with us must be difficult for them."

"They're wondering if we'd let them come out and live near us."

"Think they'll forget we're Jewish?"

"Father's begging forgiveness."

David sighed. "What do you think?"

"I'll write and tell them not to come if our Jewishness is still offensive. I'll let them know we're heading west."

"We're a strong family now but if they can't get along with us, they're on their own."

Myra kissed David's cheek. "I'll send a letter right away."

Chapter Twenty-Three: Dr. Beckham

Dr. Beckham and his wife arrived for dinner with the Kaplan family.

"We learned about North Dakota in school," Nathan said.

"How about telling us about your life up there?" Myra asked.

***

It was mid-fall in North Dakota and it hadn't rained in many months. The prairie grass which covered most of the area was dry as tinder. It would only take one lightning strike or the decision by Native Americans to burn the long grass to have fresh vegetation for their livestock, and a roaring prairie fire would ensue.

A teenager riding bareback on a chestnut horse rode up to the front of the cabin where Doctor Beckham, his wife and preschool aged children lived.

"Doc, you're got to come quick. We were out chopping down a tree and Sam Minor got trapped underneath it when it fell. His leg and head are hurt. They're trying to free him but we think he's going to need your help as soon as he's free."

"I have to go," the doctor told his family.

"Maybe your father will bring home a chicken I'll have to trade for something else," his wife Julia said sarcastically to her children.

"Shall I just let him bleed to death?"

"Certainly not! We live out here in the countryside so your family can be poor while you can tend to the country folk."

"Please Julia, not now. I know you hate living here but these folks deserve medical treatment the same as city folk."

"I agree, Gunter," she said bitterly. "Don't you think your children and I should be living on more than the pitiful barter items you earn when you treat someone? If we lived in the city, we'd have money in our pockets instead of chicken feathers!"

"I must go."

***

Two hours later their five-year-old daughter twisted her face and said, “I smell something funny.”

Julia sniffed the air. “It smells like hay burning.”

She opened the cabin door. From horizon to horizon, she saw a dull white cloud approaching rapidly.

“Children we have to leave,” she said, panicked. Picking up a child in each arm, she began running. She made a fatal mistake. Instead of checking the wind’s direction to run away at ninety degrees from the smoke, she blindly started running with the wind. Within a few minutes the smoke cloud reached them. They started coughing, followed by choking. They lost consciousness and mercifully died before the flames arrived and scorched their lifeless bodies.

Doctor Gunter Beckham commemorated the completion of his sixth year living on the prairie of North Dakota by burying his wife and children.

***

The following fall, after losing his wife and two children to a prairie fire, Doctor Beckham decided to leave North Dakota, head for Independence, and take the Oregon Trail to the Northwest. He stopped at a few of his neighbors’ farms to say goodbye.

Pulling up at the Weiners’ small, one room cabin, he noticed the fresh grave out back.

"Paul, Rivka, its Doc Beckham," he yelled as he knocked on their door. "Are you at home?"

Rivka, a plain looking, twenty-year-old woman with dark sunken eyes and short, straight brown hair opened the door to their cabin and greeted him.

"Would you like to come in?" she said, wearing a long sleeved, ragged dress which hung limply on her thin, less than five-foot frame.

"I just stopped by to say goodbye. I'm taking the Oregon Trail to Oregon's Willamette Valley."

"It's a long journey," she said as she flipped a lock of hair out of her face.

"It is but this area has too many bad memories for me. I noticed the grave."

"Paul died two weeks ago," she said, her voice beginning to quiver. "I killed him."

"What?"

"He came home drunk, as usual, and was going to beat me again because I didn't have all my chores done. I took his gun and pointed it in his direction figuring it would stop him from hitting me. He laughed at me and said he'd kill me for pointing a gun at him. He started walking toward me and I shot him. He put his hand over the hole in his chest and he fell over."

"Let's sit down, Rivka."

She walked in bare feet, limping, with her weight twisting on her right heel, over to a small table and chair where she sat down. Rivka grimaced whenever she put weight on her right leg.

"What happened to your foot?"

She sighed and said, "He came home a few months ago and I didn't have dinner ready. He slapped me a few times and stamped on my foot. It hasn't been right since. It's real painful when I walk."

"Let me examine it," he said as he kneeled in front of her.

"He broke your foot and the bones didn't heal in the right position. I can fix this, but I'll have to re-break it and you'll have to stay off your foot for a few days."

She laughed. "How am I going to live for a few days if I can't walk?"

"We'll figure something out. How long has he been treating you in this awful manner?"

"Let's get one thing straight. I haven't been a good wife. I could never do things right."

"Rivka, are you injured anywhere else?"

"My ribs kind of hurt on my right side."

"Over here?"

"Yes."

He put slight pressure on the area. She sucked in her breath as she winced.

"I don't feel a break but I should tape them. Let me get some medical supplies from my wagon."

"You don't have to bother with me. I'll manage."

"I'll be right back."

He asked her to open her dress. She unbuttoned and dropped her dress to her waist, using one arm to cover her nipples. Her upper body and arms were covered in dark bruises and angry looking welts and scrapes.

The doctor was taken aback. “Rivka, no one deserves to be treated like this.”

“I was an awful wife. I deserved whatever I got.”

Gritting his teeth, he spoke in slow, measured tones. “You’re tiny. Paul was huge. I’m horrified we didn’t know you were being abused like this so we could have put a stop to it. ” He taped her ribs. “You must be in constant pain.”

“It’s not so bad.”

He helped her as she gingerly slipped her bruised arms into the top of her dress and buttoned it for her. His eyes became teary. Rivka used her fingers to softly wipe one of his tears off his cheek.

“You don’t have to cry,” she said. “It’s over. He can’t hurt me anymore.”

He gently wrapped his arms around her tiny, bruised, and battered body.

“Rivka, I’m so sorry we didn’t know.”

She didn’t move for a moment and then leaned her forehead against his chest with an audible sigh; her hands grasped the front of his vest. She whimpered at first followed by sobbing as many years of pain and frustration came out with her tears. He held her until she didn’t have any tears left.

“We need to talk about fixing your foot. I’ll stay with you for a few days until the bones have begun to set.”

“I don’t want you to stay here taking care of me. I’m not worth interrupting your travels for. You have plans.”

“Rivka…”

"I appreciate you stopping by but you need to be on your way."

"My plans can wait a few days while one of my patients heals. The way you're twisting on your foot could damage your knee as well as your hip. If we don't get this fixed you could become a cripple. I will do my best to ensure it does not happen."

"I don't want you bothering with me. You have more important things to do."

He ignored her and returned to his wagon for more medical supplies. Doc Beckham poured a white liquid into a cup.

"Drink this; it should dull the pain and will make you feel drowsy."

While she drank the liquid, he modified a calf high boot which he would use to keep her foot from moving while it healed.

"Are you starting to feel sleepy?" he asked.

"A little."

He gently helped her move to the edge of her bed. Using a clean rag and soap, he washed her foot and leg up to mid-calf.

"Why are you washing my leg?"

"I'm really not sure but the cleaner my patients keep their wound sites, the quicker they heal and the fewer problems they encounter. I've received correspondence from colleagues in Europe, indicating better results observing general cleanliness and using boiling water on surgical instruments before each use. Oddly, no one seems to know why." Picking up a rolling pin, he said, "I'll try not to break your skin but this is going to hurt."

"Go ahead. At least this pain will help me heal."

Her entire body jerked from the sharp pain as he slammed the wooden implement into her foot. He carefully taped it and fitted the special boot.

"Thank you, doctor," she said, wiping pain-induced tears off her face.

"The medication I gave you will continue to make you sleepy. Let me guide your foot while you lay down."

She lay back and, despite the pain, quickly nodded off.

***

Doctor Beckham moved his wagon closer to the cabin, unhitched his horses, placed them in a corral, and put some hay out for them. He filled a pot with water, added oatmeal, and placed it on a hook in the fireplace. From the supplies in his wagon, he brought in brown sugar, butter, and a slab of smoked bacon. He sliced a few thick pieces from it and returned the bacon to its wheat bran filled storage barrel.

"It smells great in here," Rivka said when she woke up a few hours later.

"You stay where you are. I've prepared a one bowl meal for you."

"Thank you, Doctor Beckham. I feel guilty you're doing so much for me."

"This is what doctors do."

"I can't pay you much of anything."

"Let's get you on your way to healing before we talk about settling up."

While they ate, Rivka asked, "Tell me about your wife and family."

"We had an arranged marriage. Her family was excited she was marrying a doctor. My family was excited I was marrying into a wealthy family. I loved being a country doctor but it didn't suit her. I grew up on a farm while she grew up in town. My goal in life was to bring medicine to the countryside. Our personalities and experiences did not have anything in common. She considered me a simple minded country bumpkin with meaningless goals."

"Did she love you?"

He stared at his bowl for a while, shook his head, and shrugged his shoulders. "Not really. She loved the kids and took good care of our household, but other than getting her pregnant and providing an income, she wanted nothing to do with me. She continually belittled me in front of the children, so they didn't think I was anything useful. I wanted to believe that, with time, my son would have grown to appreciate me but I don't know if my daughter would have."

"How can a woman not appreciate a man who is bringing medicine to country folks who might not otherwise have it?"

He stopped eating for a while and said, "It sounds terrible to say this but I felt a sense of relief after I finished grieving for them. No more going home to sour faces and listening to degrading remarks about my medical practice."

"Where will you settle when you go out west?"

"I have a chum from medical school who lives where the Columbia River meets the ocean. I'll see where he is and find a place to set up an office."

They heard thunder rumbling in the distance.

"Sounds like a storm coming," Rivka said.

They talked for a few more hours while the temperature dropped. Suddenly, large rain drops beat a staccato rhythm against the cabin's two windows.

"How did you and Paul get together?"

"My number one goal in life was to have children. No one showed an interest in me until Paul came along. I knew he drank at the time we married but thought he would outgrow his need to drink. My nightmare started with an occasional slap. His drinking got worse … so did the beatings. One time I was cleaning the kitchen and left a pan on the floor while I cleaned the table top. He knocked the hell out of me."

"Life here must have been torture."

"The more I got hit the more worthless I felt and the more I believed it was my fault. Even after I've buried him, I still experience a huge drive to get all my chores done to his satisfaction. I feel the same anxiety when the time of day approaches when he would generally come home. It's as if he might walk in the door drunk again."

"You can choose a new future for yourself."

"An alone future is what I'm thinking. I feel like a worn rag ready for the garbage heap. I don't deserve to have a happy life after failing Paul."

"Bullshit. Pardon me for using an obscenity, Rivka, but everyone deserves the best life they can make for themselves."

"Kind of you to say." Her eyes gazed around the cabin. "But this is my life."

"I'll put a few more logs on the fire and go sleep in my wagon."

"No you won't. It's still raining cats and dogs outside," Rivka said. "You'll sleep in here. This bed is wide enough for two people."

"I'll sleep on the floor," he said.

"You do and I'll get out of this bed and kick you with my good foot."

He said through his laughter, "Rivka, stay where you are."

"You are a good and kind doctor, who's trying to fix my foot, who held me while I cried, and cooked a lovely meal. You will *not* sleep on a cold dirt floor. We're not children. You put out the lamp and sleep over here. I may not have much to offer but you can at least get a warm night's sleep sharing my bed and good wool comforter."

***

When he awoke the next morning, she was sitting up and smiling at him.

"Good morning, doctor."

"Good morning and please call me Gunter."

"Did you sleep alright, Gunter?"

"Your comforter kept me so warm I checked to see if the cabin was on fire!"

She laughed. "I was thinking, if you would help me, I could sit at the table for a while."

"You can sit on a chair but need to keep your foot elevated. The next few days will be critical so the bones can begin knitting together properly. I'll help you into a chair and we'll use another chair to keep your foot up."

After he moved her he asked, "Are you in a lot of pain?"

"It's not bad. I've felt worse."

He made them a breakfast of coffee, bacon, oatmeal, and corn dodgers.

"You should ride into the sheriff's office and tell him I killed Paul."

"That won't be necessary. Yesterday, while you slept, I wrote a list of your extensive injuries in a letter stating the injuries you received were inflicted by your late husband and you shot him in self-defense. Further, I wrote if you hadn't he certainly would have killed you. I'll leave the letter with you."

"Do you think they'll believe you?"

"The sheriff is a personal friend. I don't think there should be a problem. Would you like to read or something?"

"I haven't read anything since my school days."

"I mostly have medical books."

"I learned to read but not much else. Tell me, when you were in doctor school, how did you learn about the body?"

"You learn about it according to groups, for instance the bones, the muscles which attach to the bones, followed by the organs."

"Where do you start?"

"First you have to memorize the names of all the bones. I'll get a book and you can see what I'm talking about."

He opened the book. "These aren't perfect drawings and some people's bones differ slightly but it gives a good idea of the support structure of the body."

Rivka looked through the book and pronounced the names of various bones.

"Paul broke my meta … tar … sal bones. Correct?"

"That's right. See this drawing? A person's foot has a natural curve in it. The way your foot healed the curve was gone. Incorrect healing caused all the pain. I tried to put the curve back in when I set it."

"How did you memorize all these names?"

"When I would read the name from the book, I put a finger on the corresponding bone in my own body."

"Hmm, phalanges, metatarsal, calcaneus, cuboid; interesting… Just think, the next time I get angry with someone, I can be descriptive and sound real educated when I threaten to bury my foot in a person's ass up to the middle of my metatarsals!"

Gunter laughed heartily.

"Seeing I'm supposed to stay still for a few days, you let me keep reading and I'll see if I can learn these names. You can quiz me on them."

"I'll be glad to."

After a pause, Gunter added wistfully, "I wanted my wife to learn enough to be my medical assistant but she wasn't interested."

"How are you managing?" he asked when he returned from feeding the livestock and gathering a few fresh eggs.

"Well sir, if you don't take good care of me..." She quickly paged through the book. "I'll become a pain in your T5, T6, and T7 vertebrae."

He laughed again and said, "Excellent. You stay relaxed, and I'll get a meal ready for us."

The rest of the day, whenever Gunter looked at Rivka her finger was on another bone and she was pronouncing its name.

After their evening meal, Gunter suggested, "It's going to be a real colorful sunset. How about I set some chairs outside and we watch the sun go down?"

Rivka nodded, so he put three chairs outside. He gently picked her up, carried her outside, and helped her elevate her foot.

"I feel guilty with you having to take care of me like this. I'm practically a full time project for you and it bothers me."

"All my patients deserve the best care I can give them. It's part of being a doctor. Follow up care is as important, and sometimes more important, than initial treatment. Besides," he said with a huge grin, "I'm enjoying your company."

The sun approached the horizon and the sky took on a reddish hue. Daytime insects and birds quieted and their sounds were replaced by a cacophony of evening insects announcing their presence with chirps, clicks, buzzing, and occasional squeaks.

"I haven't watched a sunset since I was a child," she said while taking in a deep breath of the prairie's sweet and cool evening air. "Thank you for this."

"You're welcome. I find it refreshing just to slow down and stare at a pretty sight like a sunset."

In the fading light, she pointed out the various wild prairie flowers which were beginning to bloom.

"I love wildflowers," she said. "All they need is a little soil and a little rain. They bring a sense of beauty and peace to the world. They come up and their beauty says to us, 'Here I am, come and enjoy me.' If I could, I would have the cabin surrounded by flowers."

"My mother taught us wildflowers are God's gift to people," Gunter said.

"I never tried to beautify the cabin because there were too many chores to complete. I was a horrible wife."

"I doubt you were a horrible wife but I'm fairly certain Paul was a horrible husband. No one ever needs to beat their wife … or anyone else as far as I'm concerned."

"If a husband sets goals for his wife she should meet them."

In a pleading voice, he said, "Rivka, if he sets impossible goals, she can never meet them… He was such a cruel man. Why didn't you leave?"

"I figured I deserved the treatment I received."

"No one deserves to be treated with such cruelty. Did you ever tell anyone?"

"I told his ma once. She said, 'Oh, he's just like his daddy.'"

"Did you ever tell your family?"

"I didn't bother. They didn't think much of me. My older sister is real pretty, has a lovely figure, and she got all of my ma's attention. I was just plain Rivka; not pretty and no figure. I never heard from them after I left home."

Gunter shook his head and stared at the sunset.

Rivka gazed at the ground for a while and then looked at the rapidly darkening sky. She briefly turned toward the doctor and wondered how such a gentle, patient, and caring man landed on her doorstep.

"Tell me what it's like where you're heading," she asked.

"I'm traveling to a city in the Northwest which is surrounded by mountains. They don't get snow or real cold or real hot temperatures like we do here on the prairie. They do get a lot of rain. It's not too far from the ocean either."

"A lot of rain would be good for flowers, not to mention vegetable gardens. I've never seen mountains or an ocean. I've heard tell they're gorgeous."

"It's dark. Let's go in and get you cleaned up. It's important to keep your skin clean while all your scrapes and bruises heal. The lacerations are bad and could get infected. We need to get you bathed and into some clean clothes. We just have to make sure to keep your bandages dry. I'd also like to rewrap your ribs."

"I'm tired, Gunter. Please, let's wait until morning."

***

After breakfast the next morning Gunter heated water and gathered some clean cloth.

"Ready for bathing?" he asked.

"I know you're a doctor but if we could do it in as modest a way as possible, I'd appreciate it."

"Certainly, we will. I'll wash and dry your back, lower legs, and arms then turn away and you can do the rest."

He suggested she shut her eyes while he washed her leg and pretend a lady nurse was washing her.

"I don't think so," she said with an impish grin as she closed her eyes. "I'm going to pretend a muscular and handsome Greek God is washing me."

Gunter laughed.

When he was washing her back, she said, "Gunter this is so exciting. I'm imagining he's naked now."

Gunter laughed even harder.

Afterwards he gently rewrapped her ribs and helped her into a clean dress.

"Your family was wrong," he said. "Your tiny figure is quite feminine; it has curves in all the right places. It's sad they didn't appreciate you. And your smile has all the beauty of a sunny morning."

"Bad timing, Gunter. If you said those things to me when my clothes were off you could have had your way with me."

After another long bout of laughter, he asked, "Were you always this funny?"

"I tried to be before I married. Paul didn't think it was becoming of me to make jokes. This poor cabin must be confused because it never heard laughter until you arrived. Seriously though, thank you for saying those things about me. My anxiety's decreased since you arrived here."

"You have an uplifting spirit. You'd have been a wonderful mother. It's sad you didn't have children."

"Thank you for saying such nice words about me. As far as kids, I guess every time Paul pulled the trigger, the hammer must have landed on an empty chamber."

***

On day four, Gunther quizzed her on the nomenclature of the bones she was studying. She had learned nearly every one of them.

"What should I learn next?"

"How about the muscles which attach to and move the bones?"

"Great!" she shouted. She attacked them with same enthusiasm. She would compare her own muscles with the diagrams the same way she did with the bones. This time she kept flexing different muscles as she not only learned their names but what they did.

At dinner, Rivka asked, "You need to let me help you with things around the cabin. I feel guilty you're doing everything for me."

"No feeling guilty allowed. The only doing you need to accomplish is to heal."

"I can't help it when there's so much to do."

"You've trained yourself to feel guilty about getting Paul's chores completed. You need to think and train yourself to complete those things *you* think are necessary … and you do them on your own schedule."

"I'll never be able to pay you for all you've done and the time you've spent here."

"You've kept me laughing for the last few days which was plenty of payment. We shared a lovely sunset together and you pointed out the beautiful wildflowers I hadn't noticed."

***

On day five, Gunter said she could start taking a few steps. She was stiff from all the sitting but got around without too much pain.

"Looks like you can be on your way, Gunter."

He rapidly shook his head and said, "No. I've been thinking about it. I want you to come with me."

"What?" she said with eyes wide. Rivka plopped into a chair.

He kneeled next to her and took her hand in both of his.

"I have enjoyed our conversations and laughed more in the last five days than in the entire six years of my marriage. Please Rivka, you must come with me and you must marry me."

"I think those sunsets we watched together must have affected your mind," she said as she ran her fingers through his hair. "You're a doctor and a good man. You don't need me; a failed wife."

"I may be a doctor but you, sweet lady, are anything but a failed wife."

"Look around the cabin, Gunter. I'm the only wife in here. I don't know who you're talking about."

"Rivka, you insisted I share your bed instead of sleeping on the cold floor. You appreciate sunsets, wildflowers, good humor, and, most importantly, me. What else does a man need?"

"A wife who can get her chores done in a timely manner."

Gunter ignored her remark. "If you'll have me, we'll be married by the first judge or clergy we find. I have plenty of room in the freight wagon for all your things. We'll take your chickens, cattle, and horses. I'll buy them from you, as well as your land so you'll have your own money to travel with."

Rivka thought in silence for a while and then put her hand on his shoulder. "You don't buy anything. If we're going to be together, whatever I have becomes ours."

"We'll do things as you please. So you'll come with me?"

Rivka couldn't speak another word. She put both hands on his cheeks and nodded yes.

"I'd like to hold you again," he said.

She opened her arms to him and he held her ever so gently.

He pulled away slightly, leaned into her, and softly placed his lips on hers. Rivka's heart raced and her breathing quickened.

"Thank you, gentle man," she whispered as she kissed his cheek.

They packed the cabin's contents and moved them out to stage for placement in the wagon.

"Gunther, I think the items we won't need on a daily basis should go toward the front of the wagon."

He looked over the wagon and laughed.

"You're right. It makes no sense I placed the cooking things in the middle when they should have been at the back for easy access."

He smiled in her direction and proceeded to rearrange the contents of the wagon according to her instructions.

When they got in bed, he moved so their bodies were touching. He kissed her lips and put an arm across her. The warmth of his closeness allowed her mind to relax.

Rivka closed her eyes and listened to his breathing for a while. She slept soundly.

***

After crossing into South Dakota, they stopped at a small town to buy supplies. At the store they met two other families also headed for Independence and the Oregon Trail. They decided to travel together.

Six days before reaching Independence, one of their fellow travelers came running up just as they were beginning to get the day's journey under way.

“Dr. Beckham, would you come and look at Henry?” Mrs. Ellen Markey said. “He’s got so much pain in his belly, just above his right leg, he can hardly stand up.”

The doctor rushed over to Henry, a tall, lanky man with black hair and full beard. He found him sitting on a cot in his tent.

“I’m sorry to bother you, doc, but this pain is gettin’ fierce.”

He lifted his shirt and pushed his pants down to the tops of his legs. “It hurts like hell right here.”

Gunter put his hand over the area, which was warm to the touch and quite painful to pressure.

“I’m going to help you lay back, Henry, and we’ll need to do some quick surgery.”

“Surgery?”

“Your appendix is inflamed and if we don’t remove it, you can develop a sickness which may kill you. Mrs. Markey, will you please start some water boiling?”

“Rivka, I need you to gently wash this area where I’m going to perform an incision. I’ll get my surgical tools ready.”

With Rivka at his side, Gunter quickly opened Henry’s abdomen and removed the diseased tissue. Since she studied their names during their journey, she was able to quickly hand him the desired surgical tool as he called for it.

“Henry needs to remain lying down for the rest of the day, Mrs. Markham. I’ll come and look in on him every hour. Sleep would be good for him and, when he wakes, we have to keep him as still as possible so he doesn’t tear up his stitches. The group of us will wait a day until he feels better before we begin traveling again. Mrs. Kelly has volunteered to cook for the group while you tend to Henry."

"After-surgery care is just as important as the procedure," Rivka said, sitting down next to Mrs. Markey. "He needs to drink plenty of water and he must do what the doctor says for the next few weeks and he'll be like new."

"Thank you so much. Henry and I don't have much but when we get settled out west, we'll pay you something for fixing him."

"Fine, Mrs. Markey."

"Henry doesn't have a handsome face and has a long, lanky body, but he's as good to me as an angel. I thank the Lord every day for bringing Henry into my life. I can hardly wait to give him children."

Gunter and Rivka walked back to their wagon. "I'll clean the surgical tools," Gunter said.

"Was I a help today?" Rivka asked.

"When an appendix becomes diseased, it can burst and spread poison all over a person's body through the circulatory system we talked about. We removed it before it burst. Having you knowing the names of the instruments and following my instructions so carefully, I was able to get in, remove the diseased tissue and sew him up in less than half the time it would take me when working alone. It means he wasn't open as long so he wasn't bleeding as long. After surgery, a patient may look pale from blood loss."

"Henry didn't look pale."

"He can thank my beloved medical assistant."

"Don't be silly."

Gunter stopped walking, put down the wood box which carried his instruments, and placed his hands on her shoulders.

"We saved a man's life today. An untreated appendicitis attack is nearly always fatal. If Henry does well in the next few days, in six weeks or so he can forget this ever happened. We … and I emphasize *we* … took good care of him today."

Chapter Twenty-Four: Timely Arrivals

Sarah's left her things in her steamboat's cabin and went for a walk in St. Louis as it would be a number of hours before the same boat was leaving for Independence. She was walking near the docks when she heard a gunshot. The noise caused the four horses pulling a freight wagon to panic. They pulled hard on their traces and started to run. The wagon's driver tried to slow them and leaned heavily on the brake. With the horses going one way and the wagon pulling against their motion, the force on the rotted wood connecting the tongue to the front axle caused them to separate. With the axle unconstrained, it pivoted and the heavily laden wagon plowed onto a crowded sidewalk and into the corner of a two-story building. Part of the wall and roof collapsed. Screams emanated from those trapped under the building.

"People are caught under there," Sarah heard someone shouting.

Sarah lifted her skirt and ran to the scene. A large section of roof pinned a number of people.

"We have to lift this," a man said.

She looked around. "Over to the construction site. We need boards to lift the roof."

They ran to a pile of lumber and returned with thick boards and construction workers.

"Let's lift this side," she yelled after examining the collapsed roof. Pleas for help emanated from below the wreckage.

They slid their boards under the locations she indicated.

"Now all together… Lift!"

Sarah grunted as she jammed her shoulder against the board to lift the roof which moved a fraction of an inch. She saw a number of women and a few men watching.

She yelled at them. "Get the hell over here and help! This could be your kin."

The watchers transformed into helpers. A woman who looked to be in her late teens also jammed her shoulder under the beam Sarah was supporting. With much straining, the roof began lifting.

"You two," Sarah called to a teen and her father, "start pulling them out."

After a couple minutes, her shoulder was killing her and she could see the others were near the end of their strength.

"Hurry up," she yelled. "I don't know how much longer we can hold this."

"Last one's out," the teen yelled after another minute while pulling out a young child.

"Down slowly," Sarah called out.

A thin woman sobbed as she clung to her rescued young son. Six people were pulled free including the lifeless bodies of an elderly couple. A man with cuts on his face kneeled at the side of a woman. He shook her and yelled her name. She groaned and put a hand up to her bruised face.

"Someone get a doctor," the man yelled. Another woman, roughly his age, tried to comfort the injured woman as well.

Sarah patted the shoulder of the teenaged girl who pulled the victims out. "Good work, young lady. What's your name?"

"Rose Minton. I was kinda scared under there but tried to concentrate on getting the people out."

"You've quite a daughter, sir."

"Thank you. I'm proud of her. She evidences strong character like her mother. Rose is off to college in New York in a few days."

"She'll be a fine woman and educated as well. Work hard in college and you'll go far, young lady."

"Thank you, ma'am."

"Thank you, as well," Sarah said to the other teen. "Your name?"

"Kaitlyn."

"What brings you to St. Louis?"

"My mom and I are looking for my sister."

"Good luck in your search."

She patted her shoulder as the steamboat's whistle blew. Sarah hurried away to catch her waterborne ride for the last leg of the journey to Independence.

***

A tall and big boned woman arrived in Independence as a light snowfall began. "I'm looking for the store owned by David Kaplan and the Mandel brothers," she inquired of a tall, thin teenager.

"You'll find it about a block down on the left, ma'am. They'll have anything you need."

"Thank you, young man. I've been praying for some weeks they'll have just what I need."

"I can deliver your trunk to the store if you like."

"Please do so," she said, giving him a coin and rapidly walking in the direction he indicated.

Sarah, while still nervous about how she would be received, smiled as she looked in the direction the young man indicated. There was a large, boldly lettered sign above the entrance of a two-story building which proudly announced, 'Mandel-Kaplan Emporium'.

***

Four crudely dressed and drunk ruffians were in the store arguing with David about the total price of the goods and whiskey they wanted to buy.

"It will be another two-dollars or you can leave," David told them.

"Seeing as there is four of us and only one of you, maybe we'll beat the hell out of a damned Jew today and just take this stuff."

A tall, rugged looking woman strode into the store just in time to hear the abusive language.

"Excuse me, Mr. Proprietor!" she shouted. "Do you sell full size ax handles?"

David's head spun in the direction of the familiar voice as a knowing smile spread across his face. Abbey, Nathan, and William arrived through the back with a shopping list from Myra.

He shouted, "They're in a barrel on your left, ma'am."

The woman selected one which was about three-feet in length and approached the four ruffians. The largest of them said, "Maybe I'll just take my two-dollars out of the hide of one of these kids."

Before David could reply, the woman stated firmly, "Touch one of those children and I'll remove your head from your shoulders."

"Who the hell are you?" one of the ruffians said, laughing.

"Who I am is none of your concern, but let me assure you, engaging in aggression toward these fine people will be the last thing you do."

The largest of the ruffians approached the woman.

"I generally don't hit ladies but I'm going to make an exception just for you."

He drew back a ham sized fist to strike the woman but the last thing the ruffian saw, before he lost consciousness, was an ax handle being used like a pugil stick which the woman moved so rapidly it seemed to slam both sides of his head at the same time. The ruffian on his left started toward the woman. She twisted in his direction while using an uppercut motion with the ax handle. She jammed it into his abdomen with enough force to lift him off the ground and quickly followed with a blow to the back of his head. He joined the first ruffian in unconsciousness.

The three children looked on in wide-eyed astonishment. William pantomimed the woman's motion with the ax handle, saying, "Wham, bam, wham!"

David, meanwhile, jumped over the counter, grabbed a bottle of whiskey, and broke it over the head of one of the other ruffians who immediately slumped to the floor. The last ruffian wore a look of terror as David and the woman started moving toward him. He backed up with his hands raised. The woman put a hand on David's shoulder.

In a sweet voice she said, "We think you should leave."

"Pick up your friends and get out," David growled.

With the woman easily twirling the heavy ax handle in one hand, obviously more than willing to use it again, plus David's right hand still gripping the upper half of the broken whiskey bottle, the last ruffian quickly dragged his friends into the street.

"You arrived just in time," David said as he hugged her.

The children came running up.

"Who is she, Dad?" Abbey asked.

"Yeah, who?" William wanted to know.

"This is my sister; your Aunt Sarah. Sarah this is Abbey, Nathan, and William."

"If you're my aunt you get a hug," Nathan said as he wrapped his arms around her.

"Me too," Abbey said while also embracing her aunt.

"And me," William added.

Sarah leaned over, hugging each of them. "Now this is a fine welcome."

"Sister, you are a sight for sore eyes." He took another turn hugging her.

She kept an arm firmly around him.

"Is your husband with you?" he asked.

"No," she said in a sad voice. "It's a long story."

David nodded toward Nathan and said, *"He speaks…"*

"*I'm Aunt Sarah,*" she said to Nathan whose eyes lit up when he heard her speaking Yiddish.

"*Aunt Sarah,*" he said, also speaking in the same language, "*will you teach me to read and write Yiddish? My Aba was teaching me when he got lost.*"

"*I would love to,*" Sarah said.

"What did they say?" Abbey asked.

"Aunt Sarah said she's your aunt."

"Aunt Sarah, will you teach me Yiddish?" Abbey pleaded. "Nathan's been trying to teach me but either he's not such a good teacher or I'm not such a good learner."

"Abbey, I'd love to."

"*Aunt Sarah is here today,*" William said in Yiddish.

"Listen to this one. I *am* here today and happier than you can imagine, William. Good Yiddish, little man."

Abbey said, "If you're my aunt you need to meet my sister Ciaran because you're her aunt too."

"Ciaran?" Sarah asked, turning to David.

"Six-weeks-old," David said. "You've arrived just in time to help Myra with a newborn."

"A newborn… What a blessing."

"C'mon Aunt Sarah," Nathan said, grabbing Sarah's hand. "I can show you how to get over to our house. If you don't make a lot of noise and talk politely, *Ema* Myra will let you hold Ciaran."

Abbey was about to go with them but remembered the list.

"Mom needs this stuff."

"Go with your aunt," David said as he glanced at the list. "I'll bring these things over."

Abbey ran after the others.

***

Myra was nursing Ciaran in the parlor, seated in a rocking chair, when Abbey, Nathan, William, and Sarah burst into the room.

"Mom, Aunt Sarah is here," Abbey announced.

Myra's face lit up. She stood and put an arm around her. "I'm so happy you're here."

Sarah's eyes were riveted on Ciaran.

"I'd let you hold Ciaran but she's busy with dinner."

Sarah laughed. "She's beautiful … like your other children."

"Thank you. Please sit down. Are you hungry?"

"I'm fine."

"Nathan and I are going back to the store in case more bad guys come in," William said as they ran off.

"What are they talking about?" Myra said.

"Just a little misunderstanding; nothing to worry about," Sarah said.

"So tell me how you ended up coming out and are you going to stay? We have plenty of room."

Sarah detailed her misadventure with Alvin and said she'd like to stay.

"The fool is behind you now," Myra said. Her face brightened. "You can't imagine how happy I am to have more family around."

"Myra, I have a personal question I'd like to ask."

"Go ahead."

"When you became pregnant, did you have to pee all the time?"

"Yes, why?"

Sarah looked at her lap. "I missed my monthly and I have to pee all the time."

"You're pregnant! Congratulations!"

"I'm so ashamed," Sarah said, her eyes filling with tears as the joy of meeting with her brother's family seemed to drain out of her. "There were so many signs he was a rotten apple but I ignored them. My desire to have a family blinded me."

"Don't cry, Aunt Sarah," Abbey said, sitting next to her and putting her arm around her. She cried harder on hearing Abbey's words.

"Sarah," Myra said in a reassuring voice and squeezing her shoulder, "you're with family now. We take care of our own. I must tell you about the night I delivered Ciaran. The weather was terrible and rattled the windows and shook the house. The boys were out fishing and my blessed Abbey helped me through the delivery. I assure you, we'll be helping you when your time comes and we'll all help you raise your child."

"We yelled Ciaran out, didn't we, Mom?" Abbey said.

"Yes we did."

"Yelled her out?" Sarah said, leaning her head to the side and raising her eyebrows.

"We'll have to tell you the story," Myra said.

Sarah nodded toward Abbey. "She didn't mind seeing a birth?"

"The sight of things which would wilt a cowboy don't bother Abbey. Every time we visit the doctor, she questions him about how injuries heal or how the body works. He gave her an old text book so she can learn the names of bones."

"If I get hurt, I'm going to call Abbey," Sarah said.

In a matter of fact manner, Abbey said, "I can stop the bleeding and get you to the doctor. Don't worry."

Sarah stared at Abbey for a long time.

"Something wrong, Aunt Sarah?"

"Abbey, you look so familiar and your voice…"

"Her birth mother's name was Shayna."

Sarah's face lit up. "Oh my God. Shayna was one of my best friends until she moved to Boston with her little sister."

"Not sister; she and David's daughter," Myra corrected.

"My mom died when I was three."

Sarah said slowly, "Shayna and David's…" She rested her hand on Abbey's cheek. "We were close. I have many stories to tell you about your birth mom."

"Dad said she was intelligent and kind; just like my now mom."

"She was indeed."

Chapter Twenty-Five: Tales from the Wagon Train

"Your sister and our older daughter are a team," Myra said proudly while watching Sarah and Abbey preparing dinner. "I'm most pleased the way she teaches Yiddish to the children and helps them with schoolwork. They can't wait for her to begin their daily lessons. Even William, who seems to have as much energy as a locomotive, sits still and works hard; although our decision to encourage Nathan speak to him in Yiddish from the time we traveled here has helped immensely."

"Sarah arrived with a huge hole in her heart. William, Nathan, and especially Abbey, have gone a long way to helping her repair it."

Myra smiled thinking of the children's bright expressions and behavior when around their aunt. "The way she relates to the children, I'm sure each of them believes they're her favorite. I hope she can find a partner. Sarah is so perceptive. He must have been some inventive crook to fool her; not to mention fooling your parents."

David laughed. "I'll tell you one thing; that crook better pray she doesn't have an ax handle nearby if she ever runs into him."

"I'm glad she's traveling with us to Portland. More help with the children will be golden."

"Did you notice, William spent nearly an hour rocking, holding, and talking to Ciaran last night?"

"I saw them," David said. "He's certainly close to Abbey and Nathan but he seems especially close to her."

"I would never have predicted tough William would develop the ability to be so gentle."

Myra put her arms around David. "You usually hold me at night but the last few weeks … are you upset with me?"

David took a deep breath and exhaled slowly. "I'm hesitant to tell you … but … a family came in the store the other day. They left on last year's wagon train. After six-weeks on the trail and the loss of two family members, they returned to Independence."

"What happened?"

"Things…"

"Like?"

"Not long after you begin the journey, broken wagon parts litter the sides of the trail. Other than a bucket of axle grease, you don't need to take spare parts for prairie wagons because you can find what you need along the trail."

"That's a good thing."

David shook his head, pushed away from Myra's embrace, and began pacing.

"It also implies the wagons will need repair. I bought our wagon from a builder who assured me it was worth the extra cost to buy a wagon with tight seams for river crossings."

"Also a good idea."

"We will also be stopping occasionally to rebuild the wagons. He gave me a list of tools I'll need."

"I still don't see a problem."

David stopped pacing and faced Myra with a furrowed brow and the color draining from his face.

In an angry tone, he said, "The problem is I'm not a damn carpenter and I'm certainly not a blacksmith. Nathan, William, and I watched carpenters and blacksmiths building a wagon. They have carpentry and metal working skills using tools which I've never so much as held in my hands. I'm a man who uses math to run a business. I watched a carpenter use draw and jack planes on a two-inch by two-inch by four-foot long timber which will be used as a brake handle. He quickly rounded the square sides into a smooth round shape with amazingly dexterous hands." David shook his head. "I don't have skill like they do. I've never used my hands to build anything. What if I need to repair something on our wagons?"

"I'm sure the other men will help you."

"I may only need William."

"What?"

"He asked why the wagon wheel's spokes were angled. I've seen wagon wheels all my life and hadn't even noticed. The builder explained about the direction of the forces on the wheel. William kept asking questions from the size of fasteners to the type of wood used. By the time we left, the builder joked about offering him a job … but I'm the one who'll be responsible for keeping the wagon in good shape and it frightens me."

"We'll manage."

"I'm not so sure…"

"What else did the people who quit the journey say?"

David took another deep breath and shook his head. "They lost a two-year-old child the first day. He was playing in front of a wagon wheel when the oxen started moving and the little guy was crushed to death. They only stopped long enough to bury him and kept going."

"Oh Lord. We'll have to watch the children like hawks."

"They said it's a problem because there's so little for the kids to do when traveling."

"We'll need activities for them."

"They said there are graves all along the route. They turned around when a family with six children was lost … washed away during a river crossing. The woman said she'll never get the children's screams out of her head." David turned and began pacing again. "I may be putting the family at risk in situations which I don't have any idea how to prevent or resolve." He looked at Myra who kept biting her lip. "Am I making you anxious?"

"Yes, but each journey I've taken with you has improved my life and the lives of our children… I can't wait to meet up with Kathleen and Jack. I miss her so. I'm going to concentrate on the warm feeling I'll have when we meet again to ameliorate my worry."

"At least we know Grayson won't be following us."

Myra smiled and nodded.

"I'm thinking we should follow Kathleen and Jack's example and take a ship out west."

"If you think we should… It's a lot more money. Abbey will be a wreck once we tell her we're traveling on the water."

David stopped pacing. "I'll have some crates constructed for our things. We could be ready to leave in a few weeks."

"Dr. Beckham will be disappointed. He was looking forward to traveling with us."

"Have you heard from your folks?"

"Not yet. Maybe they've decided against coming out."

***

In the school yard, children were competing to see who could climb the highest in the trees. The children gathered as Jimmy Beasley seemed to be higher than anyone could remember. They were cheering him higher when the branch he was standing on gave way. His legs hit a branch as he dropped and turned him so he was falling head first. He screamed and tried to grab a branch but missed. He plowed face first into another branch and begin to rotate like a pinwheel. After viciously striking other branches, his body hit the ground with a sickening thump. Most of the children ran away but Abbey and Nathan plus a few of the older children ran toward him. His forehead had many lacerations and the right cheekbone was sunken.

"Somebody get Dr. Beckham," Abbey said. One of the older boys tore out of the school yard.

"Abbey, his right arm," Nathan said.

"Nearly torn off at the elbow. Only a little skin holding it on. He's losing a lot of blood there." She and Nathan looked at each other. In a nervous voice, she asked, "Tourniquet?"

He hesitated, studied the injury and said, "Yes." Nathan pulled his long sleeve shirt over his head. He looked at the boys who remained at the accident scene. "Someone with a knife cut off my sleeves." One of the boys stepped forward and did as he asked.

Meanwhile, Abbey found a twelve-inch by one-inch stick. After sliding the sleeve under his upper arm she knotted it into a loop. She put the stick into the loop and began twisting.

"Do you agree the bleeding's stopped?" Abbey asked.

"Stopped, definitely," Nathan said. He tied the other sleeve around the arm and onto the end of the stick to prevent it from rotating loose.

The school-house teacher approached. "What are you children doing? Nathan, stop that. What are you doing to him?"

Abbey said, "Mrs. Kimmel, this is called a tourniquet and we used it to stop his bleeding."

"What?"

Nathan explained, "Look at his right elbow… His lower arm is almost torn off."

Mrs. Kimmel made a screeching sound and turned away.

"Make way," Abbey yelled. "Dr. Beckham is coming."

The doctor raced up on a buckboard. One of the older girls steadied his horse as the doctor jumped off. He kneeled at Jimmy's side.

"He fell out of the tree," Nathan said.

"You two put the tourniquet on?"

"Yes, sir. We agreed it was the only way to stop his bleeding," Abbey said. "His name is Jimmy Beazley."

"Jimmy, can you hear me?" Dr. Beckham yelled.

The boy moaned. Dr. Beckham checked to see if there were other wound sites.

"Jimmy, I'm going to take you to my office." He lifted him onto the back of his buckboard. "Someone notify his parents and tell them to get to my office as quickly as possible."

***

That night, just before their evening meal, Dr. Beckham arrived at the Kaplan's home, his brow furrowed.

"Please come in," William said.

"Thank you, William. Are your parents home? I'd like to speak to them."

David invited him into their parlor where he spoke to them briefly. Abbey and Nathan were called in. William remained at the doorway.

"You two did the right thing today," Dr. Beckham said without any hint of a smile. "Jimmy would have bled to death at school if you hadn't used the tourniquet. Please tell me how you decided it was appropriate."

"You told us bleeding on an arm or a leg which has an amputation needs a tourniquet," Nathan said. "Plus you said using a tourniquet is a desperation thing to do because it can destroy what's left of a leg or arm."

Abbey said, "His lower arm was only being held on by some skin." Myra shivered. "Most of the muscle on his forearm was ripped off and the upper sections of his ulna and radius were torn from his elbow."

Myra shivered anew. "That poor boy."

Dr. Beckham sighed. "You took one huge risk. If you'd gotten it wrong you could have cost him his arm."

"He was bleeding so bad we had to make a decision," Abbey said.

"You made the right one."

David said, "Dr. Beckham is worried the little knowledge you two have might lead you to think you know something about being a doctor and make a wrong decision which could damage someone."

"I don't think we're doctors," Nathan said.

"We just used what you and Uncle Jack taught us," Abbey said. She began to fidget. "And I asked Nathan if we needed a tourniquet. I didn't do anything until we both agreed."

Dr. Beckham, unsmiling, took a deep breath. "As it happens, Jimmy died."

Nathan stared at the floor. Abbey asked, "Why? You said we did things right."

"He was injured in other places … probably internal injuries."

"How do you fix those?" Nathan asked.

"We generally can't because we can't see inside someone."

"You need a machine for that," William said.

"That would be a blessing beyond measure," Dr. Beckham said. "I wanted you to hear about his death from me, kids. Sometimes doctors do their best but patients die anyway. Because of the tourniquet, he lived long enough for his mother to talk to him."

Abbey's eyes filled with tears.

Dr. Beckham put his hand on her shoulder. "That's really what medicine is about; doing our best but knowing it might not be good enough." Abbey nodded as did Nathan.

***

Early Sunday morning, Myra said, "David, I have a surprise for you but you need to put on your suit."

Thirty minutes later, Myra, dressed in one of her finest dresses and David headed out the front door.

"You look great," Abbey called.

"Thank you, Abbey," Myra said. "We'll be back in an hour."

As they walked, Myra's ebullient expression couldn't be missed.

"Going to tell me where we're going?"

"We're almost there."

They stopped in front of Rabbi Hirschman's home.

"What's going on?" David said.

"For the last year, each time I took the children to study Judaism with the Rabbi, he also gave me things to study. I've become Jewish and today is our wedding."

David opened his mouth but no words came out. He tightly embraced Myra.

"David, I can hardly breathe."

"Sorry. You don't want the children present?"

"William believes he was born Jewish and I don't want him thinking anything else. As far as they're concerned, we've always been married. This is my present to you for being our hero, always believing in me, and providing a life for us which is far beyond anything I could have imagined as a child."

Rabbi Hirschman and his wife welcomed them to their home. As the Rabbi began speaking, tears rolled down David's cheeks.

Chapter Twenty-Six: The Storm

A few weeks later, Myra said to David, "Sarah, Abbey, and I are going down the block to the butcher. We'll only be gone a few minutes."

As they left the house, Abbey said, "Those are dark clouds."

"Yes they are … and they're moving quickly. I hear thunder in the distance. Let's hurry."

***

"We'll wait here until the rain subsides," Myra said after they completed their purchases.

A rumbling sound filled the air as the wind whipped into a frenzy.

"We have to get home," Myra screamed, trying to make herself heard over the sound of the wind. Mr. Brown blocked the door.

"It's too late," the butcher said. "We have to get to my storage room. It's the strongest room in this building."

Myra looked down the street and watched the storm pick up a horse, send it once around it's funnel, and flying through the air with its eyes wide, tongue hanging out, and legs flailing. It crashed through the second story wall of a home across the street. She watched in horror as the roof of the Kaplan home peeled away. First shingles, then framing. The walls of the second floor leaned away from the wind, disintegrated, and took flight. Wood and debris from the other buildings, already ripped asunder, pelted what remained of the Kaplans' home.

"NO!," she screamed.

Mr. Brown dragged her away from the front of the building, pushing and pulling her into the storage room. The terrified threesome sat on the floor and wrapped their arms around each other as the building shook. Sarah grabbed one of the Browns' toddlers and held him in a protective embrace. Windows imploded. Myra and Abbey felt tiny shards of glass imbed themselves in their skin.

Abbey screamed. The fierce storm lifted Sarah as the corner she occupied ripped away shortly before the balance of the building they were in came apart.

***

David and the boys heard light tapping sounds on the living room's windows.

"The sky's a funny color," William said, gazing outside. "Let's go upstairs and see what it looks like."

"Look at all this. Some big stuff is flying through the air," Nathan said as they peered out a window in their parents' bedroom.

"It must be a huge storm," David said.

"Maybe it's one of those tomato storms we talked about at school."

"I think you mean tornado storms."

"Oh yea. Is that a funnel cloud?"

"I think so."

"It's headed for that barn."

They watched as the barn was ripped to shreds by the funnel cloud.

David yelled, "Get in the root cellar under the kitchen. I'll get Ciaran."

The house creaked as the wind increased. Debris from destroyed buildings and trees began banging on the exterior. A low pitched rumble increased in intensity.

David scooped up his daughter and her blankets while the boys ran to the kitchen. They shoved two chairs aside and lifted the door to the root cellar. They were wide eyed and both jumped as a tree limb came crashing through a living room wall. David clambered in after them to the sound of braking windows and shrieking wind.

"William, hold Ciaran. Nathan, get the other board," David screamed as he put the first board into its latch to secure the door. "Get in the corner," he yelled, indicating the area furthest from the door.

The foursome's ears were assaulted by the sounds of the house moaning, the creak of nails being pulled out of wood, debris smashing into the structure above them, and the rumble of the storm as it tore across the top of them.

"I hate this," William yelled.

"Me too," Nathan screamed.

Wind noise battered their ears as did the sound of the door to their protected space which vibrated while the wind tried to rip it open.

David saw William hold tight to Ciaran as his older brother put his arms around both of them while David tried to spread himself over his children. They forced their bodies into the corner as if trying to get as far from the storm as possible. Ciaran screamed; tears running down her face. In an attempt to shield her from the noise, William positioned her so one side of her head was against his chest. His hand covered her exposed ear. The boys kept their eyes jammed shut as if not looking might decrease the danger they were in. Each time debris slammed against the door they cringed anew.

***

The noise at the butcher shop diminished as the storm moved on.

Abbey tried to move but she and Myra were pinned under a pile of broken boards. Mr. Brown pulled them off. "Are you okay?"

"I have some cuts." Myra began removing the little pieces of glass from Abbey's arms and a few from her cheek.

"We need some bandages," Abbey said.

Mr. Brown began cutting aprons into strips.

"Where's my Aunt Sarah? She was right over there."

"My boys are uncovering her. The force of the storm caused her to end up in the yard next door."

The butcher's wife bandaged Abbey's one severe cut, which was located on her upper arm.

"Let's check on Sarah," Myra said.

"We'll take some bandages in case we need them," Abbey said.

They house next door was reduced to a pile of boards and debris. The butcher's eighteen-year-old twin sons lifted a heavy beam. Sarah moaned. They removed the remaining material which covered her. Mrs. Brown lifted her screaming toddler from Sarah's arms.

Myra saw a severe laceration above Sarah's right ear which continued to her forehead. Blood covered the right side of her face and neck. Her ten-year-old daughter grabbed a length of cloth. Abbey and Mrs. Brown ran it a few times around Sarah's head, tied it, and wiped the blood off Sarah's face and neck.

"Aunt Sarah, can you hear me?"

Sarah's head lolled side to side a few times; she opened her eyes briefly, put a hand on Abbey, and quit moving.

Mrs. Brown said, "She's still breathing. We need to get a doctor over here."

Abbey looked down the street. Its former row of houses were reduced to a long pile of rubble.

"Where's my house? My brothers … Dad … and Ciaran…" She and Myra began running.

Mr. Brown yelled to his sons, "You boys go with them. There might be more folks trapped."

They stopped running and looked up and back.

Abbey said, "I think this is our house, but that's not our roof."

One of the twins said, "It could have come from another building."

Myra called her husband's name a few times. "I hear something…"

One of the boys said, "Me too. Sounds like it's coming from the back of the building."

"The root cellar," Myra said as she followed the twins to the source of the sound.

"In here," she heard Nathan yell.

The foursome ripped away the material covering the door. The teens lifted it. David, Nathan and William, who still held Ciaran, walked out to the cheers and hugs of Myra and Abbey.

"We're going to look for other people to help," one of the twins said.

"Hey, thanks!" William yelled after them.

"Nothing left of our house," Abbey said as Myra embraced them.

"Thank God you're okay," Myra said.

"Look over there," Nathan said, pointing up the street. "Those houses are okay. Maybe the store survived."

"Let's go see," David said.

"Can I hold Ciaran?" Myra asked.

"Sure," William said.

She cradled her daughter in her left arm. "Your brothers and father took care of you, Ciaran."

The boys grinned at each other as they walked to the store.

They found the store intact but for a few broken windows. Nearby they saw Dr. Beckham and others, tending to the injured who were lined up on the wooden sidewalk.

"Some people have covers pulled over their faces," Nathan noted.

"Probably the one's who died," David said.

William said, "Maybe we should go see if we can help people, Dad."

"There's going to be plenty to do. Let's go," David said.

"William," Myra said, putting an arm around her youngest boy, "Thank you for holding Ciaran as the storm passed."

She pulled him tight against her.

William let her hold him for a while then pushed out of her grasp. "Mom, I gotta go help people."

"You be careful, young man."

"Yes, Mom."

Dr. Beckham saw them.

"Kaplans," he yelled. "If you're healthy, we need help over here."

"How's my sister Sarah?" David asked.

"She's got a headache the size of Texas but she'll be fine."

***

Ciaran yawned, stretched, and opened her eyes.

Myra approached Sarah who sat back against a building. Sarah smiled at her. "Can you hold Ciaran? I'm going to see what I can do to help." She nodded.

***

Dr. Beckham called to David. "We need to get the dead off the street and over to the cemetery."

"I'll find a buckboard and a helper to move the bodies."

"Mrs. Kaplan, we're going to need more bandages. Abbey and Nathan, stay with me and I'll show you which wounds I want dressed.

Mrs. Beckham, already busy dressing wounds, said to William, "Aren't you Nathan and Abbey's brother?"

"Yes, ma'am. I'm William."

"We need to change your Aunt Sarah's bandage and get her cleaned up. Can you help me with that?"

He shrugged and said, "I'll try."

"Try?"

"I'm not so good around bloody stuff."

Mrs. Beckham removed the blood soaked bandage.

"That looks pretty yucky."

"Hold this folded cloth on the wound."

"Okay." William shivered but did as he was asked.

Mrs. Beckham quickly wrapped a long strip around Sarah's head and secured it.

"Here's a damp cloth. Gently wipe the dried blood off her face and neck." She saw a father carrying a young boy. "Over here, sir. Let me check him."

After wiping a few times, William said, "Does this hurt, Aunt Sarah?"

Sarah slowly shook her head and gave him the briefest of smiles.

"Aunt Sarah, does it hurt?"

She patted his shoulder and replied in a whisper, "Not so bad. I just need to sit for a while."

"William," Mrs. Beckham called. "Please sit over here. I need you to talk to Mrs. Chisolm." He sat next to the old woman who lay on a blanket with another covering her. "I'm told she was under quite a bit of debris. If she falls asleep while you talk to her just come and tell me."

"Hi, Mrs. Chisolm. I remember you read to us at school one time. They said you were the oldest lady in town."

"I think I am, William." She smiled, reached out, patted his hand, and then held it.

"I'm almost six. How old are you?"

"I quit counting when I reached eighty … and eighty was a while ago."

"I liked the story you read to us. You know; about the brave soldiers. Sometimes my Dad helps us write stories where my brother and I are heroes and do something great to rescue people. I used your story for ideas for our story one time."

"Glad you enjoyed it. I love reading to children." She smiled at William, squeezed his hand, and said, "Gives me a reason to get up in the morning."

"I like to get up most days … especially if I have a book I'm reading."

The old woman exhaled deeply and quit moving.

"Mrs. Chisolm? Mrs. Chisolm are you okay?"

William released her hand and walked to Mrs. Beckham.

"I think Mrs. Chisolm is asleep but I'm not sure."

"Not sure?"

"Her eyes are open but she's not moving."

Mrs. Beckham checked the old woman, closed her eyes, and put a large cloth over her face.

"Thank you, William. It was kind of you to talk to her."

"You're welcome."

"I have someone else I'd like you to talk to. Would you mind?"

"No ma'am."

"This is Celeste." She indicated a young child who was laying on a blanket.

"Hi Celeste."

"Hi William."

He looked up at Mrs. Beckham. "I know her from school." William sat next to the other five-year-old with his knees pulled up to his chest.

"Where were you when the tornado hit?" Celeste asked.

"I was home with my sister and Nathan and Dad. We got in our root cellar while the storm was on top of us. I was scared but we're okay. My house isn't. It's just a pile of junk."

"They're still trying to find my mom, dad, and brother. The wind lifted me and I didn't feel the ground for a while."

"That must have been scary."

"Yea. Very. They found me under some stuff over near the school. I feel kinda banged up. Dr. Beckham wants me to stay still until he can check me again."

"My Aunt Sarah has a bad cut on her… Celeste is this your blood?" Celeste sat up slightly. "I feel dizzy." She closed her eyes and let her head fall back. William lifted her skirt near the pool of blood and saw a bad wound roughly mid-thigh on the inside of her leg. Blood oozed out. He put his hand over the opening.

"Dr. Beckham! Over here! Celeste needs you," he screamed.

"What's wrong?" the doctor yelled.

"Celeste has a big hole in her leg and lots of blood was coming out until I put my hand on it."

"Keep pressure on it. When I'm done, I'll be right over."

Celeste opened her eyes. "What happened?"

"I think you passed out when you sat up."

"What are you doing? Why are you holding my leg?"

"I'm stopping your bleeding."

"Oh. I guess it's good you do that."

William nodded.

Dr. Beckham kneeled at Celeste's side. He examined the wound. A two inch piece of wood lay on the blanket. "The wood likely caused the puncture and the injury began bleeding when it worked its way out. I have to sew this."

"What?" Celeste said.

William said, "Dr. Beckham has to close your wound by sewing it."

"Will it hurt?"

Dr. Beckham said, "Yes, but not for long." He swore.

"What's wrong?" William asked.

"I was helping uncover some trapped people and a large beam dropped onto my hands. They're swelling. I can hardly make a fist. It's getting difficult to sew." He looked around. Everyone was occupied attending to the injured and more were arriving.

"Abbey Kaplan! Where are you?"

"Over here!" Abbey said, waving her hand. She was holding a distraught three-year-old in her lap while Mrs. Beckham applied a dressing to his side.

"When you're done, come and see me."

"Has Abbey been practicing using the needle I gave her?"

William nodded. "Mom let's her and Nathan practice all the time. Dad even sharpened the needle one time. When Mom goes to the butcher, Abbey always asks her to bring home some skin for them to sew." Dr. Beckham shook his head and grinned.

Abbey arrived and kneeled next to them.

A woman screamed. Looking in her direction they saw her collapse into her husband's arms after someone lifted a blanket which revealed three small bodies.

"Three of her children were under the blanket," Dr. Beckham said. "There'll be more of that before this is over. Abbey, my hands are nearly worthless. I need you to sew this."

She grinned broadly. "Okay. I've been practicing. Lots."

With a stern expression and measured tone, the doctor said, "You listen carefully to what I say, young lady. You do exactly as I tell you. This is not practice. This is someone's leg. Is that clear?"

Abbey wiped the smile off her face. "Yes sir."

"William," Dr. Beckham said, steadying the little one's leg, "please, hold Celeste's hands."

William held out his hands. Celeste seemed reluctant to reciprocate.

"It's okay," William told her. "Boys and girls can hold hands when it's an emergency." She slowly placed her hands in William's.

"Go ahead, Abbey." She put in the first stich.

"Ow, ow, ow," Celeste yelled and began crying. She tightly gripped William's hands.

Abbey turned to Celeste.

"Never mind her, Abbey," Dr. Beckham said. "Pay attention to what you're doing. Put the next stich right here."

Three stiches later and he said, "Now tie off with the knot I taught you."

"Good job, young lady. I'll cover the wound. William, stay with Celeste. Call me if her leg starts bleeding again. Celeste, you need to stay still. Don't move your leg or you'll reopen the wound. Abbey, you come with me."

"I want my mom," Celeste said as tears streamed down her cheeks.

"I'll watch for her and let you know if I see her," William said. "Hey, my Aunt Sarah is walking around with my mom. She looks kinda woozy."

A man walked up and spoke in quiet tones to Dr. Beckham, Sarah, and Myra. The three turned and glanced at Celeste.

William heard Dr. Beckham say, "There's going to be more than a few orphans by the time we get things settled. We need to get word out about the storm."

Myra, with Sarah using her for support, slowly walked to William and Celeste.

"Oh, oh," William said, observing their grim faces.

"What's wrong?" Celeste asked him.

William didn't reply.

"Celeste, I have something terrible to tell you," Myra said. "Your family died in the storm."

"No… They can't be… Don't say that."

Sarah said, "We're so sorry, Celeste."

She put her hands over her ears and repeated, "Don't say that."

Celeste looked at William. With reddened cheeks and eyes swelling with tears, she said, "They're liars. They're lying to me."

"Celeste," Myra said, kneeling next to her and putting a hand on her shoulder, "I know…"

"I have to find them." She tried to get up.

"No," William said. "You have to stay still or you'll start bleeding again." He held her shoulders down. Myra tried to keep her legs still.

"Let me go. I have to find them… I hate you. I hate all of you. LET ME GO!" Celeste strained and twisted against them; finally laying back. She folded an arm across her eyes, and rent the air with deep sobs.

"I'll stay with her," Sarah said. "I feel better when I'm sitting anyway. You two see who else you can help."

As they walked away, William said to his mom, "Celeste's the only other Jewish kid my age at school. She didn't like me much before but she's really gonna hate me now."

"I didn't know she was Jewish. I've never seen them at services."

"She told me her mom and dad were Jewish but didn't even celebrate *Shabbat*."

"I see."

"Celeste's pretty angry."

"She's upset because her parents died."

"Maybe … but I think she's angry at me because I was holding her down." He shrugged. "Where's she gonna live?"

"I don't know. Has she ever talked about cousins or aunts and uncles?"

"One time she said most of her family lived in France. Only her parents came to America."

***

Near the cemetery, a couple of men were busy building coffins. David arrived with more bodies.

As one of the them was placed on the ground, David noticed the man had injuries to both sides of his head. A small hole on one side and a much larger opening on the opposite side. Most of his ear was missing.

"I wonder what would cause an injury like that?" The man he was working with shrugged. They unloaded two more bodies and David returned to town.

He mentioned the odd injury to Dr. Beckham.

"It sounds like a gunshot wound but with all the airborne debris, it's hard to know for certain."

***

Myra waved David over near Celeste. In a low voice she said, "We're going to take Celeste home with us plus three teens. The three have either lost their parents or don't know where they are. Word's being sent out and relatives should be arriving to claim them … except for Celeste. William doesn't think she has family in the States. We need to load her on the buckboard without disturbing her right leg. She has a large wound just above her knee."

"I'll lift her up if you can steady her leg."

Myra sat on the back of the buckboard with Celeste. The teens sat on the seat with David.

"How's Sarah?" David called over his shoulder on the way to the store.

"Better but her head is killing her. I think she, Abbey, William, and Nathan are still working with the bandage brigade."

"Abbey sewed my leg," Celeste said.

"Did you say Abbey sewed your leg?" Myra asked, incredulous.

"Dr. Beckham told her what to do and she sewed me but I'm not supposed to move my leg for a couple days."

Grinning broadly, Myra said, "My Abbey… She *will* become a doctor."

David said, "When we get to the store, I'll bring blankets and lanterns upstairs so we can start housekeeping on the second floor again."

"I'll put a meal together. Everyone's going to be dead tired and hungry. I'll need to take some pans, dishes, and provisions from the store."

"Of course. Try to keep a list of what you take… Never mind. Take what you need. We'll worry about inventory later."

***

The following morning, David and three men pulled up to the store in a freight wagon. He jumped off and said to Myra, "We've salvaged as much as we could from our house. Some of the furniture is useable because a portion of a neighbor's roof covered them during the storm so they're dry. I also have all the food from the root cellar."

"What about clothing?"

"Anything from the second floor is probably in the next county."

Myra appeared saddened for a moment, then smiled. "I shouldn't be sad … our family is intact."

"Freight wagons are arriving from the surrounding towns with donated food, blankets, lumber, and nails. Independence is going to use the street in front of the store as a distribution area. Some folks are setting up tents and a kitchen for the homeless."

"After we get everything upstairs, I'll go see what I can do to help."

"How are the orphaned kids holding up?"

"The three teens are anxious for their relatives to pick them up now that the initial shock of losing their parents is over. They have such long faces, it's painful to look at them. Sarah has them busy at the distribution area but she'll be back in a few minutes to help get a meal together."

"And Celeste?"

"Quiet… Too quiet. Abbey keeps trying to have conversations with her. I've tried as well. Maybe you could spend some time with her?"

"As soon as we have everything upstairs."

"David, did you get any sleep last night?"

"Not really. We were digging people out of buildings by the light of lanterns until just before sunup."

"You must be exhausted."

"It hasn't hit me yet… Too much to do before I sleep."

The instant David entered the apartment, Celeste's voice called out, "Hi, Mr. Kaplan." She was sitting with her back to a wall; a blanket was pulled over her legs.

"Hi Celeste. How's your leg?"

"It kind of pinches when I move too much."

"Let me get things put away and we can talk."

"Okay."

Two men carried a couch and two side chairs into the room.

"Mr. Kaplan," one of the men said, "Dewey and I can fix your kitchen table and benches if you like and bring 'em over here."

"That would be a big help."

"My two brothers are carpenters like me and should be arriving from St. Joe. this afternoon or tomorrow. We can begin rebuilding your house in a couple days if we can agree on a price."

"Sounds great. Keep in touch and we'll do that."

"Celeste, I'm going to move you to the couch. It'll be more comfortable."

He gently picked her up.

"My dad would let me sit on his lap when I didn't feel good."

He kept her on his lap as he sat on the corner of the couch. She nestled against him. He kissed the top of her head. His eyelids seemed heavy.

"Celeste, I'm going to put my head back for a minute…"

An hour later, Myra whispered to Sarah, "Where's an artist when you need one?" She nodded in David's direction.

His head lay back on the top of the couch's rear cushion; mouth open, snoring quietly, and one arm still around Celeste. She slept curled against him.

That afternoon, and much to their relief, relatives of the three teens arrived to take them to their new homes. After teary greetings and thanks to David, Myra, and Sarah they left to begin their new lives.

***

After their evening meal, Myra said, "Celeste, you're going to sleep on the couch tonight. When your leg is better you can share Abbey's room."

The ten-year-old announced, "We'll have fun just like sisters."

Celeste nodded.

Abbey asked, "Are you okay?"

"I miss my mom." Her eyes filled with tears. She put her hands up to her face and sobbed.

"I'll stay with her," David said. He gently slid her onto his lap and held her. She buried her face in his chest and continued crying.

***

"Mom, Mrs. Kimmel is here," Abbey called out two days later.

"Good Morning," Myra said as she rapidly descended the stairs to the store level. "How did your family fare?"

"All well. They're scattered about town helping friends and neighbors rebuild their homes. Your family?"

"Happy and healthy."

"I noticed some men working on your home."

"We hired carpenters and helpers. David is severely lacking in mechanical skills. We should have our home rebuilt in a few weeks or so."

"I came by to say the school is undamaged but for two windows. However, there won't be classes for at least a week. I understand Celeste Spire is living with you. Sad about her family."

"Celeste received a bad injury to her leg which required stiches. She's uncomfortable but getting around."

"I stitched her," Abbey said.

Myra put a hand on Abbey's shoulder. "My daughter the future doctor."

"How's Celeste taking the loss of her family?"

"The first night was the worst but she's beginning to fit in with us."

***

"Celeste," Myra said, just after the five-year-old arrived from school a few weeks after the tornado, "let's have a private talk. Would you come and sit with me in my bedroom?"

Myra sat on the rocking chair she used for nursing Ciaran, and Celeste sat on a child sized chair at her side.

"I want you to know we love having you live with us. I wanted to talk to you about how everyone is treating you and if you feel comfortable living here."

"I like it here but sometimes I still cry because I miss my mom, dad, and brother."

"Would you consider staying and becoming part of our family … which means you'll continue to have responsibilities just like our other children?"

"I like 'sponsibilities."

"Really? Why?"

"I think Abbey and I are friends because I help her dry dishes. We mostly talk about girl stuff." The five-year-old seemed lost in thought for a moment. "I don't like pulling threads … and I think William *hates* pulling them… Nathan used a good 'cabulary word for work like that…"

"Tedious?"

"Yea, tedious… But you said it helps you make clothing for us; so I guess I like helping."

"You're a hard worker."

"Thank you."

"How is everyone treating you?"

"Fine. I mean I needed to talk to William just after I came here because he was pushing and poking me."

"I didn't know."

"I told him, 'William, I'm a girl and it's not nice to poke and push a girl.' Sometimes you have to tell boys things like that."

Myra laughed. "Yes you do. What about Nathan and Abbey?"

"Nathan doesn't talk to me much but, one night, I dreamed I was a flower angel and I could fly around and wherever I waved my hand, beautiful flowers would grow." Celeste motioned with her hand as she imagined flying and creating fields of flowers. "I told Nathan about my dream and he wrote it into a story for me. He titled it *The Flower Angel* and he wrote about me growing flowers and big zucchini and a sweet smelling apple orchard, just like my dad grew for us." She hesitated for a moment, looked at the floor then turned to Myra. "Nathan also put a pumpkin patch in the story. I've never seen one but he said he'd show me this fall. I have the story put away in my drawer. I'll read it to you sometime."

"I hope you will. Honey, what drawer are you talking about?"

"The bottom one in Abbey's drawer thing." While speaking she pantomimed opening and closing the bottom drawer of a dresser. "Abbey took her stuff out and said the bottom drawer was mine so I could keep my new dresses nice." Celeste smoothed her skirt.

Myra was beaming. "How about a hug?"

"Sure. Abbey told me you need lots of hugs."

After they embraced, Myra continued, "What about Mr. Kaplan?"

"He doesn't need so many hugs but he's funny." She giggled. "One time I came home from school and told him something funny. He did a little dance and said, 'Holy Balinko!' Boy did I laugh … and I don't even know what that word means."

***

As Celeste and Abbey dried dishes, the ten-year-old pointed out, "Now we have more girls than boys in this family."

Myra handed a washed dish to Celeste which she began drying. "I have two brothers and two sisters now."

Abbey said, "Sometimes I get upset with my brothers but mostly I like them."

"My brother was lots older than me. We didn't do much together." She stopped drying the dish and said, "It's different now."

"Different?"

"We were playing during recess and a boy bumped into me kinda hard. I got knocked down. He immediately started telling William it was an accident. The boy apologized to me and William helped me up." She began wiping the plate again. "That was kinda nice even though he's not really my brother. And you and Nathan read me stories while I stayed still until my leg healed."

"We help each other. That's what Mom always says."

Celeste sighed. "I still miss my family."

"I lost my first mom when I was little'r than you and I still think about her... But remember, even when we go out west, we can take our memories with us."

Celeste nodded. "I'm gonna do that."

***

"David, the last couple weeks, have you noticed..."

He laughed. "William and Celeste?"

"Yes."

David said, "When he's around her he seems ... more ... is relaxed the right word? I mean they still tease each other like any five-year-olds but there's rarely any meanness or anger between them."

"I think William feels competition with Nathan and Abbey," Myra said. "And he doesn't want to be a copy of them. They're always talking about becoming doctors and telling him that's what he should do."

"I agree."

"Did you see the five-year-olds playing with Ciaran last night?"

David smiled and said, "I don't think I ever heard our youngest giggle so much and when Celeste picks up or holds Ciaran, she's so gentle."

"It's going to be fun watching them grow."

"Did you send a letter to Kathleen telling her we're traveling by ship to Portland?"

"Mailed yesterday. I miss her. I pray she and Jack are doing well."

Chapter Twenty-Seven: Another Journey at Sea

"Tomorrow is the big day," David announced at dinner. "Everything we own is stored in a few trunks. I watched them being loaded on the boat which will get us to New Orleans."

"This is going to be my first boat trip," Celeste enthused.

Before they ate, Myra prayed aloud, "Thank You, Lord, for the food we are about to eat, and for the many blessings You have provided us," she hesitated for a moment, smiled and continued, "Please watch over us during our travel. May we complete our journey healthy and strong. Amen."

She looked at those gathered around the table and silently prayed.

Please Lord, help them watch over each other and avoid danger. Abbey and Celeste whispered to each other and giggled. *And thank you again, for blessing our family with gentle Celeste.*

***

Their ship moved away from its dock. As the ship filled its sails, it heeled away from the wind.

"Hey. Look at me," Celeste said to her new siblings. "I'm standing up straight but I'm not straight up!"

The others laughed and also played with the ship's heel.

"Here are sleeping assignments," Myra said. "Dad and I get the double bed and we'll keep Ciaran with us. Sarah gets the single bed and the girls share the lower bunk built into the wall and the boys get the one above them."

Abbey said, "Mom, that bunk is kind of small."

"If you have to, you can sleep head to toe."

The girls looked at each other and dissolved into giggles. "You mean," Celeste said, "I sleep with Abbey's feet in my face and she sleeps with my feet in her face?"

The two laughed hysterically.

"The weather's pleasant on deck," David said. "Let's go for a walk."

"But don't forget," Myra said, "Starting tomorrow morning after breakfast, Aunt Sarah and I will be conducting lessons to complete the school work Mrs. Kimmel told us you'll miss."

"And," Sarah said, "we'll be conducting Yiddish and Judaism lessons in the afternoon when your school work is complete."

"We're going to be busy," Nathan said.

"That's the idea," David said.

"Dad," William asked, "will you show me how you sharpen your pocket knife?"

"Oh, sure. Sit over here and we'll do it together."

***

As they walked the deck, Nathan stared up at the sails. "Just the wind moving this big ship. No horses, no steam. Just wind."

"And no noise," Abbey said. "That's kinda pleasant."

"I wonder how they know which way to angle the sails," William said.

"There aren't any roads to follow," Celeste said. "How do they know which way to go?"

Sarah said to Myra, "I'll see if I can convince one of the ship's officers to give the children a lesson on running a ship."

"Great idea. I'll dig through our books. I'll bet we can use Celeste's question for a number of geography lessons."

"We have enough paper and pencils. Drawing maps of the countries we're passing might be a good project for them."

As they returned to the cabin, Celeste turned to David and said, "I feel kind of yucky. My tummy feels funny."

David grabbed her, ran to the deck, and held her head over the rail while she vomited.

"I got some of that yucky stuff on my new dress," she said as tears welled up.

"We'll wash it. Let's go back to the cabin and get you cleaned up."

"Boys out of the cabin, please," Myra said. She washed Celeste and helped her into another dress. "You've got to get your sea legs, Celeste."

"What are those?"

"You and I get sick from the ship's motion. It was a huge problem for me when we sailed from Ireland to America. I kept thinking I could sleep it off. After the trip, I learned staying vertical, and walking on deck gets one used to the motion, which is called getting your sea legs."

With a pouting expression the five-year-old complained, "I don't think it's fair. My brothers and Abbey already have sea legs."

"Come sit next to me, and we'll try to get our sea legs together." Celeste sat next to her on a small couch. Sarah and Abbey were reading, while her father and the boys were busy writing an adventure story. David noticed Celeste staring at him.

"Come here, sweetness," he said. She slid off the couch and ran to him. He picked her up and placed her on his lap. She leaned her head against his chest and cuddled tight against him as he wrapped his arms around her.

"Is that better?" he asked.

"Yup."

Myra smiled at David and mouthed, "Like William."

He nodded. In a subdued tone, she said to Sarah, "When either of the five-year-olds feel ill, they want David to hold them."

"Does that bother you?"

"I have enough to do with the others… In truth, I'm proud of how secure they feel in his arms."

***

After two weeks at sea, the weather changed. Their one hundred twenty foot sail boat was being tossed about like a cork and intermittent showers drenched it.

"I'm tired of being in the cabin," William said.

"We've been stuck in here for four days," Nathan said.

"Pay attention to your lessons, please," Aunt Sarah admonished them.

David stood just inside their cabin door, talking to one of the ship's officers.

"We should have docked today to resupply with food and water. We're not running out, but we've been blown off course. It could be another four or five days to our resupply station. We're thinking about cutting the adults' food rations, pregnant and nursing women excepted, to make sure we have enough."

"A good idea. What can I do to help?"

"We'll be posting a guard outside the food storage area. We'd be looking for volunteers to take a one hour shift."

"Count me in."

"Thank you, sir. I'll get back to you about when your shift will be."

***

At two in the morning, David was standing guard in front of the supply room. A man came walking up the corridor. David squinted in the dim light to see who it was. The man's face was dark and featureless. David realized he was wearing a black hood. He raised his gun. Too late, he heard someone approaching from behind. A blow to his head dizzied him. He tried to yell while many hands tried to subdue him. David again tried to vocally signal his distress but a hand over his mouth muffled its sound. One of his assailants tried to pry the gun out of his hand; he pulled the trigger. In the confined space, the pistol's report painfully assaulted his ears which rang unmercifully. He saw the men running away but couldn't hear their hurried footsteps. David struggled to stand. The ship's officer and an armed sailor ran to his side.

"Steady, Mr. Kaplan," the officer said, taking the gun out of his hand while the sailor threw an arm around him.

"Maybe I should just sit on the floor for a bit," David said.

They lowered him to a sitting position. David reviewed what happened.

Another sailor ran up. "We've got one of 'em, sir. Found a hood in his pocket. He's being locked below."

"Find out who his mates were and get them below as well."

"Aye, sir."

"Are you steady enough to walk to your cabin, Mr. Kaplan?" the officer asked.

He nodded. David stood on wobbling feet. "I'll help you sir," the sailor said.

"I apologize, Mr. Kaplan," the officer said. "I didn't believe we'd have a problem like this."

David nodded again. By the time they reached his cabin, he was steady enough to enter and lay down on his own.

***

"David, your head's bleeding," Myra shrieked the following morning as she saw blood on his pillow.

"It's nothing. I got jumped last night."

"Sit up and let me see." She examined the back of his head. "A small cut but it's bled a lot. I'll get a rag and clean this mess."

"Does he need a bandage? Abbey asked.

"Just a cleanup," Myra replied.

"Okay." Abbey yawned. "Let me know if you decide he needs a bandage." She rolled over and went back to sleep.

"Are you in pain?" Myra asked.

"My head hurts and my right hand feels tingly like back in St. Louis."

***

"Will you tell us what happened?" Nathan asked as the two brothers and their Dad went for a walk on deck while the girls dressed.

"I was attacked by three or four men. I didn't stand a chance but I fired the gun and they knew the noise would bring help so they ran away."

"Good thing you held the gun," William said.

"They were trying to get it away from me. Heaven only knows what would have happened if they did."

"There wasn't anything else you could have done?" William asked.

"I was outnumbered. I think there were four of them. Not much you can do if you're outnumbered four to one."

"Back at the store all you needed was Aunt Sarah," William reminded him.

David laughed. "That's true."

Nathan asked, "Does your head still hurt?"

"It does. My right hand and arm feel funny. That scares me."

"Funny how?" Nathan asked.

"They tingle."

"If I was with you, we'd have beat them," William said in an angry tone through gritted teeth.

"William, that's foolish talk. There is little you could have done against four grown men."

"Yes, Dad."

"As I've told you many times, the best way to win a fight—"

Both boys said in unison, "Is to avoid one."

Chapter Twenty-Eight: Transiting Panama

"My Lord, I've never experienced heat and humidity like this. Having sweat in my eyes stings and my clothes are drenched. I would give anything for a decent bath," Myra said as their ship neared its dock in Panama.

David said, "We'll be getting on a train shortly to take us to the Pacific. We should get air from the train's motion."

They boarded a four car train whose cars looked worn and tired. The little train lurched and bounced down the uneven rails during the multi-hour journey across the isthmus. They entered dense Panamanian jungle and were greeted by the raucous hoots of Howler Monkeys, who could be seen swinging in the trees.

"Even the air coming in the windows is hot," Myra complained a few hours later.

A few hours before sunset, they heard a report like a shotgun blast and the whooshing sound of escaping steam.

"What was that?" frightened Myra asked.

The train slowed and came to a stop; David put his head out a window and saw the train crew examining one of the locomotive's cylinders.

"How bad is it?" he asked the conductor as he approached them.

He pointed to the ruptured cylinder. "These one, she dead. You know, she broke. No work no more. Need bring one new from back there," he said, pointing in the direction they came from. "You, all passenger walk same direction train going. Follow path by track. You find port where you meet steamboat. Nice town. Nice hotel."

"How far?"

"No many miles. Maybe six. You walk. Find hotel. When train fix we come bring all you things."

"How long will it take to fix the train?"

The conductor shrugged his shoulders. "Maybe two day, maybe three. You walk. You be okay. Not far. Follow path. Train bring you things when fix."

"It has a blown cylinder," David told the family after re-boarding the train. "If they get it repaired in two days, I'll be amazed. We need to walk to town." He checked his watch. "It's already three-thirty. We should start walking."

"Ouch," Myra yelled as she stepped off the train.

David steadied her. "Are you okay?"

"I twisted my ankle."

"Can you walk?" David asked.

She took a few steps. "I'll have to take small steps and go slow. You, Sarah, and the kids go ahead."

"I'll walk with you," David said.

"No, it looks like rain. You go ahead."

"You're not walking by yourself."

"I'll walk with her," an elderly woman volunteered. "When my husband was alive, we traveled this trail from before the train came through; when it was nothing but a trail for donkey carts. I'm *Señora* Maria Davila. I'm old," she said with a sparkle in her eye, "and I walk slow. We'll be fine."

"Thank you, *Sra.* Davila," Myra said and waved her family on.

They and the other passengers proceeded along the cart trail and next to a small stream which roughly followed the tracks but lay in a depression a number of feet below the level of the trail.

After an hour, the others were out of sight. Myra said, "My feet are killing me and breathing this putrid heavy air can't be healthy."

Sra. Davila laughed and said, "The scent of the swamp."

"Every time I open my mouth I can taste it. How much farther do you think we have to walk?"

"Maybe a mile or two. We could stop for a while but we should try to keep going as it's raining in the mountains over there and those clouds are headed this way."

"You seem to have traveled this trail often."

"I have children living at each end. I spend a few months with one then travel to spend a few months with the other. I don't like the traveling but I keep thinking I'll be playing with my grandchildren shortly and the trip doesn't seem so long." She grinned broadly. "You should hear them scream when they see me. They always have stories to tell me."

Ten minutes later, the clouds obscured the sun and a light rain fell. The small stream tripled its width, its former sluggishness having been replaced by a vigorous flow which crept up its banks.

"Probably run off from the mountains," *Sra.* Avila said. "Maybe we should stop for a while. We'll get under the Y shaped tree over there until the rain lets up?"

They quickly huddled under the odd shaped tree whose large trunk separated four-feet from the ground into two distinct trees as it reached for the sky.

The rain increased to a heavy downpour. They were pelted by large raindrops.

"This damn tree leaks," Myra said, trying to improve their situation with humor. "I'm starting to get chilled."

Sra. Avila moved to the edge of the stream and commented, "Look at this thing fill up. It's nearly all the way up its bank and moving like a race horse."

"Maybe we should find higher ground."

The older woman turned to reply but the bank below her feet collapsed. *Sra.* Avila twisted toward Myra, extended an arm in her direction with her faced bathed in terror as she tumbled into the raging torrent. Myra reached for her hand and caught her sleeve for an instant but couldn't hold on.

With her heart pounding so hard she thought it might jump out of her chest, Myra screamed her name. The sound of her voice was quickly absorbed by the din of volley upon volley of large raindrops falling on the jungle flora. *Sra.* Avila's head came up a few times as her arms flailed in the water.

"No!" Myra yelled. She felt running water against her feet. The stream was over its bank and rising. With her heart in her throat she hoisted herself into the tree. She clambered fifteen-feet up and hooked her leg over one branch and under another to rest for a moment when she felt the tree begin leaning over the river.

"This can't be happening," she said, as she saw the base of the tree was covered by at least three-feet of swift moving and rapidly rising water. The wind was whistling in her ears as it whipped around her. Myra was forced to use all her strength to maintain her grip on the swaying tree. The trunk she was on began splitting away from its mate. It slowly toppled into the raging flow. She closed her eyes and held her breath as the cold water enveloped her. The branches where she'd hooked her leg trapped her, keeping her face underwater. Panic enveloped her. The tree rotated which momentarily allowed her a gasp for air before rotating again, pulling her back under. Her lungs screamed for oxygen. She felt dizzy as she endured increasing pain in her chest.

Instead of struggling to get her head into the air, she worked against all the instincts which told her to strain directly to the surface. Myra pushed further below, grasped and freed her leg. She struggled through a tangle of small branches which cut and pulled at her body, finally getting her head out of the water. Lungful after lungful of air entered with a rapidity she didn't know she could achieve. The tree rotated again. She lost her grip on the branches and was plunged below the surface again.

Water entered her lungs which her body desperately wanted to cough out; but Myra knew she couldn't begin coughing or she'd drown. Once again, fighting against branches which cut and poked her body, she managed to get her face above the surface. Deep coughs racked her body. Pulling herself through the tangle of branches and onto the massive trunk, she briefly thought of her family. In the dim light she saw two iridescent eyes looking at her. Ten-feet away, an ocelot growled at her.

Stay where you are and I'll stay here, Myra thought while continuing to breathe hard and listening to a repeated low growl. She took stock of her body noting the numerous cuts on her arms, hands, and legs. She felt sickened as she discovered leeches. Feeling revulsion, she still managed to tear them off, each leaving a small trail of blood where they'd pierced her skin.

She shielded her eyes from the raindrops pelting her and scanned the surroundings for any sign of *Sra.* Avila. Her tears mixed with the rain as she shouted her name.

The rain and clouds departed as suddenly as they'd arrived. The moonlight revealed they were still being carried at a rapid rate. At one point the stream curved, bringing her waterborne celluloid conveyance near the bank. Myra thought briefly of letting go and swimming to see if she could get to the bank but, lacking all but the most rudimentary swimming skills, decided against it. Her fellow passenger felt no such compunction as it launched itself six-feet into the air and splashed down a few feet from the torrent's edge. It quickly swam out, clawed its way up the nearest tree, and disappeared into the canopy.

Myra's breathing eased as she looked around, desperate to find a way off the log and back to dry land. Even wet jungle would suffice, she thought. Every few minutes she kept checking her arms and legs for leeches. The stream widened suddenly.

I'm being carried into the ocean. I've got to get to shore. Lord, please help me.

Gripped by terror, she rolled off the log. The salt water stung her cuts as if they'd been opened by a razor.

Her memory began replaying a trip to the lake the previous summer. She remembered the children coaching her to swim like they did. Abbey said, "Kick with your legs straight and point your toes."

Nathan told her, "Make your arms kind of like a windmill but don't reach too far out above the water. Keep your hands flat like an oar."

Following their instructions, she found herself moving through the water but struggled to breathe which further frightened her.

She suddenly envisioned William, bent over at the waist while he demonstrated breathing. "Look back at your shoulder when your arm comes out when you want to breathe. Then let the air out under the water and do it again and again."

Yes, William.

"Copy the kids and me, Myra," David repeated.

Every time her left arm came out of the water she took a breath. A few times she took in salt water as well, which was sufficiently annoying to nearly ruin her swimming, but she concentrated mightily and was rewarded with the sight of lights on a beach twenty-yards in front of her. Her muscles ached. The calf muscles in her left leg were cramping when a wave lifted her then tilted and caused her to surf down its face as it carried her toward shore. Her right hand struck the sandy bottom.

With great relief, Myra struggled to her feet only to be knocked over by the following wave. Regaining her feet a second time, she heard a voice from shore, "There's someone in the ocean."

A man and woman dropped their drinks and splashed into the surf. They supported her while she stumbled onto the beach.

Myra's heart pounded. Her chest and abdominal muscles couldn't seem to move fast enough to allow her to get enough oxygen into her lungs. She kneeled in the sand.

"Do you need a doctor, miss?" the man asked.

She shook her head. Holding up one finger, she indicated they should wait for more response.

"Thank you," she finally managed to say. She smiled. "My children weren't even here and they saved me. My Lord, I love them." Myra looked up at the pair. "Have you seen a family named Kaplan?"

The man said, "What are you talking about? I don't see anyone but you. Where did you come from? What were you doing out there swimming after dark?"

"Ask questions later, Art. She sounds a bit out of her head. Let's get her inside. Poor thing looks a mess."

At the front desk she asked, "What hotels do Americans stay at?"

"This one and the one across the street," the clerk said. "Who you looking for?"

"Kaplan."

"Myra, you made it." David ran and embraced her.

"You're soaking wet and shivering. Let's get you up to our room."

"Wait." She turned to the clerk. "I was walking next to a stream which led to the ocean with another woman. She fell into the water and was carried away."

"It's unlikely you'll find her. She's way out in the ocean by now."

"I made it."

"Were you in a boat?"

"I held onto a tree."

"What was the woman holding onto?"

Myra's shoulders drooped. "Nothing. I tried to grab her but it was too late."

They proceeded to their room.

"You need to spend some time with Celeste. She's been a basket case waiting for you to arrive."

"Poor thing. I'm sure losing one mother was enough trauma."

They entered their room. Celeste took one look at Myra and made a beeline for her. Myra picked her up and held her.

"I was afraid you got lost."

"I'm fine now." She looked at the others. "I'm tired but fine."

Celeste leaned away from her, wrinkled her nose and said, "You smell like the ocean."

***

The next day the train arrived as did the sailing ship which, two days hence, would take them to Portland.

Myra, David, and Sarah, who held Ciaran, sat at a table on a large patio behind the hotel which fronted the ocean. The children were occupied playing in the sand.

"How about a glass of coconut water?" David asked.

"I'll try it," Sarah said.

"Me too," Myra said.

They watched as he walked to the bar. "The children are being good travelers," Sarah said.

"They are." Myra saw David shake hands with a man. They talked briefly. David glanced over his shoulder at Myra. His expression seemed deeply troubled. They talked longer and the two walked over to the table.

The word grim came to Myra's mind as she observed her husband's expression. She stood up.

"This is my wife, Myra, and my sister, Sarah."

"David, what's going on?"

"This is Mr. Simpson. He's traveling to South America but lives in Portland."

"Pleasure to meet you folks, and I'm sorry to be the bearer of bad news." He looked down and fidgeted with his hat. "Mr. Kaplan said you're in business with Jack Kaufman. He and his wife are good people but…" David moved to Myra's side. "I'm sorry, folks, but his friends were talking about holding a memorial service for Mr. Kaufman the day I left Portland."

"No," Myra said. She felt dizzy and her knees gave way. David grabbed her and helped her into a chair.

Mr. Simpson repeated, "I'm sorry, folks," and hurried away.

"I'll take Myra up to our room," Sarah said.

"Let me have Ciaran and I'll tell the children."

David walked out to the beach.

"Why was Mom crying?" Abbey asked.

"Uncle Jack died."

"What happened?" Nathan asked.

"We don't know."

William turned to Celeste and explained, "He's the one who taught us how to be a scout and how to stop bleeding with bandages." He looked at his dad. "How's Aunt Kathleen?"

"She's alive but deeply saddened I imagine."

"Is Mom okay?"

"She's sad as well."

William said to Celeste, "Aunt Kathleen is Mom's sister."

She nodded and said, "Mom's gonna need lots of hugs."

"Yea, lots," Abbey said.

"I'm sad for Aunt Kathleen," Nathan said.

William nodded. "Me too."

"Let's have lunch then we'll go see how Mom's doing."

***

The morning of their departure, Myra, Celeste and Abbey proceeded to the beach where she'd walked out of the ocean. Removing their shoes and holding hands, the three walked across the warm sand and a few feet into the gentle surf.

"Goodbye, *Sra.* Davila," Myra said. "Thank you for walking with me… I'm sorry I couldn't save you."

"It's sad the river took her away," Celeste said.

Abbey said, "She did a *mitzvah* by walking with you, and then died. It doesn't seem fair."

"We try to do our best," Myra said, "but life isn't always fair."

"Sometimes life is cruel," Abbey said. Celeste nodded.

Myra sighed. "I can only imagine how distraught Kathleen is." She looked at her daughters and smiled. "Let's gather the rest of our family, young ladies. It won't be long and we'll be in our new home in Portland."

Chapter Twenty-Nine: On to Portland

They sat down to dinner two days after their ship picked up passengers and cargo in San Francisco. An elderly woman with sparkling eyes sat across from them.

"I'm Edna Blaze," she said.

"We're the Kaplans," Myra said, and then introduced her family and Sarah.

"Where are you headed?"

David answered. "Portland. We have a business there. We're moving from Independence, Missouri."

"That's a long journey. I've been visiting family in San Francisco but my home is in Portland. How are the children managing the journey?"

"We've tried to keep them busy with school work but it's a challenge."

"I miss doing *Shabbat* like we did at home," Nathan said.

"Me too," Abbey said. "I miss talking about the *parsha*."

Celeste, who was sitting next to Edna, said to her, "Sometimes my Aunt Sarah helps me learn the *parsha* so I can tell the story on *Shabbat*. And Mom showed me how to light a candle without burning myself."

"I look forward to lighting candles on *Shabbat* as well," Edna said.

"You're…" David said.

Edna smiled. "Yes. We have a wonderful Jewish community in Portland which I hope you'll become a part of. We can't afford a Rabbi yet and we don't have a building but we're growing."

"Do you know a woman named Kathleen Kaufman?" Myra asked.

"Kaufman sounds familiar."

"The Kaufmans and we purchased a warehouse business near the docks."

"Oh yes. I heard old Jacob McClure sold that business. He might have sold it to someone named Kaufman. I've been down here a few months helping my daughter take care of her newborn twins so I've been out of touch for a while."

***

That evening the ship's steward knocked on their cabin door.

"The captain's asked me to report we're in for a bit of rough weather for the next day or two. Temperatures are already dropping. We'll put out food but depending on the ship's motion we may not have hot food 'till the storm passes."

They thanked him.

"What shall we do?" Myra asked.

The ship seemed to reply, as the front of it was tossed high in the air and then slammed into an oncoming wave. Their cabin followed the uncomfortable motion.

"Hold on tight?" David proposed as they heard rain begin pelting the ship.

"It must be miserable for the crew," Sarah said. "They have to work outside in this stuff."

An hour later, a shivering Sarah wrapped herself and Abbey in a blanket. "I hope it doesn't get any colder."

Early the following morning while it was still dark, they heard yelling from the deck and shortly afterward someone pounded on their door. David opened it to find the completely soaked ship's steward standing there.

"Sorry to wake you but we have an emergency, sir. Without warning, a rogue wave swept across the deck of the ship. A number of the crew were washed out to sea. We're trying to get any able bodied men on deck to help sail the ship."

"I'll help but know nothing about work on a ship."

"You'll be assigned to one of the crew. He'll work at your side but you need to be careful as the ship has ice everywhere."

David's feet began slipping the moment he was on deck. A crewman introduced himself and began explaining procedures. The weather worsened and the ship's motion increased. He yelled to be heard over the howling wind.

"When the ship comes across the wind, we have to adjust the sails. We'll try to do whatever we can from the deck. Watch where you step and do exactly as I say. If the captain decides to take in more sail, we'll have to go into the rigging to reef the canvas."

David shivered from the cold and from the thought of climbing the rigging. The storm whipped sleet soaked through his clothing. He heard the captain yell something and point into the rigging. Although not far away, his voice was barely audible.

The seaman shaded his eyes to keep the rain out of them while he gazed at the sails on the mainmast. He opened a locker, grabbed a wooden pulley, tied a short loop of line around it and put it over his shoulder. "Looks like the main moon and sky sails are secure but the pulley for the topgallant is broken. It'll take the both of us to replace it. Stay close, Mr. Kaplan."

David followed him across the slippery deck to the ship's rail where he watched for a moment as the seaman climbed. David grasped the rough, cold rope ladder and anxiously climbed into the rigging. The course fibers dug into his hands. After a few rungs, the cold temperature and wetness caused his hands to stiffen. It became progressively more difficult to get a good grip. They arrived at a small platform located halfway up the mast.

"We keep going, Mr. Kaplan," the sailor yelled to him and proceeded up a second rope ladder. David transferred to the second ladder and climbed to the next platform which was a good seventy-feet off the deck. As the mast swayed, his body occasionally leaned away from the ladder. David looked down and shivered anew. He tightened his grip on the icy rope as there was nothing but green water directly below him. He arrived at the next platform. His entire body trembled from the cold and all his muscles were getting stiffer.

"The pulley we'll be replacing..." The seaman paused and studied the men working on the deck. Even in the dim light, David could see his face turn ashen.

"No, you fools," he yelled. "LOOSEN THE OTHER SIDE FIRST." The men on deck couldn't hear him.

"What's wrong?" David screamed, fighting to be heard over the howling wind.

The seaman shouted in his ear. "They're tightening the running stays on the wrong side. When the captain changes tack, the extra pressure, along with the wind load, can cause the mast to break."

"What should we do?"

The sailor looked where the navigator stood. "THE HELM IS TURNING. GET TO THE DECK. NOW!"

With his heart in his throat, David climbed down the freezing rope ladder as fast as he could. When he was still twenty-feet above the deck, they heard the mast begin splitting.

"JUMP, KAPLAN!" the seaman yelled.

David leaped to the deck as the mainmast collapsed, cleanly tearing off the upper sections of the fore and mizzen masts with it. His feet slipped as he landed and David slammed face first onto the deck. He tried to stand but was struck in the back by a falling yard arm and became tangled under the rigging. In a semi-conscious stupor, his heart pounded as if it would leap out of his chest. He groaned while trying to struggle free of his rope prison.

***

The sound of the masts crashing woke Myra.

"Sarah, I'm going to the deck to see what's going on."

She arrived on deck to be greeted by the sight of devastation and panic with the ship beginning to list at an alarming angle. The deck hands were shouting and running about. During a flash of lightning, she saw the upper half of the mizzen and fore masts were torn away cleanly but the main, while lying on its side, was still half attached at its base while most of its length, rigging and sails were over the side of the ship.

A sailor grabbed her arm and called to her over the screaming wind, "Get below, ma'am."

"What's going on? Are we in danger of sinking?"

"Not yet. The sails and rigging are dragging in the water which is the source of the list and wild movement of the ship. We have to cut them free so we can shove the damaged sail gear overboard."

Myra saw sailors with axes chopping determinedly to sever the mast and its rigging as rapidly as possible.

She looked at the helm where two men were on the wheel desperately trying to keep the ship under control but the rudder wasn't designed to overpower all the gear and canvas dragging in the water. She saw the mizzen crushed bodies of two men, only glancing at them long enough to ensure it wasn't David who had succumbed. The sight of them caused an involuntary shudder.

"You should remain below, ma'am," the sailor said, continuing to grasp her arm as she nearly lost her balance from the ship's swaying.

She jerked her arm away, and yelled, "I have to find my husband."

With icy wind and cold rain pelting her, Myra carefully walked around the debris-strewn deck.

"Careful, miss," another sailor called. "A ten-foot section of the railing is missing down there where the main is leaning over the side."

She looked in the direction he pointed and saw a body trapped under a pile of rigging. The man's face looked like he'd lost a prize fight. Eyes puffy, nose and lips bleeding, he tried to raise a hand. Myra glanced at him but didn't recognize him at first, then realized it was David. She ran over and kneeled at his rope entombed side.

She shouted, "I've got to get you out of this." Trying to lift the heavy lines achieved nothing. Myra found it difficult to remain in place; such were the ship's motions. She heard unintelligible shouting. Myra hooked her arm around a line to prevent being washed overboard, as a wave rolled across the deck. Once clear, she saw David coughing violently. She looked around for something to help free him.

His knife, she thought, reaching into his pocket. From her knees she furiously sawed at lines the thickness of a man's wrist. Someone shouted; looking in the direction the sailor pointed, she saw another wave headed their way.

"David, brace yourself. Another wave."

The icy water slammed into her, knocking her backwards and she slid across the icy deck. Using the lines to pull herself back, Myra shivered so badly she could barely grip the knife. She hastily resumed slicing. Myra's arms ached, she breathed rapidly, and could feel her heart pounding in her chest; her body telling her it couldn't take much more. Ignoring the pain and cold, she freed groggy David. Her leg muscles screamed as she strained to lift him to his feet.

The men chopping at the mast completed their task. It started sliding off the deck. David committed a cardinal sin. He stepped into a looped line. It tightened on his ankle as it moved with the freed mast. He toppled over as it pulled him toward the sea. In mere moments he would be gone. Panicked, Myra grabbed an ax from a sailor and swung it at the line with all her strength. Just before the blade struck the line, it pulled faster, resulting in the ax blade severing it as well as slicing into David's ankle. He screamed.

In the illumination of a lightening flash, Myra saw terror in his eyes as blood poured out of the wound. He screamed again as he tried to stand on the wounded leg but instead fell to the deck. She jammed her hands over her ears to shut out his screams while two sailors assisted them off the deck. One of them wrapped his shirt around David's ankle to stem the blood flow. He screamed anew with every painful step. Myra surmised the sailor's shirt added to the pain as it likely was soaked in salt water. The ship righted itself as the freed main slid off. David's continued yells and moaning while the sailors moved him cut through her like a razor. They carried him into their cabin.

"What happened?" Sarah asked.

Her entire body shook so bad her joints hurt. "I was trying to free David. I didn't mean to… He was being pulled overboard… I cut a line that held him but my ax tore into his ankle as well…" She slumped to the floor and dissolved into tears.

"We need bandages," Abbey yelled.

Sarah started tearing an underskirt into strips.

Nathan and Abbey, with Sarah's help, wrapped David's torn ankle.

"David, I'm so sorry."

"Sorry? But for your help, I'd have been dragged off the ship."

"My clumsy help may have turned you into a cripple."

"We don't know that. You saved my life." She shook her head.

He tried to sit up but cringed and groaned. She jammed her eyes shut. He said to the children, "Your mother rescued me."

"There's a ship's doctor," Sarah said. "I'll go find him."

Myra walked to his side. He took her hand in both of his.

"You saved me. I owe you."

She yanked her hand away and folded her arms across her chest. "I've done some awful things in my life but I never damaged anyone like this."

"Have you ever saved someone's life?"

She shook her head.

"Sorry I couldn't get here sooner," the ship's doctor said while he examined David's ankle, "but there are lots of injuries. I'm going to sew some of this. It's going to hurt like hell. You're lucky you didn't lose your entire foot, Mr. Kaplan. This is a bottle of the Captain's best scotch. Said he bought it in a town called Port Ellen on Islay Island. Have some before I start. It should take the edge off the pain. You need to keep pressure off the ankle for a few days. I'll have the ship's carpenter make a crutch for you."

"What state is the ship in?" David asked. "No motion now." He downed a glass of the strong drink.

"The storm is dying but we seem to be in a fog as thick as a pea soup. The storm blew us off course. Without the sun or stars it's impossible to know where we are. The crew is trying to rig some sail but with the lack of wind right now we'll not be going anywhere."

"Are we close to Portland?"

"We should dock there sometime tomorrow."

The doctor turned to the others. "You may not want to watch what I'm going to do. I'm going to sew this."

"We want to watch," Nathan said.

"If you're going to sew him, I'll hold his hands," Celeste said. She ran to the side of the bunk.

"We'll see if we can get some food," Myra said, leaving the cabin with William, Sarah, and Ciaran.

***

Their ship approached its dock in Portland. The family was standing at the rail. Abbey's expression illuminated; she stood on her toes, waved, and yelled, "Aunt Kathleen. It's us. We're over here."

The others waved and yelled while Kathleen returned their greetings.

Myra leaned toward David and said, "She looks tired and worn."

"We've only been separated a few months and she looks like she's aged ten years."

As soon as the gangplank was in place, Abbey and the boys ran down it. Celeste hung back. Abbey noticed, reversed course, and grabbed Celeste's hand who then accompanied the others.

They embraced Aunt Kathleen.

Abbey said, "This is my new sister, Celeste. She's five like William."

"New sister?" Kathleen said, raising her eyebrows.

"We have much to tell you," Myra said, embracing her childhood friend.

"As do I," Kathleen said. "But let's get you out to your new home. Jack bought each of us a home on four acres. The properties are adjacent and the homes are but a handful of steps from each other."

"Jack?" David asked.

"I'll tell you later."

"This is my sister, Sarah. Sarah, this is Kathleen."

"Where's that goddamned bitch?" a tall man called out. He spotted Kathleen and marched in her direction. Stopping in front of her he leaned toward her, poked a finger in her chest and yelled, "You bitch. I want my cargo delivered today. Not—"

He didn't utter another word. Before Myra could say, "No David," he'd spun the angry man around and buried his fist into the his belly with sufficient force to lift him off his feet. He crumpled to the ground, gasping for air.

"Thank you, David. That should be the end of shouting at me." In a sweet voice, leaning over the man's prostrate form, Kathleen said, "Mr. Cuthbert, I was going to introduce you to my business partner but seeing as you've just met, I'll reiterate, your cargo will be delivered Friday as specified in your contract."

She uttered a deep sigh of relief, stood tall, and took Myra's arm and Abbey's hand. "Come along, Kaplans. Off to your new home. Let's pray our life in the Northwest will be as gratifying as our life in Independence."

~~~ The End ~~~

Don't miss the continuation of Richard's historical trilogy. Book 2 will depict life in Portland and the pioneers' journey on the Oregon Trail. Sign up on his website to be notified of upcoming books and book signing events and receive a bonus gift.

www.villagedrummerfiction.com

ABOUT THE AUTHOR

Richard began writing while living in the Pacific Northwest with his wife, Carolynn. Last summer they moved to Dallas, Texas. They are the proud parents of three wonderful adult sons.

Richard is a 101st Airborne Division Vietnam veteran. After an education in mathematics, a 17 year career in manufacturing engineering and a 22 year career in software engineering, Richard started a career as an author. He writes sagas about families struggling to make a life in America. His other interests range from mathematical analysis and photography to anything with an engine.

Richard's current project includes writing *American Journeys,* a series of family saga/historical fiction novels, set in 1850 – 1900, about the predecessors to the characters in his *Meant to Be Together* series and their journeys across the United States. The second book in this series will be available later this year (2014).

In addition to the extensive research for his new series, Richard is also working on becoming a Texan, exploring another part of our beautiful country, and discovering the properties of p-adic numbers.